The Monogamist

By the same author
SAIL OR RETURN

THE MONOGAMIST

John Mole

C
CENTURY
LONDON MELBOURNE AUCKLAND JOHANNESBURG

Copyright © John Mole 1986

All rights reserved

First published in Great Britain in 1986 by
Century Hutchinson Ltd,
Brookmount House, 62–65 Chandos Place,
London WC2N 4NW

Century Hutchinson Publishing Group (Australia) Pty Ltd
16–22 Church Street, Hawthorn, Melbourne, Victoria 3122

Century Hutchinson Group (NZ) Ltd
32–34 View Road, PO Box 40–086, Glenfield, Auckland 10

Century Hutchinson Group (SA) Pty Ltd
PO Box 337, Bergvlei 2012, South Africa

British Library Cataloguing in Publication Data

Mole, John
  The monogamist
  I. Title
  823'.914 [F]   PR6063.048

  ISBN 0-7126-9502-8

Typeset and printed in Great Britain by
WBC Print Ltd, Bristol

For Anne and Harry with thanks

1

Alex slammed the door on the last removal man and stormed into the kitchen where Tony was making a fresh pot of tea.

'How much did you give them?' he asked.

She lied about the tip. She increased it by a third. He always reduced the cost of things he had paid for by a third so it all cancelled out.

'Was that each?' he asked.

'All together,' she said defiantly.

'How could you be so mean?'

'They're lucky to get a tip at all. Have you seen the front door? Great gouges out of the paintwork. We should have tipped them before they started. You'd think their own houses were furnished with priceless antiques. Did you hear what the fat one said about the stains on our mattress?'

'Did you tell him they were old stains?' sighed Tony.

Tony poured boiling water into the two mugs they had left out of the packing. He kept Tony the Tiger for himself and handed her Pope John Paul II. It was her daily reminder to take the pill.

'You think you're going to a new house, a new start, and the same old rubbish comes down the drive,' said Alex bitterly. 'It's all so tatty and tired.'

'Like our mattress,' said Tony. He stood up from the box he was sitting on and scrabbled at the parcel tape that sealed the top. It was marked KITCHEN UTENSILS in Alex's writing.

'Don't do that now. I've got to wipe everything down first,' she ordered.

'Nonsense. Action. Now.'

On top was a toaster box full of photographs. One of them was taken on the day they got engaged. After ten years of marriage and two children the hopeful, innocent, radiant girl was still recognizable. The camera had caught the mischievous expression in her clear blue eyes and the slightly parted lips of passionate women and incurable mouth breathers. The photos were followed by a high-heeled shoe, a set of spanners, a wicker basket full of used tissues and cotton buds, a packet of felt tip pens, a jar full of curtain hooks, two rolls of striped wallpaper, three packets of sparklers, a lampshade wrapped in an old T-shirt, two cans of deodorant, one empty the other full, a crumpled pirate's hat, the guarantee for the dishwasher and a packet of vacuum cleaner bags. He laid these objects out ceremoniously on the kitchen table while Alex wiped down the shelves. At the bottom was a dog-eared porno magazine which he had never seen before. He left it in the box.

'You can turn round now.'

She turned round and her eyes narrowed accusingly.

'Who put all that in there?'

'If it was the same person who wrote KITCHEN UTENSILS on the top that person needs help.'

'I told you we should have thrown everything away.'

'We did. Into these boxes. And then we brought them with us. You can't escape.'

'We can,' she shouted as he carried the box out into the hall, 'we damn well can.'

While Tony sneaked down to the cellar with the porno magazine Alex looked for the kitchen utensils. She started in the sitting room. The woodwork was thickly encrusted with lugubrious brown paint. The floorboards were bare with a black stained border around the edge like a funeral announcement. The main feature of the room was a monumental marble fireplace. It was hewn out of white marble criss-crossed with dark blue veins. She promised to wear support tights whenever she saw it. The room was furnished with a blue denim sofa, two director chairs with red canvas backs, a bamboo coffee table with a cracked glass top and an old fashioned wooden standard lamp with a tasselled shade. In a couple of years they would be replaced by her parent's Japanese lacquer table, floor standing spot lights and new sofas in green velvet from the January sales that someone would spill red wine over the day after they were delivered. She would scatter salt over the stain and when that failed she would make a cushion that would be placed carefully over it when they were expecting guests.

Edwardian glazed doors opened on to the back garden. She folded her arms and peered into the dusk. This is how she would stand when she stomped out of the kitchen when they were in the middle of an argument. The Christmas tree would stand in the corner opposite the door. Every year Tony would find the cardboard box of decorations in the loft and fix the lights. One year he would put his back out standing up on the kitchen stool and Mark would do them instead. For ever after that would be his job, even when he went away to college.

The kitchen utensils were not there. She went into the front room. It was decorated like an Indian restaurant with red flock wallpaper and a brown carpet too decrepit even for the executors to have taken away. They called it the dining room although it would rarely be used for dining. It would be the room for making curtains, doing homework, laying out the electric train and the table tennis, sorting stuff out for garage sales. It would be the playroom until the children preferred their own bedrooms. The only furniture was a stripped pine sideboard with mahogany handles and oak legs. They were using the dining table and chairs in the kitchen. There were two cardboard boxes marked DINING

ROOM. One had the contents of Louise's wardrobe and the other a collection of tools, screws and nails and bits out of the car like the door to the glove compartment. But no kitchen utensils.

She went out into the hall and up the stairs. She looked for the step where Tony would trip and fall downstairs and the place where Louise would sick up the punch of her first teenage party. She looked in the bathroom. The bath and basin were pink and the walls were painted almost to match. The black and white plastic floor tiles were curling at the edges. In the bath was their old bathroom cabinet with the mirror in which they would watch their faces getting older and older and older.

The lavatory was separate, down a long corridor with a tiny barred window at the end. She wondered how many times she would sit there in the middle of the night thinking she was going to die before she turned and knelt and roared down the big white telephone. Cardboard boxes labelled CLOTHES were piled in the master bedroom. They were full of toys, records, a set of Reader's Digest condensed books but no kitchen utensils. The movers had insisted on erecting the bed, no trouble love. She was embarrassed about the stains on the mattress. Had they all come from you know what? Surely one or two must have been spilt tea or a sodden child in the middle of the night. One day they would decide that the bed was too small and the sag in the middle that made them roll on top of each other in the middle of the night was bad for their backs. They would buy a king size so they could go to sleep without touching each other. And an electric blanket.

On the landing their art collection leaned against the banisters. A poster of a Picasso exhibition in an aluminium frame. Wishy-washy imitation water colours of the Eiffel Tower, Notre Dame and the Arc de Triomphe, subtitled PARIS in case anyone was in doubt. A Dutch clog. Turner's Sunset pasted on to curling hardboard. A signed picture of John F. Kennedy in a black plastic frame. She would stand here at the top of the stairs with the doctor whispering about appendicitis and tonsillitis and three times a day and plenty of liquid. She went into the children's rooms. Nightmares. Visions. The tooth fairy. Shrieks of laughter. Adolescent fumblings. Calf love. Christmas stockings. Sulky moods. Tumbling horseplay. Please God let. Please God if you exist. But no kitchen utensils. There was nothing in the guest room. It was the room her mother would stay in just for the weekend at first, then just for a week over the holidays, then for a month or so to get over her op., then until she couldn't get upstairs and they brought her bed down to the dining room. You mustn't put yourselves out. I'll go into a Home. But we love to have you living with us, don't we Tony?

She went downstairs again, the future of the house unrolling before her. She could see blocked drains, leaks in the roof, dry rot, creeping damp, burst pipes, pigeons in the water tank, floods in the cellar. She would get to know that banister, this door-handle, that light-switch. Now alien things they would embed themselves into all their lives. She would gaze at this one, trying to find words to console Louise. Mark would fiddle with that one while he confessed to his father. Tony would grip this one with sweaty fingers while they tried to decide if his indigestion was a heart attack. The peeling paper and rotting plaster would soak up their miseries and happinesses and worries and joys and never leave a stain. She hadn't known the previous owners. Their executors had cleared out everything except the carpet in the dining room. They left no trace of the life they had lived here. The past was over and done with. Instead the house was haunted by the ghosts of the future. They were so real she could almost touch them as they crowded in on her, suffocating the present. Those would be the days.

She clattered down the uncarpeted stairs, determined not to be stifled. They had a lot of work to do. She shouted for Tony in the echoing hall. Down in the cellar Tony carefully folded the magazine and tucked it behind the gas meter.

'Coming dear,' he called, and trudged up the cellar steps.

'Why can't we buy a new front door?' asked Tony, pulling the bedclothes up to his chin.

'It wouldn't look right. All the other houses have the original front doors.' Alex put his coffee down on the carpet beside him.

'But all front doors were new once. If we were really restoring the house we'd put a new front door on.'

He knew this was a losing argument. He also knew that the front door was covered with layers of Victorian and Edwardian and Georgian and Elizabethan paint. The wood would be difficult enough but what about the stained glass that had been painted over?

'I'll take it to the strippers. They put it in an acid tank.'

'You can't do that,' mumbled Alex from inside her nightdress, 'the wood shrinks and all the stained glass falls out. Then who's going to dive for it?'

'That's what the murders-in-the-bath man was doing. The one who dissolved his wives in acid. He was an innocent pioneer of stripped pine technology. Can you reach that brass handle Dear? Careful Dear. Whoops.'

'You'll have to do it by hand,' she said firmly, sniffing her sweater under the armpits and deciding it would do one more day.

'But who cares about the front door? It's a fixation. You should see a psychiatrist. You can't go to sleep at night unless you've closed every door in the house. The children are growing up with phobias because you won't leave their bedroom door open at night. They will vandalize cat flaps and commit unspeakable acts with cuckoo clocks. What is this? Are you afraid the little man who switches the light on in the fridge is going to come and get you in the middle of the night? We must be told Alexandra.'

'That door is the first thing I see when I come into the house. And I come into it more often than you do,' she said, sneaking a pair of his socks without him seeing and putting on her trainers quickly. 'Putting the key into a purple front door colours my whole attitude to life.'

'What's wrong with a purple front door? And what sort of attitude to life will you have with stripped pine and stained glass? Cracks and gouges and white bits in the cracks that you can't get out. All unfinished looking and pseudo-genuine. In my opinion, stripped pine doors are totally bogus.'

'That's just because you can't be bothered to do it,' she said, baring her forehead to the mirror in the masochistic search for grey hairs.

'You want to show the neighbours that we are warm, natural, genuine people with nothing to hide, unafraid of our cracks, knots and blemishes.'

'So. What's wrong with that?' she asked, pulling the brush through her hair, her head on one side.

'Because we are cold and distant towards others and have no interest in anyone's personal life except our own. Personally I am embarrassed enough about my personal defects to conceal them with a thick coat of white paint. Front doors are not meant to be warm and welcoming. They are meant to keep people out.'

She inspected the inside of her gums for anaemia.

'I'll do it myself then.'
'When?'
'Today.'
'By yourself?'
'Yes.'
'How?'
'Paint stripper and a scraper.'
'What about me.'
'You can stay in bed all day for all I care.'
'What about your other jobs.'
'I'll do those as well.'
'I'll help you a bit.'
'You will not.'

'I will.'
'You will not touch that door.'
'I will.'
'You'd better get up then.' And she whipped the duvet off the bed with a triumphant smirk.

Tony stepped back from the front door to admire his work. Holding the brush at arm's length he dabbed like a pointillist painter at the blobs and streaks where the varnish had run. Despite himself he felt pride in the mellow honey colour of the wood and the glow of the stained glass. The door would bear the imprints for ever of his own hands, a witness to his craftsmanship: the gouge marks where he had been heavy handed with the paint scraper; the deep runnel where the screwdriver had slipped as he tussled with the letter flap; the hole that he had drilled too high for the peephole and had to fill up again with filler mixed with antique sawdust scraped laboriously from the underneath of the stripped pine sideboard.

'Darling. It's lovely. You're wonderful.'
'I know.'
'It's a work of art. How did you get that lovely streaky effect?'
'I forgot to stir the varnish.'
'It's beautiful. What are those little bobbles?'
'I dropped the brush on the step. I'll sand it later.'
'No one will ever see. Are those flies?'
'They'll brush off when it's dry.'
'Could I just say one thing?'
'Is it like the rest?'
'Did you mean to put the tulips back the wrong way up?'

He stared at the pane of stained glass as if he could turn it the right way up by the power of his will. But it remained resolutely embedded upside down in its leaded edging. He swore in a low voice, quietly and deliberately.

'Darling nobody will notice it, it just looks like a pattern and in any case if they did it looks like a symbol out of a tarot pack or something like that and you did it all so beautifully it's the nicest door in the whole street and now come and get changed because we're due at Joanna's party in three quarters of an hour. . . .'

He went inside muttering and cursing that he never wanted to see the bloody door ever again, from now on he would go out of the back door and round the side or he would climb in and out of the dining room window and he couldn't care less if having your tulips the wrong way up was bad luck like an upside down horseshoe. There was half a tin of varnish left but he threw it into the rubbish bin with the brush. Never again. He felt soiled and sticky all over. He had varnish in his hair and behind his ears and up his arms to the elbow and down his clothes. The soles of his shoes ripped like velcro on the linoleum floor of the kitchen. Usually when he had been varnishing he let it dry on his skin so he could indulge in the luxury of peeling it off in the bath. As they were going out he had to bathe in white spirit.

He was trying to make up his mind whether to shave when the babysitter arrived. He went down in his bathrobe to open the door, trying not to look at the upside down tulips. It was Hildegaard, the au pair from over the road. She was a small, dark, spherical girl swathed in an Indian tablecloth and carrying a large straw bag, like a refugee from a fire in a curry house.

'Hello Hildegaard.'
'You say?'
'I said HELLO HILDEGAARD.'
'Hello?'
'Mind the door. It's wet.'
'You say?'
'DOOR. WET.'
Puzzled she looked up to the clear sky.
'Wet? Is not raining.'
Clutching his bathrobe with one hand Tony stood on the

doorstep and mimed with extravagant brush strokes the varnishing of the door.

'Ah. Is nice. But why flowers upside down?'

He ushered her inside and explained in loud monosyllables and mime where to find tea and coffee and biscuits. He introduced her to the indifferent children in the living room and left the three of them watching television. Who was looking after whom? He only had time for a quick scrape with the razor round the stubbly bits on his chin and a wipe under the arms with a damp wash glove. When he went into the bedroom Alex was in her underwear bent double over the hair drier trying to achieve the windswept look. An eternity ago he would have slapped her bottom as he walked past to the wardrobe but he wasn't in the mood. She had put on the French panties he had bought her in a fit of optimism for Christmas. She was wearing purple tights over them which spoilt the effect. It was his own fault. He had chickened out of buying a suspender belt and stockings. He still felt resentful.

'Should you be wearing tights over those?'

She stood up and flounced her hair back, her face bright red.

'Where do you expect me to wear them? Round my neck?'

'You're supposed to wear old fashioned stockings not tights.'

'Respectable married women don't have time for that sort of thing.'

His mother had been a respectable married woman. She wore suspender belts. He remembered the silky feel of the stockings, the hard little nuggets of the suspender buttons, the wrinkly bits of elastic as he pushed his trembling fingers into the dark and warm and musty intimacy of the back of the airing cupboard.

The entire contents of Alex's wardrobe were heaped on the bed and the floor. Every drawer in the chest was half open, spilling its ransacked contents. They had not been worn for years. One or two mistakes had never been worn at all. They were there to give the illusion of choice. It was a foregone conclusion that she would wear the same velvet skirt and grey silk shirt that she had worn to every party for the past eighteen months. Trying on everything else first gave some kind of reassurance.

'What are you going to wear?' he asked innocently.

'I thought I'd wear my velvet skirt and the grey silk shirt. What do you think?'

'What a brilliant idea. What shall I wear?'

Again a rhetorical question. Brown cord trousers, brown cord jacket, brown suede boots, beige needlecord shirt. A green woollen tie that could be kept on or taken off when he got there depending how formal it was. When he moved from production to personnel he had adopted a warm and tactile image. I am a soft and cuddly person. He wore this outfit to work when they did sensitivity training.

'How do I look?' She stood in her stockinged feet with her hands by her sides. Same old skirt. Same old shirt. Same old windswept hair. Same old make-up. Pleading for flattery. He tried to look at her as if he had never seen her before.

'You look wonderful. Am I all right?' She ran her hand over his shoulder, smoothing out the hanger marks. He waited for her white lie. Instead she sniffed his collar.

'What's that smell?'

'My new aftershave.'

'Smells odd.'

'It's called *Je Ne Regrette Rien*.'

'Smells like white spirit to me.'

2

Joanna was Alex's best friend. They had met over the weighing scales with their first children. She was a tall, blonde girl with ringlets and a figure that was impressive even in a roomful of lactating mothers. While they waited to see the paediatrician they agreed to talk to each other about anything but childbirth, breastfeeding and Spock. Alex was flattered that Joanna talked to her. Her clothes were expensive. She wore a different pair of shoes every time she came to the clinic. Her nails were always manicured and the colour of the varnish often changed. She had a deep voice and spoke the kind of English that people only speak in American movies. Her third husband, Sam, was an airline pilot. They lived in an executive home on the Park Estate with a double garage and brick patio and through lounge for entertaining.

Sam opened the door. He was a short, muscly man with hairy arms. Tonight he wore a bright red Liberty print shirt and black trousers under a dark blue apron and brandished a barbecue fork. There was a charcoal smudge on top of his bald head. He looked like a demon at the gates of hell.

'Alex. Tony. Fantastic. Come in. Fantastic.' His friends called him Sam Fantastic.

'Sam, where did you get that shirt?'

'The sixties. Golden age. This shirt has flower power. Come in. Fantastic.'

Tony handed over the bottle of wine like an entrance fee. Sam held it up to admire it, although it was still wrapped in tissue paper. Fantastic. He closed the door and prodded them down the hall to the lounge. Alex carried on to the kitchen to deposit her donation, a lemon cheesecake. Tony took a deep breath, remembering tips for dealing with crowds from his sensitivity training but the lounge was empty. Everyone was crowded elbow to elbow on the patio. Sam dived into the huddled flesh with his fork leaving Tony to help himself to a large gin and tonic at the cocktail bar in the corner by the glass sliding doors. It was decorated with masks and shrunken heads from souvenir shops in airline hotels in exotic places. They looked like guests who had never made it home. Tony nodded to a diminutive Papuan. Cheers. First of the day.

He would happily have stayed alone on the rattan bar stool for the rest of the evening, making friends with the natives. Alex could look after herself. She would be helping in the kitchen and serving drinks and generally playing the role of hostess's best friend. He knew that sooner or later he would have to take a deep breath and join the others. He would stuff himself on little bits of celery with cheese spread and sticks of carrot dripping with runny pink stuff that would get on his shoes. He would look round in desperate hope of seeing someone he knew from the other world outside, although he knew they would behave like strangers, the men in funny shirts and the woman caked in make-up. They talked differently from the way they talked in the kitchen or the supermarket or the playground, as if it was all fresh and new, this everlasting saga of the traffic into town and last year's vacation and the new head teacher. They would marinade in the smell of tobacco and dry roast peanuts, duty-free perfume and sizzling meat. Sam Fantastic would be in the middle of it, chortling and stoking the flames with his fork. The smoke and hubbub would rise to the sodium skies and the twinkling lights of stacking 747s. Marooned on the other side of the crowd from the cocktail bar he would look up to heaven like the rich man in the middle of his torment and plead for a drink.

'What are you doing here?'

'Wishing my life away.'

'I wish you'd pour me a Bacardi and tonic.'

She was wearing a long white cotton dress full of little holes like lace, suspended from the shoulders and showing lots of freckled cleavage. Her careful coiffure was beginning to unravel around her ears and her eyes were moist and shining. She used make-up all the way down her neck. She was obviously in those first blissful moments of intoxication before befuddlement and depression set in, that taste of paradise when the world and oneself are together and it is great to be alive. It usually lasts about a minute and a half. He poured them both a drink.

'What do you do?'

'I'm in Edible Fats.'

'How scrumptious.'

'What about you?'

'I'm in fashion.'

'Are you a friend of Sam and Joanna's?'

'I'm Sam's first wife. He married Joanna for her through lounge. It's the only place he can entertain all his children at the same time.'

She wriggled on to the bar stool and leaned a practised elbow on the counter. She swigged her Bacardi leaving a perfect red kiss on the glass. Tony looked up at his Papuan friend for help. The tiny head snickered silently.

'Interesting collection of heads.'

'Heads aren't the only things Sam collects,' she said knowingly.

'Tails as well?' asked Tony.

She threw her head back and bared her teeth and laughed. She looked like the Hawaiian with the plaited straw hair behind the cocktail shaker. When she rocked forward again her hand landed on Tony's forearm. He was unsure whether this was a gesture of intimacy or to stop herself falling over.

'You're a very attractive man,' she said.

This was the moment to put his other hand on top of hers. To return her compliment. To lean over and nibble behind her ear, tasting acrid hairspray. To plant a little kiss on the nascent wrinkles of her throat or the spreading brown blemish on her nearest breast. To taste lipstick and tonic and celery dip on her luscious mouth. To memorize her phone number. Over her shoulder he saw Alex coming in, being sparkling to a florid man in a light grey suit and brown suede shoes.

'Cathy, have you met Alex,' said Tony.

Cathy held out an unsteady hand to the man in the grey suit.

'Sorry. Alex is my wife. Short for Alexandra,' he said apologetically.

'I'm only called Alexandra when someone's cross with me.'

'And I'm called Antonia when someone's nice to me,' said Tony with practised timing, rehearsed at parties since they first got married. The man in the grey suit guffawed.

'This is Gordon,' said Alex, 'he's a bank manager.'

Gordon guffawed again and the others tried to get the joke. His silver grey hair was swept back over his bald spot into a hint of a ducktail and tinted black at the temples. His dark moustache was trimmed thin across his top lip. He had Rotarian badges in his lapel and his shirt cuffs and his tie. Cathy leaned precariously over and laid her manicured fingers deftly on his shoulder.

'I've got the little dress shop in the village. We must have a chat. Deposits. Withdrawals. That sort of thing.'

Gordon put on his bank manager's face. Money was men's talk. Much too serious for flirtatious party chit-chat.

'Ah, the dress shop. My wife would know about that. My love, do you know the dress shop in the village?'

His wife's freckled face blended in with her mousy hair so it was difficult to see where one ended and the other began. She looked constantly dappled in shadow. She was wearing a little white cotton blouse over her little blue skirt and her little white sandals with the little gold buckles. She must have forgotten her rings. She twisted her middle finger where they should have been. She joined Cathy and Alex in an earnest discussion about the effect on fabric prices of China's new economic policy while Gordon and Tony sidled away into the shadows by the bookcase full of Sam's golf trophies.

'I don't believe in working women, Tony. My wife hasn't worked a day in her life. She looks after the home and the boys. You know how we could solve our unemployment problem overnight?' He tapped Tony on the breastbone. 'By making it illegal for married women to go out to work. There are plenty of people in the bank who think the same way.' He smacked his lips over his scotch and soda.

'Who would make the coffee, type the letters that sort of thing?' asked Tony.

'We'd have to make the odd exception for women's work,' said Gordon.

'Great idea, great idea,' said Tony, desperately eyeing escape routes. 'I suppose we should send the blacks back where they came from as well.'

Gordon's eyes narrowed under his bushy eyebrows. He looked over one shoulder then the other. The three women were immersed in talk and there was no one else in the room. He put his arm round Tony's waist and squeezed. Tony choked on his gin and tonic. No one had done that to him since his music master at school found him alone in the locker room. Dropping his arm Gordon whispered in his ear.

'I think we have a lot in common. Antonia.'

The temptation flashed before his eyes. Home improvement loan. Extended repayments. Gold Card. Favourable rates. No. He couldn't sell his body. Sam came in from the patio, red faced from the fire, brandishing his fork.

'Fantastic. Having a good time everybody? You look very dapper tonight Gordon.'

'He's in the mood for love,' said Tony.

'Fantastic. Where's Joanna? We need the plates.'

'I'll help,' said Tony, tearing himself away from his new friends.

'No,' slurred Cathy, 'you stay and look after me,' and she buried her upper lip in ice cubes.

Alex went to look for plates. As she crossed the hall the doorbell chimed *Plaisir D'Amour*. She opened it to a tall thin man with a black leather jacket and bright red scarf.

'Hello. I'm Derek,' he said as if it was the news they had all been waiting for. He gave her an I-am-a-dangerous-person smile, flicked his long black hair back over his ear with his right hand and kissed her on the corner of the mouth, pressing a bottle of wine into the small of her back. He kept his arm round her shoulders as Sam came out of the living room.

'Derek. Fantastic. You've met Alex.'

'I certainly have. Sam, you have wonderful taste in wives.'

'I'm not his wife,' said Alex twisting out from Derek's embrace and baring her teeth in a smile.

'Sam you have wonderful taste in other people's wives.'

'They make up for his friends,' said Alex, leaving in search of plates.

She was next to Derek in the queue for food. There was a shiny red Lenin badge in the lapel of his leather jacket. But his scarf was signed Yves Saint Laurent, his white shirt was peppered with crocodiles, his belt buckle said Levi. She dropped her plastic fork so she could bend down to see who his socks belonged to but they were hidden by the tops of his Hush Puppy boots. They bared their teeth at each other.

'Did you find any of Sam's wives?' she asked.

'A couple. Do you have any husbands here?'

'Just one. The only one I've ever had actually.'

'How unusual. You must be the token monogamist. All the other guests have been divorced at least once. Bourgeois social structures have broken down. Alimony prevents capital accumulation. Children's loyalty is to the state. It's a pre-revolutionary situation.' He tossed his head and flicked his hair behind his right ear.

'What about you?'

'I exploit the anarchy. I'm a bachelor gay.' He asked the question housewives dread. 'What do you do?'

'I'm setting up my own business,' she lied.

'An entrepreneuse. Don't tell me. Picture framing? Party catering? Interior design?'

'Guess again,' she said, playing for time.

'Cuddly toys? Fancy sweaters? Macramé pot hangers?'

'Guess again.'

'Let me think. Ornamental cherry tomatoes for the Christmas trade? Worms for organic gardeners?'

'All wrong. I'm importing medical equipment from Scandinavia. Would you like to test our anal thermometer?' She held up a salad fork in front of his face. Then she plunged it into a bowl of rice and raisins. 'What do you do?'

'I'm a college lecturer,' he said, tossing his head and flicking his hair back.

'Let me guess this time. Sociology?'

'Guess again.'

'I give up. Sociology is my best guess.'

'Accounting.'

'You're an accountant? She failed to keep the surprise out of her voice.

'Why not. It's the liberation theology of the post capitalist era.'

'What the hell does that mean?'

'Enrol on our small business course and find out.'

Both Tony and Alex went round to the passenger door. They went through the 'You're-driving-no-you-are-no-you-are' routine before they agreed that it was more inconvenient for her to lose her licence than for him. He had several stabs at the lock and once inside had to be reminded where the ignition was. Someone had moved his seat belt while they were in the house and he searched all over the floor for it before Alex pointed it out behind his ear. Bloody silly place to put it. He took several deep breaths and forced his eyes to focus before putting the car into first gear.

'Nice evening.'

'Nice evening.'

Instead of unravelling the usual string of warnings and advice about his distance from the kerb Alex was unusually thoughtful. She stroked his left thigh. He wished he hadn't had so much to drink. It always took so long when he was drunk, if he didn't fall asleep first.

'You got on well with that Cathy woman,' she said.

'I was holding her up, that's all.'

'She needed holding in as well. I wonder if all the dresses she sells are like that.'

He moved his leg so that she could stroke a bit higher. So she was jealous was she? That's why she was so amorous. It would do no harm to fan the flames a little more.

'She's an attractive woman.'

'She's available. I'm not sure about the attractive. I wouldn't go near her breath with a naked flame either.'

'If you must know, the best offer I had all night was from the bank manager. The Gay Gordon.'

'He's invited you to a Rotary meeting?'

'Sort of.' He told her about Gordon squeezing his waist and whispering sweet nothings in his ear.

'He's married. He's got two children,' she said indignantly.

'Everyone's got to have a hobby.'

He wished he had never mentioned it. It put Cathy out of her mind. She stopped stroking his thigh. He started to stroke hers but he might as well have fondled the handbrake. He concentrated on driving and then on walking in a straight line up the drive. Proud of his successful navigation he stared at the front door. He held on to the door knocker for support and began a methodical search for upside down tulips while Alex rummaged in her handbag.

'Have you got a key?' she whispered.

'No.'

'You drove home.'

'I took the doorkey off the ring when I took it in to be serviced.'

'I've left mine in my other bag.'

'Ah. Well there you are,' he slurred. 'Ring the bell.'

'It will wake the children.'

'Then we'll have to stay out here all night.'

Alex yielded to inescapable logic and gave a short sharp push on the bell. Then another. Then a long one. They heard it ring but no one answered.

'What's happened?'

'Hildegaaaard has gone to shleeeep.'

'Knock.'

Tony rapped on the door with his knuckles.

'She won't hear that. With the knocker.'

'But I'm holding on to that.'

She pushed him roughly out of the way and banged the knocker and rang the bell at the same time. Still there was no sign of life. Tony backed down the path and stared up at the bedroom windows. Alex began to panic.

'Something's happened,' she whispered, 'do something.'

'I'll look round the back.'

'Hurry.'

There was an alleyway down the side of the house closed with a six-foot gate. He stood in front of it and looked for a foothold. He found the brick that propped the gate open when he was putting out the rubbish and stood it on end. Teetering on it he reached up to the top of the gate, took a deep breath, scrabbled with his feet and managed to hitch himself up. The wood bit into his abdomen.

'Don't just stand there,' he hissed, grimacing in pain and legs waving in the air.

Alex tried the latch and the door swung open. Tony saw the wall of the house coming fast towards him. He put up his hands to protect his head and fell backwards into the garbage cans.

'Shhh. You'll wake the whole neighbourhood.'

'I thought that's what you wanted,' he moaned, rubbing his stomach and his bottom.

They hammered at the bolted kitchen door and rapped on the downstairs windows, all barred and screwed down.

'They've been gassed.'

'We're all electric.'

They ran round to the front and rang the bell again.

'Get the police.'

'Don't be silly.'

There was nothing else for it. Tony retreated half way down the path, put his shoulder down and charged. With the sound of splintered wood and falling glass the front door burst open. Tony staggered into the arms of the astonished Hildegaard emerging from the sitting room rubbing her eyes.

'Did you ring bell?' she asked.

Alex jammed the hall table up against the door and taped newspaper over the broken panes. Upstairs she helped Tony off with his socks and trousers. He was incapacitated by drink and heavy bruising on the shoulder and the coccyx and the stomach. She rubbed him with liniment and squirted him with analgesic spray. Choking on the fumes she undressed and lay beside him, fighting to keep awake. In recognition of her wifely concern he gave her chest a half-hearted grope before they both lapsed thankfully into a chaste and dreamless sleep.

Tony spent the next day repairing the damage. He replaced the splintered jamb with a new piece of pine and then fitted a new lock. He glued the splinters and stuck together the shards of stained glass. Then he set about disguising the effects of his handiwork. He always botched the basic task but long practice had made him an expert at covering his tracks with touching up and filling in. The first step was to set about the new doorjamb with light tan shoe polish and a pinch of ash from the marble fireplace.

The devil may find work for idle hands but he doesn't forget the busy ones either. There was nothing like boring manual work to encourage erotic daydreams. As he beavered away on the front door he directed his impure thoughts dutifully to his wife first and then to the lanky blonde receptionist in Edible Fats Industrial Marketing and then to a sweet little auburn-haired graduate trainee on his last course but none of them would stick. Cathy came elbowing in on the scene every time. She tiptoed through the stained glass tulips in her lacy cotton dress. It slipped from her shoulders and showed her white, quivering upper arms, the pasty flesh hanging like dewlaps. Through the peephole she fluttered long eyelashes peeling away at the corners. Mascara ran from the corner of her moist eyes like wood glue trickling down the doorjamb. Large brown liverspots swelled on her freckled bosom as he treated weeping knotholes. Her kisses planted on his inflamed flesh left a permanent imprint like the bruises of his misdirected hammer blows. She sashayed across the threshold and pressed her trembling body against his and when he pushed her away thrust her fibrillating tongue through the letter flap. When he reached for his hammer his hands closed round her thigh. Do you want a screw? she whispered, holding out the box to him. She picked one out and then a bigger and a bigger until the last, a foot long, she ran up and down herself like a vibrator.

He still had her telephone number scrawled in lipstick on a crumpled paper napkin. If you want a dress for your wife's birthday give me a call, she slurred. Letting her give it to him was the only way he could escape her. The napkin was still in the inside pocket of his cord suit. Since he had taken it in innocence he hadn't bothered to throw it away, to destroy the evidence. Evidence of what? Absolutely nothing. Then why did he cross to the other side of the street when he went by her dress shop? It would serve Alex right. She took him for granted. They hardly spoke to each other. Was this what it was going to be like for the next thirty years? One day she would come back and find a note on the table propped against the tea-pot. *Dear Alexandra. Don't expect me back this evening. Or any evening. Give my love to the children. Tony.* On second thoughts a note was a bad idea. It would only get swept away and dumped on the dresser when the table was cleared for supper along with the notes from school about the end of term concert and Louise's drawing of a mammoth being sick and the card from the window-cleaner. It could be lost for days.

'Here's that licence reminder I was looking for.'

'So that's why Aunt Ethel jumped off the bridge. She did leave a note.'

'Your swimming certificate didn't get thrown away after all.'

'Look. A note from Daddy. I wondered why we hadn't seen him.'

Running away was not the answer. But they had to put some life back in their relationship. What if she thought she had some competition. If he thought Alex was having an affair he would walk out or kill her or something. Women saw if differently. They saw it as a challenge. Everyone knew that. Look how interested she was in what he was up to at Sam and Joanna's party. It was a mistake to tell her about Gordon and what he really thought about Cathy. He should have said what a great little body she had and how she understood him. He rubbed Cathy's face away with the sanding block. If he was going to have a girlfriend she would be sexy and young and sexy and pretty and lively and sexy and interesting and funny and sexy.

He stood back from the door, held it wide open and gave it a push. It creaked on its hinges and grated against the doorjamb. There was more daylight showing round the edges than before but nothing some draughtproofing strip wouldn't cure.

But was it worth it? Little triumphs and deceptions. Phones that click off when the wrong spouse answers.

Afternoons off work, business trips, working late. Conferences in Paris and Brighton. Letters that should have been burned. Napkins searched for in panic. Revelations, discoveries, confessions, sitting on the side of the bed looking at the wall. What about the children? Of all the people he knew who had gone through that none could recommend it and few made themselves any happier. Most of them ended up with lovers who looked and behaved like the spouse they were deceiving. Then why did they all do it? Perhaps if he found the right sexy and young and sexy and pretty and lively and sexy and interesting and funny and sexy person he would find out.

Willoughby, the Crime Prevention Officer, was a big handed, big footed man whose big head hung in a permanent stoop in fear of low lintels. He looked critically at the front door.

'I would screw up that window over the door if I was you,' he advised. He had already advised them to screw all the window frames permanently closed, put a padlock on the trap door into the coal cellar, a bar across the bathroom window. Alex followed him round trying to stifle acute sensations of vulnerability and guilt. Sergeant Willoughby ran his hand up and down the new doorjamb, held it and pulled. There were cracking sounds and fresh filler crumbled on to the doormat.

'Somebody had a go at this?'

'I've just had it repaired,' said Tony.

'You didn't tell me you were already broken into.'

'I did it. It was an emergency.'

'Well you ought to fetch back whoever did this repair and have them do it again if I was you,' he grumbled. 'This wouldn't stand my old grandmother leaning up against it, know what I mean?'

Tony glared at Alex but she remained loyally silent. Willoughby looked accusingly at the doorjamb and then down at his fingers. They were covered in light tan shoe polish and traces of ash. He sniffed his fingers and frowned, trying to place the familiar smell. He took out a grimy handkerchief and reflectively wiped the forensic evidence off his hands.

'And these bolt-on locks are no good either. All you've got between you and the villains is four little wood screws. You want a deadlock that goes right through the doorjamb into the brickwork and even that won't hold a really good kick. What you want is what we call in the business a three point purchase. A simple bolt top and bottom, know what I mean?'

'How do you get out then?'

'There's your problem. You're at your most vulnerable when you aren't here. Ninety per cent of your villains come through the front door, same as you and me and your missus. There you are.'

'Thank you very much, Sergeant, you've been very helpful.'

'Yes well there isn't anything you haven't been telling me about is there? Lots of people don't like to tell us you know for some reason. Silver, stamp collections, valuables you keep in a safe or under the floorboards, know what I mean?'

'Sorry. No hidden secrets in this house. What you see is what they get.'

He looked disappointed.

'Ah well. Don't forget your front door. That's how your unwelcome visitors will come in. Know what I mean?'

'Thanks Sergeant. I know what you mean.'

3

'Where are you going?' he asked in mock surprise.

'College,' said Alex as carelessly as she could, damping down the excitement in her voice.

After she came out of the bath she plastered her wet hair down over her head, willing it to her shoulders and brushing out its natural curls. She applied the contents of a new make-up kit in as close an imitation of last month's *Cosmopolitan* cover as she dared. She sprinted up and down stairs from the bedroom to the drier with clothes she had spent all yesterday afternoon trying on in front of the mirror. She had finally selected a tweed jacket she had worn before they were married, dark blue baggy trousers from the London Road Surplus Stores, a white shirt, open at the neck, a college tie with a loose knot where her cleavage used to be before she had children, a dark green velvet waistcoat with pearl buttons from the children's dressing-up box, meticulously defluffed with adhesive tape, short black boots with pointed toes and slender heels. Over it all she slung a heavy dark black overcoat that she had been promising to take back to her father since they came back from Auntie Doris's funeral last November.

'Is it an audition?' he asked innocently.

'No wonder you're in personnel. Tact. Charm. Encouragement. You're wonderful for a woman's confidence.'

Tony's mother had foolishly bought him the tie when he

got a conditional place at university to study microbiology. When he failed to get good enough grades to take it up he put it in the back of the wardrobe. He sometimes came across it when he was having a clear-out but did not throw it away, although he had long given up the ambition to take the exams again and wave the distinctions in their face. Was this what he had been saving it for?

'What do you need your father's winter overcoat for? It's May.'

'So what? It's as cold as November.'

'It's because your bottom sticks out of the back of that old sports coat isn't it?'

'What I wear is my business.'

'Not when they're other people's clothes.'

(This is what he really wanted to say: Ahem. Seeing you wear that tie has brought back many memories of my hopes and ambitions and disappointments. I was on top of the world when my mother bought me that tie and on the bottom of it when I threw it in the back of the wardrobe. I have kept it in the slender hope that I can recapture one day some of that feeling. I don't mind you wearing it but please give me a hug to soothe away the pain. New paragraph.

Ahem. I can understand how nervous you must be feeling about going to college for the first time with people who are fifteen years younger than you are and unmarried and exuberantly youthful. I wish I could help, by saying how marvellous you look, but I am afraid it's something you have to cope with yourself. If I think you look a bit odd in those clothes it's only because I'm not used to seeing you in them. New paragraph.

Ahem. I admit that I am envious of your being able to make a fresh start on something new and ambitious while I am stuck in my same old dead-end job. But I can easily suppress the envy, like my mother did when she gave me that tie, as long as I can share just a little bit in it. New paragraph.

Ahem. Good luck and don't forget me and let me give you a big hug. You look great.)

'Who's taking the kids to school?'
'Louise's already gone. She went with Alice!'

'She didn't say goodbye to me.'

'Mark. Are you ready for school?' she yelled out of the kitchen door. Mark came in, his Mr T satchel slung over his shoulder. The front of his head was neatly combed, the back a bird's nest. The cuffs of his grey sweater, chewed into holes, hung down over his wrists. String hung from the pocket of his baggy trousers. His shoes, originally black, were scuff grey.

'Dinner money. Brick money. Stamp money. Chip club money. Here. Did you clean your teeth? Go and wash the marmalade off your cheek. And your tie.' She straightened it and tightened the knot to where the top shirt button would have been if she had remembered to sew it on last night. He reached up and did the same to hers.

'Thank you dear. Say goodbye to your father. He wants to be loved.'

Tony stood up and gave him a peck on the cheek, avoiding the marmalade. He walked over to Alex who was rummaging in her bag for car keys and loosened the tie so the knot was half way down her chest again. She ignored him. He shrugged his shoulders and took his mug and toast plate over to the sink and rinsed them under the tap.

'I'll load the dishwasher before I go, so it won't be a mess when you get back. I hope it all goes well today. Actually that outfit looks all right. There are plenty of girls dressed like that at the office. You look just great.'

But when he turned round she was not there. He heard the front door slam. Of all the bloody nerve, walking off like that, without even a goodbye. He walked quickly out into the hall but hesitated with his hand on the latch. He couldn't make up his mind whether to shout 'Good Luck' or 'Bugger off then.' He peered through the peephole. She was at the gate and looked very far away through the fisheye lens.

Alex flogged the engine into life and accelerated down the street in first gear so the engine screamed. The car compass glued to the windscreen gyrated wildly as she turned into the main road. Bloody Men. She had heard him start to wish her luck as she left the kitchen but she wasn't going to give him the satisfaction of knowing she had heard him. Too late boyo. And he didn't even have the decency to come to the front door she had slammed behind her. All right. If that's the way he wants it, that's the way he gets it.

At the junction with the London Road she gunned the car away from the lights in second gear, causing a packet of tissues, a nibbled chocolate biscuit, two felt tip pens, the top of a yoghurt pot and a can of fly spray to cascade out of the glove compartment on to the rest of the debris on the floor. Stuck at the beginning of a bus lane she leaned over and picked up the biscuit. She had not had time for breakfast and bit into it hard. She eyed the rest of the rubbish on the floor but there was nothing else to eat. No doubt if she had cared to rummage in the cracks and crevices of the back seat she would have found among the sticky chocolate papers, banana skins, chewing gum wrappers enough half-eaten apples, sandwich crusts, sucked licorice sticks and crumbled biscuits to make a filling meal but she wasn't that desperate and in any case the seat belt stopped her turning round.

It was her first day on the small business course. She had left early so she would not be rushed but she could not find a parking space outside the college. She had to use a multi-storey half a mile away and arrived hot and out of breath, wishing she could take off her velvet waistcoat. The college occupied a fifteen storey purpose-built tower-block that looked as if it should have housed one of the less favoured government departments. She stood confused in front of the board showing what rooms the classes were held in.

'Hey Miss,' asked a spotty youth in jeans who did not look much older than Mark 'where's the toilets?'

'Sorry. It's my first day too,' she replied, trying not to sound maternal and sounding crusty instead.

'Oi Miss. Where are the lifts to the basement?' This time it was a girl with a shock of pink hair and white make-up that successfully eliminated all facial features except eye sockets and nostrils.

When Alex found her classroom on the tenth floor she was the last to arrive. It was furnished with tubular steel tables with plywood tops and matching chairs. Derek was already speaking at one end in front of a large blackboard, pristine for the new term. He wore his red scarf and leather jacket with the Lenin badge over bright green jeans and jodhpur boots. He stopped when she came in and the whole class looked round at her. In one nervous glance she took in bleached hair, shaven skulls, black T-shirts, a tattooed shoulder. Derek tossed his head and flicked his hair back.

'OK Gang. We've got a touch of class. Middle class,' said Derek looking at the rest of the class for laughter which they obediently supplied in ragged titters. Alex sat down at the back and glowered at him, hoping he would interpret the colour in her cheeks as anger. Most of the thirty or so students were recognizably male, a few female and the rest indeterminate. They were about eighteen or nineteen years old, conventionally clad in baggy clothes and T-shirts and mops of coloured hair sprouting from otherwise shaven skulls. If Tony thought she was grotesque in her present outfit wait until she came downstairs dressed to blend in with this lot.

'. . . want you to pay attention to this course because whatever you end up doing you're going to find it very, very important. You'll learn how the bosses pickpocket the purses of the working class without them even knowing it. Know your enemy. Accountants are the enemy's storm troops. Unless we understand the tools of exploitation we can't break them, we can't turn them to our own advantage. Suspense accounts, trial balances, T accounts. That's how *they* understand reality, that's how *they* enforce the class system. . . .'

He went on like this for about half an hour. Then he wrote on the blackboard the name of a textbook.

'. . . I know it's expensive. You'll find secondhand copies

if you're lucky in the students' union shop or they may have some in the library if they haven't all been nicked. Don't give up hope. The system can't keep knowledge from us. If you really have a problem come to me and I may be able to dig something up. . . .'

Alex covered her brand new copy with her notebook. At the end of the lecture the other students rushed for the door leaving her alone with Derek.

'When do we get round to book-keeping?' she asked.

'Instead of the real world? I wondered when you were going to ask that. Everything is political. Accounting is pure dialectic. Double entry. Thesis and Antithesis. It's all based on exploitation. We all exploit each other. But you wouldn't see that.' He shoved the class rosta in his Moscow Olympics Tote bag. 'How about a cup of coffee? We can talk some more. I'll take you into the staff common room.'

'What about the class war? Don't you hobnob with the proletariat?'

'To each according to his needs. I need real coffee.' He gave her a toothy smile.

Tony dawdled across the playing fields with his jacket slung over his shoulder. From a distance the children sounded like a flock of starlings gathered for migration. Their twittering drowned every other sound. Other parents trooped across the damp grass dragging camping chairs and baskets and toddlers and blankets and umbrellas. A thunderstorm hung muttering in the sky behind a grey canopy of clouds ready to drop on them all like a fire blanket. The children sat on one side of the track in neat rows with their legs crossed. The head teacher fiddled with a large stop watch, trying to make sense of the buttons. He strutted in grey flannels and a blazer with a large crest and a stripy tie like the Olympic officials on television. Fathers eyed each other and wondered who was unemployed and who had taken the afternoon off. Children too young to go to school rampaged between their legs. Babies and toddlers slept or cried or made a game of running on to the track with nappies round their knees to be scooped up and brought back wriggling. Earnest ladies circulated in the crowd looking for black people to be nice to. Tony wandered to the parents' side and peered over the front rows to see Mark. His first duty was to catch his eye to show him he was there. As soon as he waved back Tony could devote himself to sizing up the bums in the jump suits the young mothers were wearing. They hung like luscious, ripe fruit, from plums to watermelons, each a temptation to cupped and greedy hands. He felt fingers grasp his arm above the elbow. It was Joanna.

'Hello Tony. Where's Alex?' she asked.

'College.'

'Ah,' she said knowingly. 'Sam's in Dubai.'

She was dressed in a white jump suit unzipped almost to the waist and a long pink scarf and red shoes whose heels sank into the grass so she walked as if she had something wrong with her knees. She carried a red camping chair and a large designer bag. There were tiny beads of perspiration on her top lip. He unslung his jacket from his shoulder and folded his arms to hide the damp patches under his armpits.

'I loathed sports day when I was a kid,' he said. 'Even today when I see whitewash on the grass it makes me feel ill. I'm not the competitive type.'

'I like a bit of sport in the afternoon,' said Joanna.

Class One egg and spoon was announced. Four boys and four girls lined up, fidgeting and looking forlorn. One boy stared at his feet. Another waved sheepishly at the parents. A girl with long brown hair to her waist, shampooed and conditioned and carefully dried the night before, stood with her hand on her hip brimming with confidence. They were given their wooden eggs and wooden spoons, put under starter's orders, and were off. The twittering from the children's side rose in a crescendo matched by the screaming and baying of the grown-ups.

*

'Carn Alex!' 'Run Livvy!'
'Pick it up Damian!' 'Way to go Ben!'
'Wrong way Jamesie!' 'Don't drop it Dommo!'
'Nairmind Anna!' 'Go Marty go!'

The children ran the howling gauntlet stooped over their spoons, running from the knees down like little Groucho Marxes. Livvy was disqualified for holding her egg on with her thumb. Ben dropped his egg three times in a row and burst into tears before fleeing from the mob. Alex ran diagonally across the track, barging his competitors and was swallowed up by the crowd. Anna, her dark hair flowing behind her like Atalanta, swanned gracefully to the tape without once dropping or stumbling, pursued by little Damian, his face screwed up in determination. It was chilling how you could tell their futures from the age of five. The successes and failures and comedians and the accident prone, the plodders and triers and the indifferent. And there were those who malingered or were ill and refused to be part of the crowd.

'Training for life. I can't stand this, Joanna. I'll buy you a cup of tea.' Tony fetched two polystyrene cups of milky tea.

'There's Pam. She's just moved in with Jack Truelove. Do you know the Trueloves? She's talking with poor Nancy. Her husband left her before Christmas. Cathy's over there with Humphrey. She'll eat him alive. Still, it serves him right. . . .'

Tony let her gossip flow past his ears. Her information was like gale warnings in Rockall and Shannon and Finisterre, exotic happenings of great interest and danger to those concerned but irrelevant to him. He had no desire to take part in their games of musical beds. The pain was out of proportion to the small amount of pleasure. But why was Joanna telling him all this? She was standing close to him, one hand on the arm that was carrying his jacket. He could smell perfume, heavy in the sultry air. Was this how gossip started? It wouldn't be hard. She could leave first to avoid suspicion. Then he would look at his watch, wave good-bye to Mark, and saunter back to the car. What a simply ridiculous notion. Fancy messing up the whole of your life because you had nothing better to do on a hot afternoon.

'I think it's Mark's race. That's him, isn't it?'

'I suppose I'd better watch. That's what I've come for after all.'

He left Joanna and pressed his way to the front of the crowd. He waved to make sure Mark saw him and was rewarded with a watery smile. Thank goodness it was just ordinary running – no eggs or bean bags or pyjamas or buckets of water to perform with. Mark looked small and vulnerable out there with his hair sticking up at the back and his spindly legs and bulging knees. Don't worry son. The yapping and roaring began. Mark ran towards him, his thin arms pumping back and forwards. Tony couldn't help himself. Something took over his lungs and his larynx and his tongue. He could resist his instinct and the rest of the crowd no longer. 'Carn Mark' he yelled at the top of his voice, knowing full well that his cries were lost in the din round him. He was behaving just like everyone else.

Brooding on infidelity Tony admired himself in the mirror on the back of the bedroom door. To show that underneath the pinstripe suit and white shirt he was really lovable and furry and tactile he wore a pink woolly loose knit tie. He left other little clues that inside the uniform there was a real human being. He teased the curls at the back of his head over his collar. He put a pink silk handkerchief in his breast pocket, tucked down almost out of sight. I AM REALLY AN INTERESTING PERSON announced his gestures in a still, small voice.

One train was cancelled, two others were delayed. Drizzle damped the scent of after shave and toilet water and hair spray that hovered over the press of commuters. Tonight it would be damp polyester and sweat and tobacco. When the train at last arrived Tony was caught in the rush for the doors. He wanted to hang back from the humiliating scrum. Why were they all so desperate to get to work? On the train his arms were pressed to his sides so he couldn't read his paper. He felt the perspiration building up in his armpits, challenging his deodorant. The bespectacled man on his left was also in a dark pinstripe suit and white shirt. He had a sober maroon tie but in his breast pocket was a flamboyant gypsy red handkerchief. A younger man on the other side had a dark grey suit, red striped shirt and white collar. His tie was covered in kangaroos that he stopped from escaping with a tie chain made from tiny shark's teeth. A solemn lady in front of him, shielding her breasts from casual encounter by holding a civil servant's crested briefcase over them, wore a white blouse and black jacket. Around her neck on a gold chain were a star of David and a crucifix and the Hand of Fatima. I AM REALLY AN INTERESTING PERSON they all said in still, small voices. He smiled at the solemn lady but her ecumenism did not embrace strange men on trains.

At the terminus they were disgorged. On the same cue umbrellas sprouted into a black and shiny carapace over the sinuous creature flowing like a brainless worm on the bridge over the Thames. There was a technique for being in the procession. If you were in a hurry you escaped the procession by skipping in and out of the gutter or slipping elver-like through the ranks. Most people marched at the same pace not looking at each other, not touching each other, trying not to walk in step, trying not to make straight ranks that would imply that they were all part of the same mindless army moving under unspoken orders. Most of them did not know that this is how armies do indeed cross bridges, breaking step so their rhythmic tramp does not shake them down. Sometimes, although he tried to think happy thoughts, Tony indulged in the delusion that at the other end of the bridge a black and bottomless pit waited for them and without speaking or crying out or breaking step they all poured into nothingness.

Instead of the pit there were office blocks. The cortège separated, its strands going different ways as if the funeral was over and not just beginning. Edible Fats' headquarters was a monolithic granite block built in the thirties. Niches in the wall had sculptures of horses and pigs and sheaves of wheat and horny handed sons of toil. The company crest was emblazoned in bronze over the studded iron doors. Inside only the directors' and senior managers' suites were preserved in thirties monolithic style. For lesser employees the high ceilinged offices had been divided horizontally into two low ceilinged offices, the windows of the upper ones beginning at floor level. They felt like squatters in the remains of a grander civilization, monkeys in a ruined jungle palace.

Edible Fats' training centre was at the end of the east wing. Tony's office had the luxury of a window overlooking the Embankment. His view was obscured by a granite balcony covered by guano and strips of jelly to discourage pigeons. He had to stand on tiptoe to see the river but he could always see the sky. His secretary, Dot, had already arrived. She was a tall lanky woman with a frizz of blonde hair around her head like an out of focus halo. She dressed in undyed linen and wool clothes that she wove herself. Some mornings she looked as if she had been baled for shipment. She had two children and a husband who was a potter. She fed them on whole foods and home grown vegetables. The top of her desk was covered with sprouting alfalfa and fava beans. The shallow drawers were full of germinating pulses. The deep drawer, lined with polythene, was for mushrooms. Filing cabinets and cupboards were nurseries of vegetables. She collected pigeon droppings to fertilize them. Tony had forbidden the dedication of waste paper bins to compost. The buildings maintenance supervisor regularly ordered her to dismantle the miniature allotments, covered in chicken wire, that she established on the balcony.

'Dot,' said Tony early in their relationship, 'do you realize that all round you in this massive fortress men and women dedicate their lives to the synthesis and manufacture and marketing of processed foods. And here you are growing beansprouts in pigeon droppings on your desk.' Whenever a new product was announced, with self-righteous fanfare and time off for tastings and free packets to take home and tell friends about, Dot's reaction would be the same. 'I wouldn't use it for mulch.'

Dot was busy in the audiovisual store pricking out fenugreek. He patted his hair in the reflection of the window, straightened his tie, and forced his face into a how-to-win-friends-and-influence-people expression. Apart from a trial packet of boil-in-the-bag cauliflower cheese there was nothing of interest in the in-tray. He settled down to the crossword in the *Telegraph* that lay on his desk. He had never asked for the *Telegraph*, he didn't know who delivered it or ordered it or paid for it and he never asked. Why rock the boat?

'Morning Dot. Dying for a cup of coffee.'

'Morning Tony. You'll have to get it yourself then.'

Dot's job description described her as secretary. This implied a mutual dependence and cooperation with her boss that she went out of her way to undermine without actually being accused of insubordination. She pointed out on her first day that she did not make tea or coffee or run personal errands. She did not answer his phone unless he was out of the room. She did not take dictation or type from handwritten drafts. He would have to use the dictating machine. By the time she had finished her list of proscribed activities it was clear that she did not seek job satisfaction in the sharing of tasks or accomplishment of mutual goals.

'Dot. Why do you come to work?'

'Money.'

He pretended not to notice when she came back to her desk with a steaming mug of herbal tea. He tried to concentrate on the crossword but infidelity distracted him.

Surely there was someone in the building who was hungry for adventure and passion and excitement. How would he find her? Where did he start? Most of the affairs on the office grapevine were between bosses and secretaries. The contractual subservience of the relationship had the same appeal as traditional marriage. He looked over the top of his paper at Dot and winced. The thought sent a shudder down his spine.

4

Alex woke early as usual. She had never been able to shake off the habits of a childhood spent in a family of newsagents. Early to rise. Catch the worm. Rise and shine. Sort the newspapers. Pencil in the addresses in the top right hand corner before the boys arrive. At least once a week one of them failed to come so she had to hump round the green sack in the dark streets. Early to bed. Even at parties her eyes grew heavy at ten at night. She was twenty-one before she saw the New Year in. Once she had cried on her mother's shoulder.

'There there. Don't worry. There are plenty of boys who get up early too.'

'I don't want to marry a milkman or a greengrocer.'

'How about a nice farmer?'

She promised herself she would marry someone who never went to bed before midnight or got up before eight, someone who came down to find the newspaper on the front door mat, someone who did not turn into a pumpkin before the ten o'clock news. They would see the dawn at the end of the day not the beginning. They would lie in bed together until noon. Instead of having to go to the movies in the afternoon so she stayed awake to see the end they would go to the late shows and come out blinking into neon light instead of daylight. Tony fitted the bill. Although he was a management trainee in a large company he had the biorhythms of a croupier. On her first visit to his bedroom she was astonished by the number of alarm clocks he needed to get up for work. On her third visit, when she let herself in with her own key, she was even more astonished to find him slumbering away in what sounded like a swarm of angry bumble bees. She was wooed surrounded by clocks. For months the words Alarm Set would induce a tingling in the base of her spine. Her sexual awakening was accompanied by the insistent ticking of clockwork and the sensual purring of electric motors. The magic had faded with the silence of quartz.

After two years of marriage she was convinced she had thrown off the habits of childhood. With the maturity of womanhood came the ability to stay awake until after midnight and sleep in until at least eight o'clock. This had not been achieved without a struggle. Their courtship had been marred by unpleasant incidents such as her falling asleep in his arms on the dance floor at Edible Fats' Christmas dance and his oversleeping her parents' silver wedding gala luncheon at the Montego Steakhouse in Dollis Hill. There was a particularly acrimonious exchange of views when she fell asleep while they were making love.

'What do you think I am? A necrophiliac?'

'Next time I'm at the butcher's I'll order you a side of beef.'

'It probably wouldn't move any less.'

'What about this morning? I kissed you all over and it didn't even stop you snoring.'

'I was tired.'

'What the hell do you think I was last night?'

'You just want it when it suits you.'

'I don't want *it*. You always think about it as *it*. It it it.'

For the first couple of years they managed more or less to synchronize their timetables. Then she became pregnant. By the third month she was waking up with the delivery boys again. Wide awake she would put her head under the blankets to shut out the repellent cacophony of the dawn chorus. The only consolation was that she had time to get up, have breakfast, get dressed, be sick and have breakfast again. When her mother told her it was Nature's Way of preparing her for the early morning feed she burst into tears.

'Nature's Way. Nature's Way. You sound like a laxative advertisement.'

Mother was right. She would sit up in bed at five in the morning sipping lukewarm tea with little Mark clapped to a breast and try to feel contented and drowsy while Tony snored beside her. But it was no good. She stayed wide awake all day until nine o'clock in the evening. For years she had worked on sleeping later but she still woke before everyone else and went downstairs feeling like a thief in the night.

'Don't worry, darling,' Tony would say 'there are A People and B People. A People naturally wake early and sleep early. B people wake late and sleep late. We're born like it. There's nothing you can do.'

'But B People are having all the fun.'

A People got to be healthy, wealthy and wise on a diet of fresh worms. They went jogging in the morning. They bounced downstairs with their hair combed and their faces washed to eat cornflakes on the television. They were never late for school and work. They were glowing and successful. And when they went to bed the B People went to jazz clubs and discos and watched late-night movies. They had bags under their eyes but they were happy. Like Tony.

It was still dark when she woke up. She started to stroke Tony's soft, hairy stomach, letting her fingers wander under the waistband of his pyjamas. He grunted, pushed her hand away and rolled over with his back to her. Mentally notching the rebuff on the bedpost she got out of bed and put on the jogging suit she used as a dressing-gown. She crept down to the kitchen. The sink was piled with dirty dishes. The dishwasher had not yet been emptied of yesterday's cleans. The remains of a lemon meringue pie were taking on a life of their own next to the boiler. She put the kettle on and fished a tea bag out of the packet. She put a slice of bread in the toaster. She found Pope John Paul under the pudding bowls in the sink and rinsed him under the tap. She bared her teeth at his paternal smile and stood on tiptoe for her pills which she kept in the top of the dresser. A couple of months ago she would have started to clean up. By the time the others came down she would have finished the kitchen and put the first load of washing in. No more. The early worm had turned. She poured water on her tea bag, smeared butter on her toast, popped the pill in her mouth and reached up again to the top shelf of the dresser where the recipes and washing machine instructions were kept. She took down a severe-looking hardback entitled *INTRODUCTION TO BOOK-KEEPING*, pushed last night's cocoa saucepan and a pile of underwear to the other end of the kitchen table and sat down to read.

Tony slouched in the doorway of the kitchen in his bathrobe, his eyes puffed up with sleep, the Sunday paper under one arm, reflectively scratching his stomach.

'What's for breakfast?'

'Whatever you like.'

'What did the children have?'

'Whatever they liked.'

'You didn't clear up.'

'Very observant.'

'What happened last night? You were asleep when I came up again.'

'Sorry.'

'You'll sleep enough when you're dead.'

'You weren't exactly alive this morning. Have you gone off sex?'

Tony pursed his lips. This was the first watershed in their Sunday. He could start an argument or he could let it pass. He decided to ignore it. It was like all the other little compromises and white lies and deceptions that made cohabitation possible. Heart-to-hearts always end in tears.

She still had not looked up at him. She was concentrating with furrowed brow on her book, knotting her hair. There was a message here somewhere. What was she trying to tell him? No one could be that interested in book-keeping on a Sunday morning. He stifled a yawn and idled over to the table. He looked over her shoulder, still noisily scratching his stomach.

'Must you do that? You sound like a monkey.'

'Speaking of which don't forget your mother and father are coming to tea. Who's this girl your father wants Edible Fats to hire?'

'No idea,' she said. 'Would you mind grooming your body hair somewhere else?'

'Shall I do lunch?'

Would she look up if he tipped the gangrenous lemon meringue pie over her head? Not worth it. Let her get on with it. There was a chicken in the fridge. He poured off the watery blood, fished out the polythene bag full of nasty bits and gave the inside a quick rinse under the hot tap. He cut the crusts off the half loaf of bread he found by the toaster and put the rest into a tupperware bowl. Among the jams and peanut butter he found an old jar of French mustard. He scooped the greenish crust off the top and threw it away. The rest he spooned into the bowl with the bread. He added salt and pepper, a long squirt of lemon juice and half a glass of cream sherry from the bottle he had got in for his mother-in-law. He squidged it all up between his fingers like playdough for half a minute, rolled it into a ball and stuffed it inside the chicken. He rinsed his hands and switched the oven on. He opened the freezer and took out a bag of oven chips and a packet of spinach.

'That's that then. Chicken à la Dijonnaise. Pommes frites. Spinach dauphine. Ready in an hour and a quarter.'

He had put over his own message. Loud and clear. Sunday lunch took seven and a half minutes. Women's work was a piece of cake. And a cake out of an Edible Fats mix at that.

*

'Mittens off to eat.'
'Go and wash your hands.'

'Go back and wash the backs.'
'Use a handkerchief.'
'Now go and wash them again.'
'Don't pick with fingers.'
'Elbows off the table.'
'Sit straight.'

'Stop rocking the chair.'
'Go and get a cloth.'
'Don't slurp.'
'Use a fork.'
'Use a knife.'
'No not like that.'
'It's nice gravy.'
'You've never tried it.'
'You don't have to like it.'
'You have to eat it.'
'Use a napkin.'
'We say napkin.'

'Think of the Ethiopians.'
'Get up off the floor.'
'It's on your ear.'
'Don't shovel.'
'Don't scoop.'
'Stop that.'
'Who flicked that?'

'Don't like spinach.'
'Why can't we have hamburger?'
'Washed them this morning.'
'It's clean dirt.'
'I did wash them. Smell.'

'What's for dessert?'
'Is this custard?'
'Louise ate a worm in the garden.'
'Wannagotertheloo.'
'Kanigo?'
'Dad just did a squeaker.'
'It wasn't his chair!'
'Poo poo.'
'Poo poo.'
'Mark jogged me.'
'This is disgusting.'
'What's the funny taste?'
'But I hate it.'
'I hate it too.'
'Miss says serviette at school.'
'Can't we have TV dinners?'
'Why is it rude to say fart?'
'Ow.'
'Ow.'
'He kicked me.'
'She kicked me.'
'Dad. What's a deathbed?'
'What's a deathbed?'
'Where do you buy one?'
'Granny's going to get one.'
'Do hamsters have them?'

'No darlings it's just an expression. When you're on your deathbed it means you're dying. Any bed can be a deathbed. There's nothing special about a deathbed. Just a normal sort of bed. And when someone has died in a bed it goes back to being an ordinary sort of sleeping bed.'

'You usually change the sheets.'

'Tony!'

'You talk about a marriage bed as well. It's the bed that married people sleep in. There's nothing special about a marriage bed is there Mummy? It can be a little camp bed or a bunk or a straw mattress or a double bed like Mummy's and Daddy's. It's just any old bed. There's nothing special about marriage beds. They are usually very ordinary. Sometimes it's impossible to tell the difference between a marriage bed and any old bed.'

'Do you have to change the sheets Dad?'

'If you're lucky.'

'Tony!'

'Like deathbeds you change them when it's all over.'

'Tony!'

'Do Granny and Grandad have a marriage bed?'

'Of course they do. They're happily married.'

Granny and Grandad had been sleeping in separate beds for twenty years. Ever since the day Granny came home early from her mother's and found Grandad on the stockroom floor with Veronica, the part time shop assistant. A week before his fortieth birthday Phil walked out, leaving a note on the kitchen table. Alex was ten years old. Gloria did not tell her where he had gone. Daddy's gone away. Alex first assumed he had died. That's what happened to people when they died, they just disappeared. The grown-ups kept it a secret. Sometimes she hoped he was still alive but in prison or the Foreign Legion. Other times she did not think of him at all. They did not talk about him at home. It was as if he had never existed. Now you have a Daddy. Hey presto! Now you don't. Gloria's mother came to stay at weekends and help look after the shop. She slept in the main bedroom where the marriage bed was exchanged for two singles. Otherwise life did not change very much.

They heard nothing from him until he walked into the shop on the following Christmas Eve with his suitcase and a doll's house. Everyone had a good cry for half an hour and then life resumed as before. Gloria's mother went home but the single beds remained. It was as if he had never been gone. Hey presto! Soon it was as if that year had never been. Any reference to his absence was treated with a puzzled stare. Over time, by confusing dates and anecdotes the year was papered over with spurious memories of holidays and birthday parties and illnesses that had really happened in other years. Veronica was expunged from the family record.

But Alex had put two and two together. One morning she had come back early off the round for a *Titbits* for number 44 and seen them kissing in the stockroom. Lying awake she had heard snatches of tearful conversation. She picked up chance remarks between her mother and grandmother. After he came back to them she heard her father say that he had no idea where 'she' had gone. Back up north probably. The only time she had asked her mother outright about it was the night she got engaged to Tony.

'Your father had a fling. Then he came back to us. Don't ever tell a soul. Shhhh. . . .' whispered Gloria, lightheaded with sweet Sauternes.

Alex had never told a soul. She had never told Tony. There never seemed any point. Or the time was not right. Why rake over old ashes? It was the family secret. Father had had his fling and come back to them. Sort of.

'Kanigedown.'

'Kanigedown.'

'Karndad. Let's play football.'

'Karndad.'

Alex got up from the table and put her arms round Tony's neck from the back. She kissed the top of his head.

'Go on. I'll clear up in here. You go out and play with them. That was a lovely meal,' she said.

Sometimes, thought Tony to himself as he followed the children outside into the garden, her changes of mood are totally inexplicable.

Phil peered through waving palm fronds at Tony on his knees before the front door.

'Here. Before I rupture myself,' was his greeting.

Tony turned with a start to see his father-in-law lurking behind a feathery tree rooted in a pot that he cradled in his groin. It seemed to spring from his overhanging belly like the tree of Jesse.

'It's your house warming,' he added graciously.

Phil was in his Weekend Break outfit. Bright green golf jacket, yellow polo neck sweater, brown trousers, sandals and yellow socks to match the sweater. His silver hair was plastered back on his head to show off a tanned forehead. A touch of his wife's make-up hid the tracery of broken veins over his cheeks.

'Wonderful. Alex will be thrilled. Another palm tree. How exotic. We'll put it with the others.'

'Gloria knows you like them. I'll go and help her out of the car. Her back's playing up.'

Tony put the sandpaper down on the front door mat and pulled the rubber gloves off his sweaty hands. He transferred the pot to his own groin and manoeuvred it into the house like a recruit on camouflage exercise. Phil went back to the car for Gloria. He wondered what they did with the plants. They should have enough by now to fill a conservatory. This one would probably die of cold and neglect like the others. Who cared as long as he got it out of the Metro? It would take hours to vacuum the grains of soil off the carpet. It was worth it to see poor Tony pretending to like it.

'Come on dear, rise and shine,' he said, opening the brightly polished door of the car. Today Gloria had adorned her fleshless body with various shades of violet and mauve to match her rinse, with the exception of her flatties which were bright red. She was of the generation whose taste in clothes had been formed when the world was heady with the excitement of artificial fibres. She had had a lifelong love affair with nylon. She shimmered with reflected light and crackled with static electricity. Phil was glad he wore rubber soles as he took her hand.

'I don't know how they can bear to live in this place I really don't I'd be frightened for the children did you see those coloureds they'll be broken into within the month . . .' she said, pausing only to put a breath sweet in her mouth.

Phil put the top back on her empty flask and put it in its place in the glove compartment. He took an aerosol from its place in the map pocket and drowned the sweet sherry fumes with the smell of new car leather. In one hand he took his wife's capacious straw bag, a souvenir of Majorca, and in the other her bony arm. He helped her out of the car, down the path and into the hall.

Mark and Louise came tripping to greet their Granny and Grandpa. Phil and Gloria beamed at their traditional heart-warming welcome.

'Ello watchergotme.'

'Ello watchergotme,' they bellowed. Without waiting for a reply they began to rummage in Gloria's straw bag while Alex tried to beat them off.

'Mind the milk,' shrieked Gloria as it glugged over the floor. With an agility surprising for someone who was such a martyr to her back she skipped backwards towards the front door. While Alex smacked the children Tony went to the kitchen for a cloth to wipe the floor. Phil stood at the bottom of the stairs, holding the dripping straw bag at arm's length as though it might explode. The children escaped with their prizes, disappointing beach balls. Alex belatedly held an empty milk bottle carefully upright.

'We do have milk you know Mummy.'

'You know I like to be sure it's fresh,' said Gloria, 'you don't know how long this London milk has been hanging around. Oh look at Tony on his hands and knees aren't you good. . . .'

They went on the Tour of the House. Phil noticed how tidy it seemed but he was not deceived. He knew that clothes had been bundled under beds, dirt under carpets, newspapers under cushions. He listened to the plans for rewiring and redecoration and renovation and bet with himself that it would still be the same the next time they came. Even when Tony started things he never finished them. Like that front door. He would take any money that the wood would stay bare. Tony would never get round to painting it. Alex was more organized, after all she was his daughter, but now she had started this college nonsense she wouldn't have time. There were still cardboard boxes in the dining room although the table had been laid for high tea: ham and tongue, hard-boiled eggs, tomato, beetroot, lettuce, piccalilli, Heinz salad cream, bread and butter, a jam sponge her mother had brought with a yesterday sell-by date. In the centre of the table was a cut glass bowl. Through the facets glowed a pale yellow sludge.

'Trifle. Your father's favourite. Is it sherry?' asked Gloria hopefully.

'Tony made it. You know I'm hopeless at that sort of thing. It's my job to put the little silver balls on.'

'You are lucky. You'd never find your father doing anything like that.'

Tony forced a smile and avoided Phil's leer. He led the way back to the sitting room.

'And this is the drawing room,' said Alex.

'Nice lounge,' said Phil.

'We had a living room like this,' said Gloria. 'I always did like a nice coal fire once in a while but I was glad when we had our fireplace taken out and the gas fire put in because of all the work I used to have to dust twice a day and I never did like the marble we threw it out and put in those beige tiles do you remember Dear but these days I bet this house takes a lot of cleaning I never did like that plasterwork in the ceiling either real dust traps they are but these old houses need doing up all the time your father was good at that sort of thing he would have been up at crack of dawn scraping and painting that front door he would have done half of it by the time I made him his breakfast I never missed making him his breakfast you know from the day we were married that was something my mother your grandmother told me always do a good breakfast and a good tea for him and make sure you've changed into something nice for when he comes home from work and I always made sure I had something nice to wear when he was in the house of course that was before jeans came in and men's sweaters that you young ones wear all the time and we had just as much work to do round the house if not more but I suppose that's what you want these days although living in this sort of area I suppose you have to be very careful about the schools round her although I shouldn't worry about that accent they've picked up they'll soon lose it when they go to a decent school. . . .'

Only the men went down the rickety steps into the cellar. Tony span tales about workbenches and wine racks which Phil took with a pinch of salt. While listening to the potential for a nuclear shelter Phil noticed the porno magazine tucked behind the gas meter. He pulled it out and examined the centrefold at arm's length. Tony blushed.

'Good Lord. What's that? Must have come with the house. Mustn't let the children see it.'

Phil tucked it back behind the meter. Perhaps Tony was normal after all. That's what he really used the cellar for. Lucky for him. Phil had to keep his own pornography collection in a beach hut at the end of the promenade.

'Everything all right with you and Alex?' he asked and gave a man-to-man wink.

'Great. Never been better.'

After tea Tony did the washing up to while away the time

before his in-laws left. He was surprised when Phil sidled up with a tea towel and picked up the cut glass bowl from the draining board. There were still bits of angelica stuck to the rim so he slid it back in the bowl.

'There aren't any jobs going in Edible Fats are there?' asked Phil.

'I thought you'd retired.'

'Not for me. A young kid I know. She's been trying to get a job for a year. She's a graduate.'

'What does she want to do?'

'She wants to deal with people.'

Tony bit the inside of his cheeks to stop himself snickering. When he left school he had told the careers guidance teacher that he didn't mind what job he got as long as it didn't involve meeting people. He wanted a job to do with things. When he didn't get high enough grades to take up his university place he was taken on by Edible Fats as a trainee in production management. He was so hopeless that they transferred him to personnel. From there it was a short step to a day release course at the Institute of Personnel Management. Now he was the training officer in the Edible Fats Division.

'Tell her to apply for production engineering.'

'You're joking.'

'No one wants to do that. Especially girls. There are always vacancies. After she's stirred margarine for six months she can apply for a transfer.'

He had never been able to whip up enthusiasm for margarine or frozen pastry or any of the other company products. He felt guilty when young people asked his advice about applying for a job or when he went round universities to recruit. He was tempted to tell them to do something interesting and useful with their lives. Think of what it will be like on your dying day, he had once told a fresh-faced history graduate, when you look back on your life and with your dying breath tell yourself you made it to the top of the tree in edible fats. The graduate just thought he was testing his determination and executive potential and tried even harder to get hired.

When he wanted to feel depressed he sometimes asked himself what he would whisper to himself on his own death bed. But I'm not really in edible fats, he weaseled, I'm in people. I make the same contribution that I could make anywhere. I make sure people do the things that they are best at and make them even better at it. That makes them happier. If someone really wants to sell more arrowroot biscuits than anyone else, who am I to criticize? I heip them realize themselves. But he didn't really believe that either. Perhaps he should have gone into computers. What the hell. It was a job.

5

At five o'clock Tony stabbed himself symbolically in the navel with his paper knife. Another wasted day. His search for the all consuming passion of an illicit love was getting nowhere. His heart wasn't in it. There was no one he fancied enough to be worth the gossip and the innuendo, the trouble and the expense. It would have to be a stranger, a beautiful, mysterious stranger bursting into his life. She would bowl him over while he swept her off her feet and in the resulting tangle of arms and legs they would consummate their ecstatic desire. It had happened to him once before, why couldn't it happen again? He had ended up married to the woman but the next time he would know better.

He watched Dot gather pulses among the cabinets and cupboards for her family's supper. She transferred the daily compost collection from her top drawer into a recycled paper bag. Two banana skins, an apple core, three herbal tea bags, other scraps of rind and skin and the crusts off Tony's corned beef sandwiches. Her day had not been wasted. She would go home and bathe her family in low calorie, high fibre love. He would go home to a frozen steak and kidney pie, Mark's homework and an evening in front of the television while Alex pored over her textbooks in the dining room.

'I'll teach her,' he exclaimed, slamming his hand down on the desk and rattling his pot of paper clips. Dot jumped.

'Teach who?'

'What? Ah yes. Em. Alex and I are taking up badminton Dot.' He fussed over his blotting pad and pencils, waiting for her to make a final tour of the smallholding. He waved goodnight and picked up the phone.

'Hello darling. I'll be home late. I have to go through job applications. Of course it's urgent. About nine. Don't keep supper. I'll get a sausage.'

But what was he going to do for the next three hours? He should have made plans. He would certainly not go through job applications. He could scarcely summon up the enthusiasm to deal with the small amount of work he did during normal working hours. He had never felt the attraction of workaholism. He preferred domestic stress any day. Alcoholism was preferable but he wasn't ready yet to join the ranks at the bar of those who needed Dutch courage to go home. Outside on the pavement he bought a paper to discover that any film he wanted to see at the cinema would have already started by the time he got there.

It was a nice evening for a stroll. He turned west along the Embankment towards Westminster. Everyone else seemed purposeful, commuters, joggers, theatre-goers, lovers, even tramps shuffling off to night shelters. The only other people with nowhere to go were the down-and-outs lying under Charing Cross Bridge, making up their cardboard beds for the night and passing cider bottles backwards and forwards. As he walked he tried to remember what it was like to chat up a strange and exciting and beautiful girl.

'I tell you what Marcella, let's look out for dead pigeons. How many pigeons do you think there are in London? There must be at least five million. The life expectancy of a pigeon must be about five years. That means, my love, that if five million pigeons live for five years a million must die every year. Are you with me? That's nearly two a minute dropping off the perch or out of the sky. We should be knee deep in dead pigeons. Corpses should be raining down on us. WHERE DO THEY ALL GO?' He would have to brush up his technique. This was not the romantic badinage that drives a woman into a man's arms.

He plodded on pondering seduction. He misdirected a couple of French tourists who asked him the way to Ze Peeca-deely Seercus but it gave him no pleasure. On the way down Whitehall he fell back on funny walks to pass the time. He ran through his repertoire from the difficult double hernia (experts only) through steel kneecaps, amputated big toe, floppy ankle and fallen arches. He did both versions of wooden leg, the above the knee and the below the knee. For old times' sake, he did the beginner's pigeon toes followed by the all purpose limp. He stopped for a beer and watched a repeat of the Eurovision Song Contest until at last it was time to go home. He arrived just after nine. He was pleased that he felt guilty since he would not have to pretend so much. Alex was putting the children to bed. He made a cheese sandwich and ate it quickly before she came down. He switched on the snooker and slumped in the chair with a can of beer.

'Hello darling.'
'Hello darling.'
'I saved you some supper.'
'That's all right. I had some.'
'I thought you were working.'
'I was. Working supper.'
'I called your office. You weren't there.'
'Must have popped over the hall. Group personnel.'
'The doorman said you left at five.'
'Popped out to get something to eat for a working supper. What's the matter? Why are you checking up on me? What is this? Do I have to report in every half an hour. Shall I get a radio pager? Bleep Bleep.'
'I couldn't remember if you wanted me to save you some.'
'I didn't. I don't. Thank you darling. You're too good to me. I'll go and say goodnight to the children.'

He went upstairs with a smirk on his face. So far so good. She was very curious to know where he had been. But in future he would have to find something to do when he was pretending to do what he hoped she thought he was doing.

He walked up to the perfume counter where a blonde, her face caked in what looked like an orange mud pack, lounged contemplating her long green fingernails. He picked up a sample bottle and looked at the label. At the risk of cracking her face the blonde bared her teeth.
'That's a lovely one.'
'Smells a bit sweet to me.'
'Is it for your wife?'
'No. It's for someone sexy and young and pretty and lively and interesting and funny and sexy.'
'This is what I wear,' she simpered. Her nose looked about to break out of its make-up like a chick out of an egg. She picked up a silver atomizer. Tony sniffed the nozzle. He gave a couple of puffs over his lapel and one under his right ear. 'Thanks,' he said, handed it back and walked out of the shop.
'Pervert,' muttered the blonde.

It hadn't been a bad day, reflected Tony, hanging from the ceiling of the crowded railway carriage. He had nearly finished the crossword, had avoided confrontation with Dot, had earned the credit for volunteering for a task force on employee benefits as soon as he was certain the places had been filled. The evening stretched uninvitingly before him, starting with the pandemonium of supper with the children, nagging them to do homework, putting them to bed and then settling down to catalepsy in front of the television while Alex did housework and buried her head in a textbook. But nothing threatened that could not be anaesthetized with a little gin while he planned his secret life.

He edged nearer the door as he would be getting out at the next station. He was pressed up against the back of a wishy-washy young man in a snappy dark suit and white shirt whose only distinction was a mane of fine blonde hair, streaked and curled over the collar. The opportunity was too good to miss. Tony let go of the strap and pretended to scratch his chin. As the train slowed down he selected the longest blonde hair in front of his face and tweaked it out by the root. He grabbed the strap again and looked innocently up to the ceiling as the young man turned his head. He was dismayed to feel the young man's hand on the front of his thigh, the fingertips softly palping. Jammed against the others Tony could not move his legs. Without looking at him the young man let his hand wander up and inside. He looked disappointed when Tony lunged for the door.

He scurried home, hoping he was not being followed and scratching his thigh to drive out the sensation of being groped. What sort of a kick did men get out of that? Before he opened the door he carefully arranged the blonde hair on the shoulder of his suit jacket, tucking one end under the collar so it would not blow away.

'Darling. I'm home!'

He made sure Alex was busy with her accounting and Mark and Louise were watching television. He went silently up the stairs two at a time and into the bedroom and closed the door. He picked out a shirt from the laundry basket. He unwrapped a lipstick from a Woolworth's paper bag and took the top off. It was a deep, violent scarlet, the kind that shines out from darkened doorways in Soho. He poised the tip over the collar and hesitated. He would have to make a proper job of it. He went over to the mirror, smiled at himself, and smeared the lipstick all over his lips. It was greasy and perfumed and brought back kisses on dark porches and the tops of buses. He held up the shirt collar, planted a kiss on the side, and threw it in the basket. He did not want to take the lipstick off. He admired himself in the mirror, checked his front teeth for smears, blew himself a little kiss. It was an improvement. He liked his mouth and gave himself a sultry, pouting stare. There was a strange, old excitement like when he tried on his mother's bras when he was a little boy. Carried away he did not hear Alex come up the stairs with a pile of clothes out of the drier. When she came in he fell on all fours, his nose near the carpet.

'What are you doing down there.'

'Saying my prayers. Allah is good. What do you think I'm doing?'

'What have you lost?'

'A contact lens.'

'You don't wear contact lenses.'

'That explains why I can't find it.'

'Can I help?'

'Don't worry. I know what I'm looking for.'

Keeping his face to the ground Tony pushed his head under the bed. He found an old sock and scrubbed away at his lips, choking on the dust. By the time he came out Alex had gone away.

When she bundled the dirty washing into the machine Alex did not notice the purple kiss on her husband's shirt collar. But she was intrigued by the red stain on an old tennis sock. It smelt like lipstick. She shrugged. It was another of the mysteries of daily life.

'How is it going, my love?'

Joanna followed Alex into the sitting room and put the tray down on the coffee table in front of the varicose-veined white marble fireplace. It gave the room a sepulchral air. Despite the pot plants and flower vases scattered round the room she had the feeling there was something missing, a wreath of lilies perhaps. 'Until death do us part' she thought. Alex poured tea into the china cups and slipped a slice of lemon into each. She would rather have had milk but since the days when they had nothing in common but post partum depression and thought each other terribly smart they drank tea with lemon together, although neither of them liked it. It had now become a special mark of their friendship.

'Our general studies lecturer always tells us how she went to Cambridge. She thinks she's doing voluntary service. Preaching to the great unwashed. They burn her effigy when there's a demonstration.'

Joanna sipped her tea, trying to avoid the lemon bobbing against her top lip.

'The economics Professor looks like Albert Schweitzer. He reads out his lectures as if we weren't there.'

'They sound awful,' said Joanna, putting her cup down and looking for her cigarettes in her handbag, 'no dishy men?'

'The accounting lecturer is all right. He's got nice curly hair. He think's I'm too middle class and just looking for an excuse to get out of the house. He wants to start a revolution. His name is Derek but everyone calls him Ché.'

'A revolutionary accountant?'

'We did intangibles and the capitalist conspiracy yesterday. It makes you think.'

'Intangibles? What are they?'

'Things that cost money but aren't really there.'

'Ah.'

'They treat me as a mother figure. Some of the girls talk to me but all they want is advice on birth control and abortion.'

Joanna flicked her ash deftly on the slice of sodden lemon in her saucer.

'What does Tony think about it?'

'He doesn't seem to mind.'

'You're lucky. Most husbands spend half their time telling you to do something useful and then when you do, moan because you're not at home doing the housework.'

'I told him I was doing extra accounting to catch up. He said "It's your life dear," and went back to the crossword. More tea?'

'Is everything all right between you two?' asked Joanna.

'We're fine. Tony's frightened we'll be broken into. He's screwing all the windows shut.'

'Nothing you can do my love. I should know. I've been broken into often enough.'

Joanna looked solemnly at the memorial fireplace and observed two minutes silence while Alex went out to the kitchen for more tea. She scented something. Usually it was Joanna who poured out her marital problems on Alex's sensible shoulders but now she sensed that the roles might be reversed.

'Alex and Tony are going through a rough patch. How awful for her,' said Joanna to herself.	'Complacent madam had it coming to her,' was the reply.
'I should help her like she's helped me. She needs a friend.'	'I wonder who he's seeing?'
'I know just what it feels like. Poor thing.'	'Must be someone at work. Usually is.'
'She'll feel better if she talks about it.'	'Unless it's someone round here. Sam saw Cathy giving him her phone number at our party. How delicious!'
'Such a sweet couple. It's probably not too late for marriage guidance.'	'Perhaps it's her and not him. Still waters run deep. She's changed her make-up and she doesn't wear those frumpish clothes any more.'
'She's so brave to go back to college.'	'The crafty bitch is planning a break. Good for her.'
'I'm her only decent friend after all.'	'Who though? It had better not be Sam. I'll murder her if it is.'
'That's what friends are for.'	'Or it's someone at the college. Who did she talk about? Only that loony accounting lecturer. Wait a minute. She said she was doing some extra accounting.'

'The poor darling. It must be such a strain.'

'She mustn't go through what I went through.'

'I hope I can help. Poor dear.'

'I bet he hasn't got two pennies to rub together.'

'You see? It happens to everyone. Everyone. I'm not such a whore after all.'

Mark and Louise, shouting at each other with mouths full, cheek pouches bursting, struggled for possession of the honey knife. Alex, immersed in *Business Week*, pretended not to notice. She continued to read when Tony walked into the kitchen, shaking rain drops off a large black plastic bag.

'Watchergot Dad?'

'Watchergot for us?'

'Where have you been? I've got to go to the supermarket,' snapped Alex.

He tested the furniture for sticky patches and found an unhoneyed chair. He proudly took out of the bag a light blue summer suit and a lemon short-sleeved shirt. He held them up defiantly.

'What on earth is that?'

'It's not a leotard. It's not a tutu. It must be a ser-yoot.'

'You don't say. Who gave it to you?'

'I bought it.'

'With good money?'

'You think I shoplifted it?'

'Dad's going to a party as a parrot.'

'Are you going to America?'

'I needed a change of image. Gone is cuddly Tony. Pinstripes to work and furry cords to parties. I have decided to be the predatory male. I'm going to flaunt my sexuality with provocative wit. That's what it said in the colour section.'

'I don't want to be seen with a predatory twit.'

'Prederry Twit.'

'Prederry Twit.'

'It's just a blue suit and a pastel shirt. The man in the shop thought I looked fantastic. And I got these.' He pulled out of the bag a pair of white leather shoes, a white belt and a white silk tie.

'You know what they call this in the trade? High Casuals. I'm going to buy a track suit too. Body awareness. Macho man is back. The Peacock Male. Look in the colour section. *L'homme fatal.*'

'It's certainly fatal.'

'It makes a statement.'

'It does that.'

'Sort of provocative.'

'It provokes me.'

'You don't like it do you? You want me to take it off and take it back. You want me in a brown suit and grey socks with clocks on and a woolly tie because that's nice and safe and predictable. Hard luck, is all I can say. This is the new me.'

'Hello new you.'

'You women want us sober-sided and gentlemanly. You don't want to be threatened. Then Macho Man comes bursting through the swing doors with designer leathers and his shirt open to the waist and you all fall over.'

'Laughing.'

'You needn't take that patronizing attitude. Just because for the first time you didn't come with me to buy it.'

'I'd love to meet who did.'

'Just going out for a walk Darling.'

'Where?'

'Around the block.'

'But it's dark.'

'It usually is at eleven o'clock at night.'

'You never go out for a walk.'

'Pretend I'm taking the dog.'

'We haven't got a dog.'

'That's why I suggest you pretend.'

'I don't mind. I'm just surprised.'

'Who can know the mysteries of the human heart, even after ten years of marriage? Listen Poppet: I AM GOING FOR A WALK. ALL RIGHT?'

He slammed the door on the way out. Lucky they didn't have a dog. She wouldn't have thought it was odd. He walked briskly round the corner to the telephone. It was vandalized. So was the next. He had to walk to the Parade and use the one outside the post office. It only took a minute. He strolled slowly home nursing a quiet glow of satisfaction.

Alex was already in bed. She was sitting up with the newspaper. That meant something was on her mind. Otherwise she would have been asleep or pretending to be asleep. He took time over flossing his teeth and dusting his athlete's foot. Let her wait.

'Tony, did you phone when you were out?'

'Me? We have a perfectly good phone in the house. Who would I want to phone from outside?'

'I don't know. That's why I asked.'

'Besides, all the phones are vandalized. I'd have had to go into the village.'

'How do you know?'

'What?'

'The phones are vandalized.'

'Ah. Well. They always are, aren't they? And anyway, how do you know someone was trying to phone?'

'A feller came from the post office and banged a gong outside the front door. How do you normally know someone's trying to phone?'

'Who was it?'

'If I knew that I wouldn't be asking if it was you.'

He got into bed and took his book off the bedside table. He lay on his side with his back to her. He read half a page before she broke the silence.

'Do you love me?' she asked.

She'd fallen for it. He felt the excitement of the hunter

with the prey in his sights, the angler with the fish nibbling round the hook.

'Ow.'
'You ought to do exercises.'
'Ow.'
'Wonderful.'
'Don't do it like that.'
'Why?'
'Just be tender.'
'You'll like it.'
'How do you know?'
Gotcha.

The affair took a predictable course. He sometimes wore his sharp suit to the office. He left early in the morning and later and later in the evening and sometimes had meetings and seminars that lasted until nine or ten. He mentioned that he might have to go over to Paris for a few days to visit the French affiliate. He spent all Saturday afternoon shopping for a pound of nails or a can of paintstripper. He went out for walks in the evening with ten pees jangling in his pocket. The frequency of wrong numbers when he wasn't in the house increased. He deserted the barber's behind the station, and will there be anything else sir, for the unisex hairdresser in the Parade, blow waves among the palm trees. He did exercises in his new tracksuit, working on thin arms and sagging stomach muscles. They were obvious ploys. He was embarrassed by their innocent childishness. But they seemed to work. Alex kissed him goodbye in the morning and made an effort to stay awake when she went to bed.

'Poor Joanna,' she said one evening, sitting up in bed while he got undressed. 'She thinks that Sam is having an affair.'

'How does she know? Lipstick on the collar. Blonde hairs on the jacket, that sort of thing?'

'He's being nice to her. He must be up to something.'

'Ah.'

When he came back on Saturday afternoons with nails or paint-stripper he brought a bunch of her favourite flowers. He asked out of the blue if she would like tea or coffee when she was studying. He offered to get the children off to school so she could get herself ready for the all-day seminar on business policy. He brought back a copy of *Business Week* from the office because he thought she would be interested in one of the articles. He gave her, for no reason at all, a bottle of scent with the special offer label scraped off. He forced himself to speak to her when there was nothing to talk about, over coffee when they had finished loading the dishwasher or on a Sunday morning before they got up.

'Look at this, Alex,' he said one evening, leafing through one of his management training bulletins, 'there's a three day study trip to electronics factories in Scotland. Silicon Glen. It hardly costs anything. It's for day release people. Why don't you go? I'll take care of everything here.' That should get her really worried. Why does he want me away from the house? 'Oh Darling you are sweet. But that's Mummy's birthday. I promised I would take the children down.'

So he derived all the benefits of the gesture without the consequences.

He was cheerful and smiled at her. He combed his hair and shaved and put on a clean shirt even when he wasn't going out. When he came back late from the office in the evening, instead of churlishly refusing the supper she had kept for him and skulking in a corner of the sofa with the crossword and the racing results, he was lively and debonair. He asked her what sort of a day she had had and how the children had been. He kissed the back of her neck when she was at the sink for no reason. He gave her cuddles and little kisses and spoke to her even when she was having a period. If all that didn't make her suspect something nothing would, short of coming home and finding him in bed with his girlfriend.

It was very hard work. It demanded an effort. It is difficult being lively and interesting and considerate with someone you've been living with for ten years. But it was worth it. His plan worked like a dream. It was obvious to him that she wondered why he was suddenly behaving like this, why he was guilty, what he was trying to hide. It was clear that she suspected his eye and even something else was wandering far from home. She did not say so in so many words but he could tell from her body language and things she said and other little clues.

She acted surprised and pleased when he gave her scent and flowers and put her arms round his neck but he knew she was wondering what he was up to. She talked back to him when he started conversations about nothing, trying to worm out of him the reason for his sudden attentiveness. He caught her looking at him with a funny smile on her face while he read the paper. When he 'worked late' she asked him about his job and his boss and what he did all day and did he really enjoy it and what was on his mind. It was the first time in years they had talked about the office. Of course she was trying to find out what he was really up to.

Her behaviour changed too. She started to have her hair done every week at the unisex hairdresser in the Parade. She bought new jeans just for slopping round the house. She wore the scent he gave her when she wasn't going out. She bought a whole packet of disposable razors just for herself. She deliberately did not wriggle away when he tried to kiss her just after she put make-up on. At odd moments he felt her long fingernails scratching the back of his neck and making shivers run up and down his spine or her lips brush his cheeks when he wasn't expecting it. All this touching and feeling and talking excited more than her suspicions. She didn't pretend to be asleep when he came in. Sometimes he would be nodding off to sleep when he felt her hand insinuate itself inside his pyjama jacket and play round-and-round-the-garden-like-a-teddy-bear on his lower abdomen. He had to remind himself that she was only trying to win him back from the Other Woman.

6

Tony reversed into the parking space. Alex waited while he got out with the umbrella. He sniffed. He bent down and sniffed the back wheels. He went round to the front and sniffed the bumpers.

'What's the matter?'

'I think the brakes are rubbing. Or there's something burning in the engine.'

'It was all right on the way down. You didn't smell anything then did you?'

'It smells like asbestos. Sort of sweet and acrid.'

He went round to the passenger door and held the umbrella for her. As she got out she looked up over Tony's shoulder. He followed her gaze to the crematorium chimney. Smoke swirled and was borne down by the rain towards them. She bit her lip.

'Breathe through your mouth,' he said by way of advice. 'At least it's not the car,' he added by way of consolation.

Her father had arranged everything. He had ordered only one mourners' car, which is why Alex had volunteered to go in their own. He chose a pine casket with plastic handles, a ten pound wreath, 'Abide With Me' and a two o'clock funeral so it would be too late for lunch afterwards. They could get away with tea and biscuits and the bottle of Bristol Cream sherry laid by in the bottom of the writing desk.

Tony held Alex's arm as they walked over to the

crematorium, as much to keep the umbrella over his head as to support her in her grief. They followed the rest of the family into the chapel while the previous party left by a side door. It was three minutes past two so the priest had already started the service. The two fifteen was already queuing up outside and the two thirty was on its way through the cemetery gates. Alex took her rightful place in the front row closest to the stage where the coffin lay. Apart from immediate family there were few other mourners. Her father didn't want many people there.

'They only gloat that they're still here and not in the box,' he used to say, 'I don't want them bragging over me.' He was very clear about what he wanted and it was his funeral. As the curtain swished across the stage to the strains of 'Abide With Me', Tony could see what he meant. He was glad he was in the audience. The front house might be dead but not nearly as dead as his father-in-law.

'Who was that at the back?' he asked Alex as they were hustled out of the side door into the rain.

'I didn't see.'

'Blowsy woman. Fat. Black veil.'

'I didn't see. Must have been left over from the lot before. Let's get in the car. I don't want to see that chimney.'

Phil had no inkling when he woke up that this was his last day. He was born on Saturday and therefore condemned to work hard for his living, a fact that he never tired of telling his daughter over Sunday lunch. But there was no rhyme about a meaningful deathday. He had often wondered what day it would be. He hoped it would not be a Wednesday. Wednesday was early closing. He associated it with pleasure and not depressing things like his last breath. At a specific minute of a specific hour of a specific day his heart would cease to beat, his brain would cease to function and only his toenails and fingernails and superficial body hair would continue to attest to life. There would be one morning that would be his last, one last read of the paper, one last toasted cheese sandwich, one last rootle in the ear with the little finger. Those things would be special but only in retrospect and he would be the one person not to appreciate their significance.

Tuesday was the day. It was an ordinary summer's day at the English seaside. The sky was grey, the sea breeze was chill and drizzle swept the promenade. He was woken up not by the gale warnings for the south coast on the radio/digital-alarm/bedside-lamp/tea-making-machine that automatically sprang into life at seven twenty-seven but the urgent susuration of boiling water piddling into the teapot. It made him get out of bed to go to the lavatory, thereby undermining the whole point of the thing which was to provide the courage to get out of bed in the first place. He took off his hairnet, took his bottom dentures out of the electrolytic cleanser and made for the bathroom. He was not to know it was his last wee wee but two, not counting wetting his trousers simultaneously with his last breath.

By the time he came back Gloria was awake and the tea was brewed. She sat up with a mauve nylon bed-jacket tossed carelessly over her pink brushed nylon nightdress, a pillow between the headboard and the rollers in her hair. He poured two cups, added milk and sugar and passed her one. He would have sipped his own more deliberately had he known it was his last cup of tea but one. This was when they made plans for the day. He should have decided to sail to Honolulu or climb the Matterhorn or play a round with Arnold Palmer. As he only had a few more hours to live it didn't matter what his plans were so they might as well have been ambitious. Instead he told Gloria that after breakfast he would replace the rubber grummet, a stitch in time, on the revolving clothes line. That should take him until lunch.

'What are you doing this afternoon, Popsicle?' he asked Gloria.

On the answer to the question depended his plans for the

rest of the day. If she was staying at home he would take a little walk down to his beach hut at the end of the promenade.

'Nothing Hubbie.'

'No bridge?'

'Tomorrow Hubbie.'

Gloria drained her cup and got out of bed. She put on her artificial mink slippers and went downstairs to cook his breakfast for the last time. Phil poured the last of the tea into his cup, waste not want not, and listened to the end of the news of robberies and hijackings and tornadoes and other horrors and disasters afflicting the world outside, feeling safe and comfortable in his cosy home. Little did he know. He got out of bed for the last time and went to the bathroom. For the rest of the morning he left behind traces of his passing: a ring of bristles in the washbasin; a damp toothbrush; dirty underwear in the plastic wicker basket in the corner of the bedroom; a packet of pipe cleaners by the paper next to the armchair in the living room; a worn rubber grummet, might come in handy, next to the bread tin in the kitchen. Sighing, his widow would potter round the house gathering these relics in the days to come.

After lunch, his last meal, a nice piece of boil-in-the-bag-cod-in-parsley-sauce, he put on his summer boots and his summer waders and his summer anorak and summer rain hat and left the house. Gloria would long treasure the memory of his last words: 'Nice weather for ducks.' He walked down the street between the immaculate bungalows to the promenade, ducking his head to the wind and spray that came off the sea. It was worse when he got to the promenade. Breakers crashed against the sea wall sending spray high in the air over seafront hotels. The gale whistled in the strings of fairy lights and rocked the illuminations. Stripy awnings cracked and ripped. The road was awash with water, ebbing and flowing under the railings. He thought of going back. Press on regardless, he admonished himself sternly.

He pressed on half a mile to where the promenade petered out into a rocky, shingle beach and the cliffs started. Indifferent to breakwaters and other puny man-made obstacles, thundering breakers dashed against the cliffs. He felt clammy inside his waterproofs and licked salt off his lips. He suddenly felt insignificant, a rare emotion. 'God help us,' he said, his words swallowed up by the roar of the gale. At the end of the promenade, with their backs to the rising cliff, was a row of green-painted wooden huts with pointed roofs. They were windowless and narrow, rented out for the storage of fishing tackle and boating gear and beach equipment. He pulled out a bunch of keys attached to his trousers by a leather thong. He opened the end hut, slipped inside and slammed the door behind him. It was pitch dark. With practised fingers he turned on the battery-powered lamp hanging from the roof. He took off his waterproofs, hung them on the door, sat down on a wooden chair and reached underneath it for the bottle of Stone's ginger wine. He took a swig, smacked his lips and looked over the floor-to-ceiling shelves that took up most of the space in the tiny hut. They held probably one of the best private collections of pornographic magazines on the south coast. He had not bought a single one. They were samples given by eager suppliers throughout his newsagent's career. He had kept them in garden sheds and beach huts since he began the collection on his return to the bosom of his family after the Veronica episode twenty years before. During that time he had never been unfaithful to his wife.

The police came for Gloria at seven o'clock. She was watching at the window and saw them park outside. The policewoman made a cup of tea before they left to identify the body. It was stretched out under a tarpaulin on the beach at the foot of the cliff. The gale had abated and the tide was out. They had prized his fingers from the inside catch of the door lock. The remains of the shattered huts were strewn on the beach along with beach equipment, boating gear, fishing tackle, sodden Playmates and Bunnies and Pets. The freak waves had sucked them out to sea and thrown them back up again.

'Oh. Look at his little smile,' she said.

That night the nine o'clock news reported the deaths of three yachtsmen, an old-age pensioner and two poodles in the worst gales the south of England had experienced in a decade. Gloria wrote indignantly that her late husband was not an old age pensioner but a retired businessman. She did not get a reply.

Alex and Tony collected the ashes from the crematorium the next day. They were in a shiny brown plastic container with a screw top like a thermos flask. The attendant put it in a white cardboard box.

'Do we really have to do this?' he asked.

'Mummy remembers him saying that's how he wanted to be buried when they went on their retirement cruise.'

'But he's already had one burial at sea. Surely that's enough. The sea spat him out. It looks churlish.'

'It means a lot to Mummy. What else do you suggest?'

Tony could think of lots of places where his late father-in-law would prefer to be sprinkled in view of the hobby that had come to light in the wreckage of the beach hut but he was too diplomatic to suggest them. Burial at sea it would have to be. They picked up Gloria from the house. She was wearing her black coat and hat and spotty veil. She sat in the back with her hand on the white cardboard box. They drove at funeral speed down to the promenade and looked for a place to park.

'I've told the police I shall take them to court. They have no right to bring up that beach hut at the inquest. It's not true. Your father would never have done a thing like that. It's libel. None of those things belonged to your father. It was someone else's hut. They should come out and confess and clear your father's name. It's disgusting. He was a decent man, your father. We were married thirty-five years so I should know. He was a pure man. Pure. I've told the papers I'll sue. It's not for me. It's for him. He'd turn in his grave. If he was here now he'd have something to say, you mark my words.' She drummed her fingers on the white cardboard box.

Although the sun was still hidden behind a blanket of grey clouds it was not raining. Holidaymakers flocked to the beach to take advantage of the fine weather.

'Does it have to be here?' asked Tony, 'shouldn't we go somewhere more private?'

'This is where he came for a walk every day. Not down by those dirty huts. He liked it here, bless him,' said Gloria, dabbing the corner of her eye.

They cruised slowly up and down the seafront looking for a parking space and building up a cortège behind them. Finally they found a slot next to the pier. Gloria had fifty pee in her purse for the meter. After calming her down when she realized that she was intimately related to the white cardboard box on the seat next to her, Alex led the funeral party across the road, past the candy floss and down the steps to the beach. In their mourning clothes they threaded their way through deck chairs and sand castles and ball games. They stopped as close to the water's edge as they could without getting their shoes wet. Alex was already carrying her high heels.

'I'll paddle out then,' said Alex.

'The tide's blowing in. He'll drift back over those people paddling,' said Tony.

'We'll have to go further out,' said Alex.

'I didn't bring my swimming shorts,' said Tony.

'We should have gone to the end of the pier,' said Gloria.

'It's too windy. He'd have blown back all over the ghost train,' said Tony.

They stood before the lapping waves, listening to the hiss as they ran back to the undertow, gazing at the limitless horizon, a *memento mori* among the carefree holidaymakers round them. Tony felt a craving for an ice cream.

'We'll have to get a boat,' said Alex.

They walked up and down the beach, plodding through the sand in single file, looking for boat-owners. There were plenty of boats but they were all abandoned above the tidemark.

'Isn't there a trip round the bay?'

'That's not very private.'

'We should have gone along to the marina.'

But the facilities of an English seaside resort are not to be underestimated. Children, pets, burials at sea, all catered for.

'We can't do that.'

'Why not?' she insisted, 'perfect for the job. Look, that one's even painted black.'

Tony gave his shoes to Gloria to hold while the boy dragged the pedalo to the water's edge. She remained on the beach, a lonely and perspiring figure, while her daughter and son-in-law performed the very last rites.

'Pedal, come on,' shouted Alex, pulling her skirt up to her thighs.

'My legs are killing me.'

They thrashed out to sea until they were clear of swimmers. Gasping for breath, sweat pouring down their faces and arms, they drifted while Alex took the urn out of its box and unscrewed the lid. The sea was choppy and Tony gripped the side of their craft.

'Should we stand up, do you think?' she asked.

'We'll capsize if we do,' he replied, swallowing hard.

'Should we say anything? I mean, what are you supposed to say?'

'Ashes to ashes. I don't know. Goodbye Dad. Get on with it.'

She started to tip the urn but she was on the windward side. The breeze blew a fine white dust into her eyes and over her black dress.

'Quick. Turn round,' she spluttered.

Gingerly Tony stood up and gripped the back of her

chair, facing the back of the pedalo with his bottom in the air.

'Not you, you fool. The boat.'

They pushed their protesting legs on the treadmill again with the tiller hard over. Facing the right way at last Alex emptied the urn, smacking the bottom with the flat of her hand like a ketchup bottle. They bobbed up and down in a grey-white slick.

'What shall I do with this?' she asked, shaking the urn like a cocktail shaker.

'We'd better put that in too.'

She unscrewed the lid again and dipped it in the water, soaking her dress up to the armpit. She replaced the lid and tossed it a couple of yards. It floated upside down.

'We can't leave it like that,' she said, 'it'll get washed up.'

'What's wrong with that?' he asked.

'It's not right. Who knows what it would be used for.'

'Flowers? Picnics? Martinis?'

'Get it back. We'll have to bury it if it won't sink.'

Afficionados of the pedalo will be familiar with the game of 'Man Overboard'. This consists of churning round and round in circles trying to pick up a floating object like a ball or a bottle or a plastic bag. It is fascinating how the object seems to have a malevolent life of its own, swirling near to the side and at the last moment bobbing away out of reach. So Tony and Alex, in their best formal clothes, chased the recently vacated urn of her late father round and round in circles in the choppy water watched by the bemused widow on the shore and carefree holidaymakers in deckchairs.

7

Tony managed the induction programme for the new graduate trainees. For the first two days he lectured them on the history of the company, its organization, its world mission, and the trainees' role in carrying Edible Fats forward into the future. Then they were preached at by department heads, chosen not for their relevance but their ability to keep the attention of his class. The last part of his course was an 'In-basket' exercise. They were all given a sheaf of memos and letters and asked to write brief replies to each one. Although they would know nothing of the subjects, the exercise was designed to illustrate the political and social complexity of the organization. Don't write to the head of another department without copying your own department head. Always send a copy to file to prove that you wrote it so when they try to pin the blame on you you can prove it wasn't your fault. Some things were dynamite and shouldn't be touched with a barge pole. And so on. For Tony this was the most important thing he could teach them at the beginning. This is how they would spend the rest of their careers and it was never too soon to learn the law of the jungle. While Dot wasn't looking he patted his hair in the reflection of the window, straightened his pink woolly tie and forced his face into the benign-but-authoritative-I-am-an-old-hand-at-this-game expression.

'I'm off to face the lions,' he said.

'Good luck.'

He never knew whether the spasm in his stomach every time he faced a new class was an attack of nerves or a pang of compassion. He stood before them in his dark suit and tactile tie, the beaming face of Edible Fats, about to launch them on their new careers. For some of them, the lucky ones, it would be short lived. As soon as they found out it wasn't for them they would leave without hesitation and try something else. For a few others, also lucky, it would be the start of an illustrious and satisfying career. They would revel in their ambition, loving each little victory, each little step up the ladder. How they would feel when they reached their peak and there was nothing else to try for was another matter but at least the getting there would be fun. But the majority would neither enjoy it nor find the courage to leave until it was too late. Coming to work would be a dismal burden, shouldered for the children's sake, borne with lethargy and inertia. They were the dead wood, fodder for heart attacks and alcoholism. They would live in fear of redundancy, which would, if they only knew it, be their one hope of saving something from their lives. If only one could tell them apart before it was too late.

'Good morning and welcome again to Edible Fats. My name is Tony and for the next week. . . .'

He listened to himself speak the practised words, the practised jokes, the practised pauses. There were seven women and five men. They sat bolt upright in their chairs, fresh faced and groomed, new haircuts and blow waves, white shirts and blouses, interview suits still pressed. As he spoke Tony examined them and began to tell them apart. A good looking fellow with curly hair and flopping handkerchief. Brand management. A plain girl with black spectacles and grey suit. Finance and administration. A fluffy blonde in a pink dress. Market research. A girl at the back had short black spiky hair growing out of an abandoned punk cut. She was wearing the sort of suit he remembered his mother wearing, charcoal grey, long tight skirt tailored over the hips, pinched waist, pointed lapels, padded shoulders with a cream blouse and a single string of pearls. There was a mischievous expression in her clear blue eyes and she had the slightly parted lips of passionate women and incurable mouth breathers. There was something familiar about her he could not place, something that troubled him, put him off his recorded speech.

'What was I saying? Ah yes. Now I've introduced myself, why don't we all introduce ourselves. Just stand up and tell us who you are, why you joined Edible Fats, what side of the business you're interested in. . . .'

Tony had developed early the facility of teachers and parents and politicians to listen with only a tiny part of the brain. The feedback techniques that assured the speaker of rapt attention came automatically – nods, uh-huhs, repetition of the last word of a sentence, all the things they teach at Dale Carnegie and human relations seminars. The drivel he heard washed through a mental sieve that held back only the unusual words and phrases. He had learned to steel himself against the touching descriptions of their young, optimistic lives, their doomed hopes, their innocent ambitions. If he really wanted to show he was listening he asked questions.

> How exactly does selling more margarine in inner cities alleviate undernourishment in the third world?
> What did you say the connection was between quarterly dividends and creative fulfilment?
> Tell us again how TV dinners liberated your mother from male chauvinist exploitation. By giving your father an ulcer?

He tried not to be too sarcastic. In any case they only thought he was doing it to test their dedication to their new employer and their tenacity and their performance under stress and they would get a rotten evaluation if they did not stick to their guns. They would have to find out for themselves how silly they sounded, by which time it would be too late. Too bad. Let them get on with it. What really disturbed him was that he remembered himself saying the same kinds of things that they were saying now, quoting from the curriculum vitae that he thought had landed him his first job.

'School, College, Male/Female, Degree, Home Address, Driving Licence, Unmarried/Married/Divorced, Health Excellent, Reasonable French, Guitar, Reading, Current Affairs, Squash, Summer Jobs, Travel in Europe, Interest in Marketing, International Finance, Production Management, Self-fulfilment, Needs of Society, Rewarding Career, Rhubarb, Rhubarb, Rhubarb. . . .'

Young lives. What would they make of them in the next fifteen years? The same sort of life he had made of his?

The girl in the back with spiky hair and clear blue eyes had a Midlands accent, flat 'a's', baths and paths to rhyme with maths.

'My name's Georgina but everyone calls me George. I come from Acocks Green near Birmingham. I went to a comprehensive and then to collidge where I did Economics and English and I mean it was pretty useless wasn't it? Nobody got jobs afterwards. I went back to the supermarket where I used to do weekends and holidays. Edible Fats didn't recruit at collidge. My mom found out who to write to. I'm in production engineering. I mean I've never been to London before. That's all reely.'

The brand manager, who had been at Sussex University, smirked. The market researcher, who had studied in Geneva, looked at her long fingernails. The finance and administration manager, who played the oboe and had been articled to a chartered accountant fixed a smile on her bland face. Tony wanted to take her in his arms and give her a big hug.

'So you want to be a production engineer,' he said, praying he didn't sound sarcastic.

'I'd rather deal with people reely,' she said and blushed.

'What did it feel like to fall in love?' asked Tony.

'What a funny question,' answered Alex. She handed him a red plastic pail brimming with socks like some hideous eel catch. She swung it at him so he was forced to catch it.

'Here. Most of them are yours.'

'So?' he said gruffly, playing dumb.

'Put them into pairs.'

When Alex started college they had agreed he would take more of a share of the housework. All his suggestions as to how it could be done more efficiently had been ignored. Alex jealously guarded the secrets of the washing machine controls but expected him to do more of the skivvying. With loathing he tipped the pail out on to the table and spread out the contents. Not all of the catch was this week's. The sock pail was kept on the floor of the airing cupboard, half-full of those which had failed to be paired the last time. It was topped up with the latest wash and the whole lot re-sorted in the hope of one day pairing them all off. Fat chance.

'I don't know why you women want to go out to work when there are fascinating things like this to do at home,' he grumbled as she picked up the rest of the laundry to take upstairs. He eliminated the easy ones first, Mark's football socks and Louise's dayglo pink for parties, school socks with purple bands on the top, two pairs with clocks on the side that Phil and Gloria had given him for his birthday. The feelings of rebellion and resentment at this futile task only began when he started on the hard core of dark blues and greys that had such subtle differentiation of stitching and colour that they looked identical until he crossed his legs in front of the boss or hitched up his trouser legs to sit down at a dinner party. Odd socks were the beginning of the end, the first sign of going off the rails, losing grip, going to pieces, falling apart, worse than a fraying collar or a missing cuff button or unzipped flies.

Upstairs Alex dumped the washing on the bed in their room and started to sort it into piles. What did it feel like to fall in love? Might as well ask what it felt like to eat a chocolate éclair or go off the diving board for the first time. She remembered that she had fallen in love, she remembered incidents, she remembered words like elation and fear and vulnerability. But the feeling of what it had been like had completely evaporated. Pity. Even worse was wondering if she would ever recapture that feeling again before she died.

Downstairs Tony scowled at the pile of misfits on the table and dumped them back in the pail. He should throw them all away right now. A fresh start. Clean sweep. An empty bucket. He stomped with determination out into the side passage where the dustbins stood surrounded by eggshells and tea bags and potato peelings. He lifted the lid, releasing a large bluebottle and a fetid smell. No. It was a waste. Perfectly good clean socks. You never know, he might have made a mistake. One of the pairs on the kitchen table might be a fraud and the genuine partner lying in the bottom of the pail. He put the lid back on, maliciously trapping a wasp, and went back into the kitchen. Alex had come back from the airing cupboard.

'Marriages aren't made in heaven,' he said, 'they're made in the sock pail.'

'What made you suddenly think of that?' she asked.

'I dunno. Just a joke. Pairing socks makes you think of that sort of thing.'

'No. I mean what it was like to fall in love.'

'Oh. Nothing reely.'

Alex abandoned the exercise Derek had set, a trial balance of the Armaments, Ballistics and Cannon Company, or the ABC company as it was abbreviated in their text books. He had told them to think of them as suppliers of riot shields, tear gas grenades and weighted truncheons to South Africa, Chile and the Philippines. It was an ingenious idea. The frustration and anger and feelings of inadequacy engendered by not being able to make the thing balance at the twentieth attempt were all vented on the international arms trade. She stood at the sink rinsing her coffee cup and looked out of the window. It was her turn to do the garden. They said 'do the garden' as if they going to inflict harm on it, which was usually correct. Half an hour's gardening would put her back in the mood for the ABC company. She put on Tony's boots. Her own were expensive green ones that fitted round the calves for walks in the country and going to the shops in the snow. She wasn't going to spoil them with gardening. She put on the pink rubber gloves usually reserved for cleaning the lavatories, a chore ranking about equal with gardening. She clomped out of the back door to the outside lavatory and unhooked the rusty bit of wire that held it shut. She knew from experience to jump back a pace as two deck chairs, a rake, a hoe, a besom, a garden fork with a broken handle, a grass encrusted hovermower handle and a pile of plastic flower pots, most of them cracked, tumbled malevolently out of their oubliette and cascaded round her feet. She looked in grudging admiration at so much mess crammed into such a small space.

'Somebody ought to clean this up,' she muttered to herself. Good old Somebody. Gardener, maid, handyman, factotum, valet, servant, the faithful Somebody.

'Somebody ought to mend this light.'

'Somebody ought to go to the supermarket.'

'I wish Somebody would clean up this broken glass.'

The careless Somebody was usually responsible for creating the mess in the first place.

'Somebody knocked over the bottle of milk in the fridge.'

'Somebody's used up all the toilet paper.'

'Somebody's stuck chewing gum under the dining room table.'

Somebody had not been very diligent in the outside lavatory. In addition to the stuff that leapt out when the door was opened there was a jumble of old shoes; a burst football; the grass box from an old hand mower; several watering can roses without the essential perforated discs; a rusty fireman's axe; a tennis trainer in a cat's cradle of aluminium poles and string and minus the tennis ball. There were also the remnants of passing fits of gardening enthusiasm. Plastic trays which might come in useful one day; special offer seed propagators which had never propagated anything more than fine green mould; a thing for jabbing holes in the lawn; three of the four necessary sides of a compost bin, the fourth having been used to block up the fence so the guinea pig couldn't get out of the garden. Compost was another story. Sometimes for as long as ten days there would be a disgusting bucket in the corner of the kitchen and a stinking little pile of refuse at the bottom of the garden until the craze wore off. In the middle of the lumber lurked the lavatory bowl, cracked round the edge and with a sinister puddle of greenish water in the bottom that got only filthier when it was flushed. When the children were puking over their pillows Alex would blame the outside lavatory and its fetid little pond breeding typhoid and cholera and make Tony promise to do something about it in the morning. He never did, so she had to be content with pouring bleach down it when she remembered, making the water browner and more noxious than before.

Wrinkling her nose at the smell of mould and rotting grass and bleach she dragged the hovermower from the wreckage and yanked at the cable that was entwined around the other tools like convulvulus. She reached up for the shears hanging on the handle of the window, stepping on a flower pot with a satisfying crunch. She went back into the kitchen and transferred from the window ledge to the draining board the washing-up liquid, a bottle of hand-cream, Louise's saucer of damp blotting paper and mouldering cress, Mark's half-painted plaster rabbit, an avocado stone impaled with toothpicks and balanced on a jam-jar, a plastic cup of old toothbrushes and a long dead begonia so she could pass the mower cable through the window and plug it into the electric kettle socket without knocking them all over. Instead she knocked half of them over from the draining board into the sink but at least they didn't have so far to fall.

She clomped back into the garden and surveyed the task ahead. The rectangular garden was taken up mainly by a rectangular lawn, pockmarked with bare patches from football, dotted fairy rings and variegated with brown moss. Tufts of rye grass struggled against creeping alopetia. The only place the grass grew with abundance was round the edges over the borders, out of reach of the mower. Down both sides of the lawn were strips of earth they euphemistically called flower beds. Their colour alternated between green and brown, depending on whether they had been weeded. At the bottom of the lawn was a privet hedge that blocked off the rubbish pile and bonfire and the remains of a wooden shed that had blown down several years before and now housed a thriving colony of woodlice. Not even the hedge was safe. It was the sole source of supply of food for Louise's class's stick insect collection and was regularly pillaged for the choicest leaves, leaving the rest in holes and tatters.

Just after they moved in Tony had succumbed to his annual fit of horticultural mania and bought a tray of bedding plants from the garden centre. He got half of them into the ground before the enthusiasm wore off. The rest were wilting in front of the French windows, their leaves brown and etiolated and their roots, white and wormlike, bursting out of their flimsy plastic containers. The ones in the ground did not seem to be doing much better. Unwatered, trampled, perforated by slugs and caterpillars, spaced a foot apart to fill up the bed so that it looked even more barren, they wilted disconsolate: an alyssum, then a lobelia, then a salvia, then the sequence remorselessly repeated in a straight line equidistant from lawn and fence.

When they first married they promised each other a long stripy lawn sloping down to the rhododendrons, a rose covered pergola, wisteria over the stable wall, a wrought iron table and chairs, a labrador at her feet. She recalled this vision from time to time when she was struggling over inflation accounting or monetarist theory as a promise of the reward to come if she persisted. The only embellishment she added was a full-time gardener called Somebody. She pressed the trigger and began to cut, hoovering the mower backwards and forwards with the suppressed resentment she reserved for the iron and the mop. They laughed about gardening when they were first married. He used to joke that he would never grow fruit or vegetables when they had a garden, that he hated the idea of it all growing in the earth, crawled over by worms in the dirt and filth. All that pollination and fertilization and germination going on. He wanted none of that promiscuity in his back yard. We live in a decent neighbourhood. Did she know how many things you have to have male and female plants for before they grow anything? He came out with this nonsense the first time he came to Sunday lunch and her mother had taken him seriously. For years she would only serve them tinned vegetables. Perhaps he had not been joking, perhaps he really meant it. He didn't say that sort of thing any more. When was the last time they had lain in bed and rabbited on about nothing in particular, joking and teasing? There hadn't been time for that sort of thing since they moved house. Either the children came in and the bed became a rough house or she would slip silently out to make the tea while he huddled under the duvet trying not to wake up. Life had become solemn. They were too busy to talk to each other any more.

She carried the mower back to the lavatory across the shorn and lumpy grass. She wound the cable round her hand and elbow and threw it over the mower handle. With a disgruntled sigh she picked up the shears and clomped back to the lawn, scuffing at the blade-resistant tufts and sprawling plants in her path. Somebody ought to get weedkiller. Stooping so she would not get grass stains on her new jeans she hacked at the edges. The dull, rusty blades masticated the grass and chewed into the turf. Halfway along the border she straightened up and stretched her aching back. She peeled off the pink rubber gloves. Her hands were sweaty and wrinkled. Enough for one day. She went back to the lavatory and put the shears back on the window handle and balanced the mower on the fetid lavatory bowl. She looked at what she had done. She had made the bare patches barer and the brown patches browner. The trails of grass cuttings were already turning yellow. The fringes lay where they fell on the border like hair on a barber's floor. It wasn't Nature's fault. You only get out of anything what you put in. She scooped up the tools that were scattered on the concrete, threw them in the lavatory and slammed the door on them to fall out on the next person who opened it. For reasons she barely understood she beat on the door with the palms of her hands and then her fists, drumming faster and faster, as if she were on the inside trying to get out.

Alex thankfully closed her book on the subtleties of accelerated depreciation and packed it away with her pad and pencils. Derek meticulously wiped chalk dust from his leather jacket with a yellow handkerchief and shouldered his Moscow Olympics tote bag.

'I don't believe a word of it,' she said as he walked past.

'Accounting? So you shouldn't. It's all a mirage. But it's handy until something better comes along.'

'I mean your Trotskyite interpretation of depreciation. A capitalist conspiracy to conceal assets from the workers.'

'You have your opinion, I have mine.'

'What I mean is, you don't believe it either. It's just a way to keep us interested.'

He mimed shock and horror at the accusation.

'Come along on the next Stop The City Demo. See how sincere we are.'

'No thank you. I have no wish to throw stones through windows.'

'There you are. Bourgeois respect of property over lives.'

'You're twisting everything again.'

He gave her his I-am-a-dangerous-person smile.

'Let's talk about it over a drink. And perhaps a bite to eat afterwards?'

Tony was at home looking after the children. She had left a shepherd's pie in the oven. She was free to be witty and intelligent and captivating, to banter about monetarism and Marx, to show that she was not simply an appendage to a husband and children and a house.

'I have to rush. The children are waiting for their supper.'

'Another time then.' His smile turned from dangerous to mocking.

Alex hammered the steering wheel with the palm of her hand all the way home. There was no reason at all why she shouldn't have gone at least for a drink. If she was going to make it on her own she had to stop feeling guilty every time she left home.

8

Where had he seen her before? He saw her face everywhere, on passers-by in the street, on his secretary Dot, on a poster advertising toothpaste. Spiky, black hair, clear blue eyes, set wide apart, lips slightly parted. It was as if he had known her face for ever, imprinted in his memory from birth. He saw her in his own tired, pasty face when he looked in the mirror in the morning or took sidelong secret glances at himself in shop windows or passing cars or the polished aluminium of the lift at work. But most disturbing was seeing her in Alex's face. He had forgotten how Alex used to look before. Now he only saw George's blue eyes, the same straight nose, the same dimple in the corner of her mouth as she smiled. Alex's hair was different and the face was older, more laugh lines and frowns, but to his deluded mind her features and expressions were the same. Sometimes when he looked at Alex it was like seeing George as she would be in fifteen years time. Nothing he could do, no amount of gazing at their wedding photograph on the mantelpiece, recalling old memories, picking out differences between them, could cure the hallucination of seeing one face superimposed on the other.

He would suddenly look up from his paper on the train as if he had caught someone looking at him and catch a glimpse of her getting off or hiding behind a book. He would see her in the next carriage through the swaying window of the connecting door but by the time he forced his way to the end of the aisle she had disappeared. As he walked over the bridge he would see a familiar figure twenty yards ahead in the crocodile and force his way through the ranks of mute commuters but by the time he had reached her the shape of her head, the colour of her hair would have changed. But at the office, where he could see her every day for the next two weeks, he avoided her. He savoured the contrary deliciousness of finding urgent work at his desk during coffee breaks or pressing appointments at the end of a session when he usually stayed behind to answer questions and chat. When he was speaking to the class he looked at the plain girl with glasses who always stared down at her notepad or the bland smile of the brand manager. When he did catch George's eye a palpitation in the chest, a squeeze in the stomach put him off what he was saying. Like her face, the feeling when he saw her was old and familiar, not as though it had suddenly come upon him, not as though it was fresh and new and spring-like as he thought he remembered it from years ago but as if it had been alive within him forever and it just needed her to come along and take off the cover, open it up to the light, peel away the encrusted indifference and boredom that had overlaid it for so long. The feeling when he looked at her belonged to him, *was* him.

    She said she wanted to deal with people. He could arrange for her to transfer from production to personnel. He could make a case for taking her on as an assistant. If necessary he could get rid of Dot and her market garden and replace her with George. He buried and reburied the thought every time it resurrected, fought it off with the shield of self-righteousness and the sword of common sense. If George were in the same room with him day after day who could tell what might happen, except the obvious? The edible fat would be in the fire.

One afternoon Tony stayed behind to gather up the remains

of the in-boxes scattered round the classroom. Sometimes he imagined what would happen if some of the mock memos he used for training got into the system outside. It was his ambition to send them to the directors and union officials on his last day at Edible Fats. He would be like the hero escaping from the baddies' headquarters and watching it explode into flames behind him. He thought he was alone but George was hovering by the door.

'Can I talk to you about personnel?' she asked, fixing him in the spotlights of her blue eyes. There was no escape. She helped to stack the wire trays. He tried to be cool although his heart was pounding.

'Of course. You still want to be in personnel? After what you've seen so far? You'll never be managing director, you know.'

'That doesn't interest me.'

'The pay isn't very good. It's the same now but in twenty years the others in the class could be earning twice as much as you.'

'I know that. Reely.' From her mouth the Birmingham twang was not as ugly as its caricature on TV. It seemed genuine and unpretentious. You could look down on an accent like that but you would trust it. She had a lovely voice.

'Why do you want that sort of job?'

'I saw so many people like my Mom and the permanents at the supermarket and lots of others who were lucky enough to have jobs who were so bloody miserable at their work. They make a fuss about unemployment but so many people can't wait to get away from work when they have it. It would be nice to do something that made people a bit happier at work.'

'Sort of prison chaplain?'

'Perhaps we can talk another time.'

'Please don't go. I didn't mean that.'

He picked up a paper lying on the floor under a desk. He had said almost exactly the same thing to Alex when he transferred from production to personnel. Making people happy and motivated and fulfilled while they filled plastic bags with frozen peas and drove round supermarkets filling shelves with cans of beans and pored through print-outs looking for unpaid receivables.

'You know the best job I ever did?' he asked. 'I sampled inner tubes at a tyre company. I had to fit the tube to an air hose and put it in a tank of water. If I saw bubbles I rang a bell and someone came with a pad and wrote the tube number down. I did it for three months and I was sorry to leave. Can you explain that?'

'All of us hope that something's going to happen, don't we?' she replied. He pondered the simple truth of her remark.

'If we didn't think something was going to happen, even if it never did, what would be the point of it all, reely?'

'George?'

'Yes?'

'Can I buy you a drink?'

He put the in-baskets back in the cupboard they shared with the sub-arctic bush tomato seedlings while he waited for her to get her things and come back from the loo.

'Easy, wasn't it?' he told himself.
'You've done it hundreds of times before.'
'Like what? She's one of your trainees.'
'Rubbish. What do you know about falling in love? You're old enough to be her father.'
'One little drink. A chat about personnel and home in time for supper.'
'The pub as usual.'

'I shouldn't be doing this.'
'Not with anyone like her.'
'But I've fallen in love with her.'

(Does some mental arithmetic.)
'I'd have been a precocious fifteen year old.'
'Where can we go?'

'Impossible. The rest of the office will be there. I might as well put it on the notice-board.'

'Put what on the noticeboard? All you're doing is Relating to Subordinates. You teach a seminar on this to middle managers. The pubs in the City are full of middle aged men Relating to pretty girls who work with them.'

'Achievement. Recognition. Job Interest. Responsibility. Personal Growth.'

'But that's what you give them all day.'

'You've got to think about your own Objectives with her. What are the Success Criteria?'

'All right then, if you don't like Motivational Theory, what about selling techniques? What are the Features of this encounter? What are the Benefits? What are the Incentives?'

'What's the matter now?'

'We'll go to the wine bar under London Bridge. It's on the way to the station. But what are we going to talk about?'

'Don't give me that rubbish.'

'I'm paid to.'

'Belt up.'

'Oh Lord. Oh Dear Lord.'

'I'm wearing odd socks.'

'My God. Look who's just come in,' said Robert, the trainee brand manager, tucking his tie back in his jacket as if he had been caught in a state of undress. Debbie, the trainee market researcher, squashed next to him in the corner behind the small upturned barrel, flicked a blonde tress over her ears and squinted through the dark and smoke of the subterranean wine bar. Her contacts were starting to feel gritty.

'Who?'

'Our Tony and that little totty from production engineering.' He put his hand back on the thigh that was squashed against his own, a few inches higher up than it was before.

Tony shepherded George as close to the bar as he could

and left her standing while he nudged and sidled his way through the drinkers to place his order. She stood with her arms by her side, staring up at the blackboard over the bar advertising vintage ports and champagne concoctions like a bewildered traveller in front of the departure board.

'Bit of a smoothy, our Antonio,' said Robert, simultaneously taking a swig of his chablis and stroking his hand up and down her thigh under her pink dress. His palms were warm and sticky against her damp, soft skin and she thought of two pigs rubbing up against each other but she did not stop him.

'You think so? What about those ties of his? I think his wife knits them for him.'

'No. It's that vedgy secretary of his, Dot. She weaves them out of carrot tops and dyes them with beetroot. If you can't eat it, wear it.'

She put her arm on his shoulder and teased the curls on the back of his head. He thought of a monkey grooming for fleas but he did not stop her.

'You know why only men wear ties?' she said. 'The way a man wears his tie reflects his image of his own penis.'

'No wonder you're in market research.'

'Let me see yours,' she said. 'Your tie I mean.' She put down her glass and reached inside his jacket. She waved his tie in front of his nose. 'Look at this. Covered with little purple spots.'

'I don't believe it. She's having a snowball.'

'Why not? That's what they drink in the north of England. Snowballs and scampi and melon balls flambéd at your table,' she said, dipping the tip of his tie into his glass.

Tony stood in the middle of the floor, holding two glasses to his lapels and fending off jostling drinkers with his elbows. His hand was wrapped around the glass of advocaat and lemonade as if to shield it from the mocking gaze of the *maîtres du vin* round him. They looked round for somewhere to sit.

'He always looks so glum.'

'When he's not putting on an act for us.'
'What a life.'
'You wonder what's on his mind.'
'Probably the same as on everyone else's,' she said, putting her hand on top of his.
'What was that garbage this morning? Matzo's Hierarchy of Needs?'
'You can't be happy unless you've satisfied your basic physiological needs.'
'Like I said. It's on everybody's mind.'
She gave his tie a jerk making him bang his bottom lip on his glass.
'You think he's trying to score, do you sweetie?'
'Stranger things have happened. I bet he lives on his own in a little flat south of the river somewhere. He's paying the kid's school fees and the wife's maintenance and the mortgage on the four bedroomed semi in Finchley. She does picture framing. He had to buy his wife the Renault 4 but luckily he still has the company Sierra. He's waiting to meet someone just like his ex-wife but meanwhile picks up totties from his training course on a Friday night. Poor bastard.'
'He may be gay. Have you thought of that? There are plenty of gay married men.'
'Well I'm neither,' he said pushing his hand as far as it would go and squeezing while he nibbled her ear. 'Let's go.'
He put his tie straight and she smoothed her dress over her knees. They stood up as far as the sloping cellar roof would allow and edged round the upturned wine barrel. Robert led the way to where Tony was standing, shouting something in George's ear.
'If you're quick there's a table in the corner,' said Robert.
'Oh ullo,' said George.
Tony started and briefly wiped his mouth with the back of his hand as if he had been caught eating sweets. He forced a jovial smile and folded his arms defensively across his tie.
'Ah. How nice. Can I buy you a drink? George and I were discussing hydroponics.'

Sorry they had to go. They were in a hurry. They had another appointment. Their eyes were shining with wine and lust. Robert's tie was hanging out again.

'Have a nice evening,' said Tony unnecessarily. He led the way to the barrel in the corner, threading his way through the press of bodies, looking round to make sure George was following. She sat in the corner under the lowest part of the roof where Debbie had been sitting and he squashed in after her. Their chairs were jammed up against the wall behind and there was hardly anywhere to put their feet. He had to sit with his knee pressed close to hers.

'What are hydroponics?' she asked.

'You grow things in water instead of earth. The company makes the chemicals you put in the water. Great idea. I hate the idea of my greens growing in earth. I go miles to buy things wrapped in cellophane. Comes of growing up in the city I suppose,' he gabbled.

'Reely?'

'All that dirt and filth in the country. Who wants to eat stuff that worms have been crawling over? And the smell. It's unhygienic.' (Why do I always say these things? Is this what Robert and Debbie were saying to each other? I mustn't talk about dead pigeons.)

'You're having me on.'

'I hate gardening too. All that pollination and fertilization and germination going on. All that filth and sex. It's disgusting. Promiscuity, that's what it is. I'm having none of that in my back yard. We live in a decent neighbourhood.' (What the hell am I saying? Am I going mad? I'll laugh so she thinks it's a joke. It is a joke, dammit.)

George laughed. She had a captivating chuckle and she showed her teeth and the corners of her mouth turned up. (That's how Alex laughs.)

'You're ever so funny. You'd never guess in that classroom. You look ever so serious in the office. Reely.'

'When I talk about the company's mission? Edible Fats and personal self-fulfilment? It is serious. It's bloody serious. It makes me cry sometimes, it's so bloody serious. Margarine is an integral part of western man's image. It means hardship in the war and a flat stomach and a beautiful bottom. We're making history at Edible Fats, you know.'

(This can't be me. She'll tell everyone what a nutter I am. How much of this wine did I have?)

He fingered his tie. 'Can I get you another drink?' praying he wasn't going to have to run the gauntlet of the wine tasters with another snowball.

'I did ask for a Chateau Saint Baule. It's on the blackboard. It's a Côtes du Rhône. I didn't reely want one of these. I don't like the cherries either.' She pushed over her half finished snowball.

'You don't like those?'

'Not since I worked in a pub once. The glasses are the worst to clean. And they've always got thick lipstick round the edges. Me mom likes them though.'

'Why on earth didn't you say?' he asked.

'Didn't like to. Anyway, you were being funny about the vegetables. I like people who make me laugh.'

His thoughts and emotions in a turmoil Tony went back to the melee at the bar for two glasses of Saint Baule. Was he expecting her to ask for a snowball? Did he want her to ask for a snowball because she looked the kind of girl he used to buy them for when he was twenty years younger?

'Two glasses of Saint Baule, please, without the cherry.'

Her knee was not in the same place again when he sat down but his foot touched hers. He adjusted his position on his chair as an excuse to give it a little nudge. She didn't move it away. He felt a tightening about the groin. Had she noticed? He nudged her foot again and still she kept it there.

'I've told you all about my hang-ups, you tell me about yours.'

He tucked his tie firmly back in his jacket.

'Me? I get up early in the morning and go for a run. That's daft, isn't it? . . .'

Tony nudged her foot. She did not take it away. He fondled it with his toecap and insinuated it underneath her sole. He jiggled it up and down and it followed his rhythm. Unless this pretty girl has a wooden leg I'm away. Right now I shall put my arms round her shoulders and tell her what beautiful eyes she has. Or should I put my hand on her leg first? No, first the declaration then the foreplay. Then she might stroke my ear, here in the dark or gently tease the hairs at the back of my head. I love that. These days I have to pay for that at the hairdressers. Then her place. A phone call to Alex. Sorry dear, I forgot to tell you. I'm having dinner with the new recruits tonight. How the hell can I get my arm round her? There's no room. Help. My arm's stuck. . . .

'. . . thanks ever so for the drink. I have to go now. I hope you get used to the garden. You could put trousers on the sweet peas.' She picked up her handbag from underneath the table and held it up to the candlelight. 'I shouldn't have left this on the floor. It's got footmarks all over it.'

Tony stood on the platform and waited for the next train, breathless from the sprinting walk over the bridge he had prescribed for himself to consume the adrenalin and lust engendered in the past hour. He had a headache from the smoke and wine but still felt restless and excited like a dog smelling distant heat.

On the tube between Bank and Euston Georgina took a tissue out of her handbag and carefully wiped away the footprints and wine and sawdust with a little spittle when she thought no one was watching her put the tissue to her mouth.

Debbie tugged impatiently at Robert's tie while he undid the buttons on the back of her dress, fingers shaking. The air was heavy with the scent of stale hyacinths. They both went down on their knees simultaneously, thinking the other would remain standing up and burst into giggles. Here then.

On the carpet. 'I wonder if Antonio and his totty are having a good time too?' he asked with his mouth full.

Alex and Tony were in the kitchen folding sheets that had just come out of the drier so they would not need ironing. Not so you really noticed. She passed him the double sheet off their bed. It was one of their oldest, brown stripes faded to yellow, fraying along the seams. They had had it since they were married. He imitated her movements, folding his end lengthways, finding the fold with his thumb, leaning back to stretch it again, holding his end up for her to take and add to her own. In the old days he would tease her by folding it the wrong way or twisting it anti-clockwise or backing away so she had to follow. She would pretend to be cross and tickle him to make him behave. They didn't do that any more.

'Who is George?' she asked.

Tony dropped the sheet. 'George? I don't know any George. Why should I know a George?'

'You were talking to George in your sleep this morning.'

Tony dropped the sheet again.

'What did I say?'

'I couldn't hear. But you definitely said George.'

'Impossible. You were dreaming.'

'You were talking to him.'

'Him?'

'Yes. George.'

'Oh *him*. George. Of course. Silly me. I must have been dreaming about the office. He's a new trainee at Fats. Nice chap.'

As soon as the sheets were folded Tony went upstairs to the bedroom. He had got out of that one by the skin of his teeth. He had to make sure Alex suspected nothing. He took his suits out of the wardrobe one by one and like a jealous wife inspected them for hairs on the collar and lipstick stained tissues in the pockets and matches from the wine bar and any other scraps of incriminating evidence. He squirted deodorant on the lapels to remove traces of scent. He searched the rest of the wardrobe and his drawer in the dressing table for clues to destroy.

9

Alex did not know what to do with her father's urn. Although it was empty and washed clean by the sea it didn't seem right just to throw it away or bury it in the garden with the hamsters. When they got home she put it on the top shelf of the wardrobe with her wedding veil, old handbags, Mark's first feeding bottle and other relics she was too sentimental to throw away. She also brought back from the seaside a black metal cash-box. The police phoned the day after the cremation to say it had been found in the wreckage of the beach hut and would someone come and collect it. Alex went without telling the others. If the rest of the contents of the hut was anything to go by, what was in the box would not reflect well on the memory of the dear departed. There was no key. She smuggled it home and slipped it under the bed.

One morning she came back from taking the children to school and before clearing away breakfast brought down the box. With a screwdriver and pliers from the saucepan cupboard she prized open the lock. She expected to find the jewel of the pornography collection. Instead she found a sealed plastic bag containing a bundle of letters bound with a rubber band, an envelope with a curl of fine hair, a baby's bootee and a Swiss cotton handkerchief embroidered with forget-me-nots. She pushed the cereal bowls to the other end of the table, wiped the plastic cloth with kitchen paper, sat down and started to read.

'My Darling Darling Philander. . . .'

Some were written by Veronica, some by her father. They were the most tender, sweet, loving words she had ever read. They wanted none of their love to slip between their fingers. They were passionate and sensual, reliving their moments on the stockroom floor, on the settee upstairs when Gloria was at her mother's, on Wednesday afternoons in the park. Each was consumed in the other, beside themselves. They were graphic and uninhibited but no more pornographic than memories of honeymoons. As Alex read them her lips grew dry and her palms grew moist and her heart began to pound. The first few letters were misspelt, ungrammatical, awkward, but written in a flood of passion. They became slower, more contrived, peppered with phrases and emotions that came from the magazine shelf in her father's shop. They started to play roles, look for emotions they thought they ought to feel. She also read through misted eyes about his worried, busy wife, his gawky, distant daughter, the remorseless treadmill of the shopkeeper's life. They described their longings and regrets and the meagre satisfaction of doing the right thing by not running away together. When they did run away the letters stopped.

Veronica wrote one more letter. It was the plainest, the least embroidered, the most moving. There was no room for posturing. It was written a month after Phil came back to his family. It said simply that she was pregnant, that she was moving away to her sister's in Birmingham, and it would be best if they never saw each other again. She would be grateful if he could spare some money for the child. At the end a touch of True Life Romances crept in. PS Please send back the letters we wrote each other. When he grows up I'd like our baby to know he was a love child.

Alex wished the box had contained pictures of blowsy, women in extraordinary underwear committing unnatural acts. What she had read was not fantasy, not deviance, not perversion. It was natural and real. She cleared the table. She put the cereal bowls in the fridge, the butter in the bread tin and tipped the contents of the sugar bowl in the sink. Her mother must never know. In any case Gloria would not believe the letters were genuine. Beatification had already begun. The police had made a terrible mistake. He would never have a beach hut. He must have been trying to rescue someone else. He gave all in life, he would have given all in death. Tony must not find out either. She had never told him before of Phil's missing year. Something she could not put her finger on made her reluctant to tell him. She was afraid of opening a Pandora's box much bigger than the black metal container sitting on her kitchen table.

She went into the living room and knelt in front of the monumental marble fireplace. She threw the letters on to the grate. Three matches broke as she tried to strike them. As she broke the fourth she felt tears drop on her hand. 'Daddy' she cried out loud. She sobbed great retching sobs. When she finished she picked the unharmed letters out of the grate. Burning things just left ashes. She would hide the letters where no one would find them. The cash box itself was too bulky to hide. She threw it on the skip outside number fourteen.

'OK Gang. Car keys in the middle of the table. Fantastic.'

'Let the ladies put in tonight,' said Gordon, adjusting his cuffs so the rotarian badge showed, 'June's driving. She's got the keys.'

'Fair enough. Sign of the times, eh girls?' said Humphrey.

'I don't let Humphrey drive the Alfa anyway,' said Rachel.

The women picked their handbags up off the floor by their feet and started to rummage. One by one they dropped their keys with a clatter on to the chrome and glass coffee table. Rachel's had an Alfa Romeo tag, June's a little gold pencil, Joanna's a leather thong and Alex's a twist of yellow and red plastic that Louise had given her for Mother's Day.

'Right. This is going to be fan-tas-tic. This is your first

time, isn't it Alex? Never mind, you'll soon pick it up. Easy days, eh gang?'

The others snickered politely.

'Fantastic. Mix them all up. No peeking now boys. Come on Humphrey take your pick. If it's Rachel's you have to throw it back into the pool. No husbands and wives. I'll get the drinks.'

Humphrey looked sheepish and buttoned his blazer. He had worn a blazer on every social occasion in his life since he started secondary school. He closed his eyes and took out Joanna's keys. She winked flirtatiously and he patted the cushion next to him. Gordon closed his eyes and drew out the red and yellow plastic. Alex forced a smile and went to sit beside him. Tony made a play of shielding his eyes and picked out Rachel's Alfa Romeo. She blew smoke from her cigarillo into his eyes. That left Sam paired off with Gordon's wife June. He came back from the bar with a tray of drinks, careful not to spill anything as he stepped down into the recessed lounging area, and put it on the chrome and glass coffee table.

'Fantastic. Fantastic. Dim the lights, start the music, let's have fun fun fun. . . .' He leaned over a control panel set in the corner table between two of the three sofas and turned up *The Hollywood Bowl Strings Bring You Frank Sinatra*. '. . . I'll do it my-ee way. . . . Rachel, here's yours.'

Sam put Rachel's large whisky and water down in front of her while she lit another cigarillo. She was a successful woman. She had built up her estate agency in five years from a tiny office in a side street to a prime corner site with house details revolving in the windows like doner kebabs. She blew smoke up to the crystal light fittings. The fluffy ringlets of dyed corn blonde hair round her face failed to soften her prominent nose and emphatic jaw-line. Rachel had bones. They not only stuck out of her face but out of her arms and her hips and her massive knees. Her bosom tried to burst out of its shocking pink silk shirt so she chained it in with heavy gold links and ropes of pearls that clanked and churned over her chest. Her shirt hung out over a voluminous Liberty print skirt. She wore ankle length cowboy boots in sculpted leather with pointed toes and straps for spurs.

'. . . and this is for Humphrey. Bianco and soda, right Humphrey? Fantastic. Sooner we start the sooner we get the fun and games.' Humphrey was Rachel's third husband. She called him 'Pet'.

'Well I hope we're all in the mood this evening. Fantastic. Who knows what will happen? June, yours was the sweet Martini and Gordon's was the gin and tonic. What a memory.'

June was wearing her little white cotton blouse over her little blue skirt and her little white sandals with the little gold buckles. Silly her, she had left her rings by the side of the sink again and twisted her middle finger where they should have been.

'Fantastic. White wine for Alex and Tony and a Bacardi on the rocks for me. What will you have my sweet petal? Come on, they're panting to begin.'

Joanna came into the room with a tray of dips and roughage. As she tripped down the step Sam deftly caught the tray as if they had been practising. They were a wonderful couple. Joanna had put her hair up for the evening. She was wearing a low cut white summer dress, trimmed with lacy stuff round the hem.

'The usual, Sweetheart. Campari and orange.'

Sam went away to the bar. Tony was the first to plunge into the dip, craning over his shoes and cupping a hand under his chin so he wouldn't dribble on his party cords. Rachel made Humphrey pass the tray to the ladies. Sam clapped his hands and opened the board on the table. Then they all settled down with their partners to a game of Trivial Pursuits.

'What did Zsa Zsa Gabor say was almost as silly as getting married just because you love a man?'

'Come on Humphrey.'

'Have a guess.'

'Getting divorced just because you don't.'

'Humphrey's cross because you're using new questions. He goes through ten cards a night swotting up the answers. That's why he's so usually so good at it, aren't you Pet?'

'That's a lie. I just happen to be good at general knowledge.'

'Who said married men make the best lovers?'

'Marilyn Monroe said that.'

'Come on June. Your throw.'

'Give us a red doodah.'

'We're winning.'

'Naughty naughty. Can't give your husband clues.'

'A six. Which way shall we go?'

'Who's asking the questions?'

'I am.'

'What sociable marital practice is the primary topic of the John Updike novel, *Couples*?'

'Never read it.'

'Have a guess.'

'The answer is "Wife swapping". Come on Joanna. Get moving.'

'What does cunnilingus mean?'

'It's on the tip of my tongue.'

'What did Robert Louis Stevenson define as "at its lowest, a sort of friendship recognized by the police"?'

'I don't like these questions.'

'Alex don't be a spoilsport.'

'They're silly questions.'

'That's the whole point. They always are in Trivial Pursuit.'

'She means they're serious questions, don't you Alex?'

'What's the answer, anyway? I bet it's marriage.'

'Dead on. Marriage it is. Give them a yellow doodah.'

Alex stood up, her face red.

'Count me out. I'm not playing. It's trivial and silly and nasty and I'm tired of all this play-acting and innuendo and stupidity. Have we got nothing else to think about? Nothing else to do? This is nothing but bourgeois decadence and we shall reap the fruits in the whirlwind of the class war as our social structure disintegrates.'

'Shh Darling,' said Tony, 'it's only a game.'

'All right, all right,' said Sam, 'we'll change the boxes.'

Alex sat down, took a swig of her glass and hummed to Frank Sinatra while the others busied themselves with roughage and dip.

'OK Fan-tas-tic. Humphrey. History. How many wives did Henry the Eighth have?'

'Then what will you do?'	'I'll take her back home.'
'Then what?'	'She'll ask me in.'
'You should be so lucky.'	'Cup of coffee before you go, wink wink.'
'Coffee keeps you awake. You'd better have a nice cup of tea.'	'I'll help her off with her coat in the hall and then she'll take me into the lounge. Stoke up the fire. A little soft music, a couple of table lamps. In the mood.'
'I bet she lives in a tatty bedsit.'	'A little drinkie-poos on the velvet sofa? Here, you open it. You're so strong Tony.'
'She'll give you instant brewed up on a ring. And creamer out of a cardboard tube.'	'Why don't you take your jacket off? I'll slip into something more comfortable. Throw another log on the fire. Make yourself at home on the bear-skin rug.'
'Have you got fifty pee? Ten pee will do. The meter's run out.'	'Do you like this kimono? Feel how soft the silk is. You like soft things, don't you Tony. I can tell from your lovely ties. Let me loosen yours.'
'I just have to go down the hall to rinse the mugs out. Back in a sec.'	'She'll be so tender and innocent and fragile. She'll cry just a little bit. Then she won't be able to help herself, she'll be

        all over me, a tigress, a frenzy, help, I'm melting, oh no, oh no, oh oh oh. . . .'

'You dreamer you.'

Tony leaned back his chair and stabbed the letter-opener into the side of his desk. Over the past five years he had bored a hole about an inch deep, just like his desk at school. The letter opener was a brass dagger, a present from an Indian trainee whose vocation in life was now marketing pot noodles to the Tamils of the sub-continent. It must have been a terrible weapon, ripping and gouging the flesh round the incision if its performance on envelopes was anything to go by. Tony kept it to bore holes in his desk and simulate *hara-kiri* when he felt depressed. Was he going to ask her or wasn't he? If she refused how would he ever be able to look her in the face again? The consequences of her accepting were even more horrendous. It could change his whole life. And George's whole life. And Alex's whole life and Mark's whole life and Louise's whole life. Everybody's whole life. On the other hand it could be a total non-event. Thanks for dinner. Bye. See you in the morning. What could be more innocent?

 He picked up the invitation. The Institute Of Management Training. Park Lane. Annual Dinner. Dress Informal. Seven-thirty for eight. What was wrong with bringing a colleague from work who was interested in the profession? They always put 'and Guest' on invitations now instead of Mr and Mrs so that people could either bring their own husbands or wives or other people's husbands or wives. They would all wonder who that young girl was with him. It would be round in no time. Let them gossip. Who cares?

'How are you going to tell Alex?'   'You're not coming to the annual dinner this year. I'm taking someone else.'

'You haven't got the guts.'
'Are you mad?'
'You are mad.'

'You'll get animal passion all right.'

'If I were you I'd tell her it was the Edible Fats Social Club bingo and snooker night, employees only.'

'I think I'm having an affair.'
'I want an open marriage.'
'I still hanker after animal passion.'

'So there you are, my dear. My mind is made up. I shall not require your companionship on this glittering pinnacle of the social calendar, this *succès fou* of the *beau monde* of *le management training*.'

'And as for you, you namby-pamby creep, you bleating coward, I'm sick and tired of your moaning and snide remarks and pouring wet blankets and throwing cold water in the works and chucking spanners over everything I do. You were the one who stopped me going off the top board and buying a motorbike and joining the paras and emigrating to Canada and taking up parachuting and buying Australian mining shares and asking Bo Derek for her autograph and everything. Why do you think I'm here right now with nothing to do except jab holes in my desk? Because of you. What have I got to show for it all? A wife who doesn't give a shit and two kids who need me for my pocket money and a mortgage and a wreck of a house and two hundred British Telecom shares. Big Deal. Well this time I'm

'OK OK. Have it your own way. We'll see. We'll just wait and see.'

going to stand up and rip my Marks and Spencer's fifty per cent dacron shirt open and you'll see a bloody big S that's what you'll see. And no frigging around in telephone booths either. This is it. I.T. Will the real Tony step forward please and take a bow? I'm going to tell it like it is. I shall tell her straight and I shall tell George straight and I shall tell everybody straight. So sod off! Sod off with your nasty little ways, your conniving and cheating and weaseling, your petty little *compromises*. I have had enough. N.U.F. do you hear? I have decided to be a MAN from this moment on.

10

Tony couldn't make up his mind which tie to wear. His friendly, woolly ties were not the thing for a formal dinner. Besides, he was out to make a bold, definitive statement. He ignored the best dark blue silk with the little white dots. Alex had given it to him for Christmas. The maroon with little crests that looked regimental from a distance was too staid for seduction. All his colourful, devil-may-care psychedelic kippers were symptoms of acute sixtyitis and advancing age. The blue silk would have to do. Serve Alex right.

Alex ran into the bedroom clutching a towel, drops of water on her back, hair in rats' tails on her shoulders.

'I'm going to the Training Association meeting after work. I'll probably stay out for a drink afterwards,' he said casually.

'Fine.'

'I mean, I ought to fraternize a bit.'

'Fine.'

'You needn't wait up.'

'Fine.'

'Don't bother to save dinner. I'll get a sausage.'

'Fine.'

Didn't she care where he was going? Why didn't she comment about his best tie? Didn't she remember that he never ate pub sausages? Why didn't she offer to come and meet him after the meeting? WHY DIDN'T SHE STOP HIM?

He stood in front of the mirror to tie his tie. The front bit was too short. He unravelled the knot and tried again. This time the front bit dangled down over his flies. He unravelled it and tried again. Alex let the towel fall to the floor and stepped between him and the mirror. She opened her mouth so she could put mascara on her eyelashes. He had to stand on tiptoe and peer over her shoulder. He looked at her reflection. There were a few dimples and wrinkly bits but it wasn't a bad body to be intimately associated with. His hands hovered over her bottom but thought better of it. What was the point? This time he got it right, the tip just touching the top of his trousers. Don't wait up then. Don't wonder what I'm up to. Don't ask where I'm going and who I'm going with.

He paced up and down the lobby looking at himself sideways in the mirrors that decorated the pillars. Every few paces he tightened his tie and looked at his watch. This was madness. They should be huddled in a corner of some discreet little bistro, sipping house white and picking bits of candle grease off the bottle between them. Instead they were about to spend the next three hours under the bright chandeliers of the Tudor Suite, fiddling with the menu card, praying for the wine waiter to come round and herding breadcrumbs backwards and forwards across the tablecloth with the back of the dessert knife. Was this the seedbed of an adulterous passion? He wished he'd had the guts simply to ask her out to dinner.

He did not recognize her when she came through the revolving door. Her hair was tousled up into a tangle of spikes and sprinkled with glitter. Each cheek was split in two by a vermilion gash, the same colour as her lipstick. Her eyes were set in panda rings. She wore a loosely fitting satin buccaneer shirt slashed into tatters over a tight Band-Aid T-shirt. Below this were black cotton harem trousers decorated with little silver moons and stars and pointy toed high heeled ankle boots. Instead of a sensible handbag she had a khaki canvas knapsack slung over her shoulders. He steered her into the Tudor Suite feeling more like her father than her lover, embarrassed and proud.

They didn't even sit next to each other. George was on the other side of the long table, two places down, too far away to talk to. On her right was a middle-aged queen with a sweet little pink bow tie. Her other neighbour was several years younger than Tony. He looked American with a jogger's gaunt features and bottled tan and short black hair brushed back and a gold pin that pinched together the two wings of his collar and gave his yellow tie a permanent erection. After the first glass of wine George's eyes were shining. She shrugged and giggled and bit her bottom lip and nudged her companions with her elbow and tugged their sleeves and whispered things into their ears that made them smile. Tony strained to hear what she was saying but caught only the occasional 'reely'. On Tony's right was a large lady covered all over in large black plastic sequins like a mussel bed. She was in recruitment for one of the big banks. She spent the first half an hour telling him what a good listener she was. On his left was the mousy wife of a redundancy consultant whose passion in life was the preservation of rural bus services in East Anglia. This topic took up the grey beef and selection of waterlogged vegetables. Opposite was a lecturer in organizational behaviour, an authority on motivation in Arkansas pyjama factories in the fifties. Hell must be like this, Tony thought. But no, only purgatory. Hell came with the speeches.

After dinner Tony found himself next to the American at the urinals.

'I enjoyed your colleague.' It sounded like a biblical euphemism for what Tony was planning to do later.

'Refreshing, isn't she?' he replied.

'She said you'd both join me for an after-dinner drink.'

Burt worked for a computer company in California. He was over with their UK subsidiary on a six month assignment. He exuded health and youth and jogging and aerobics and decaff and bran and low cal and positive additood. He looked as if he could keep going all night with girls like George. He let her order a small brandy and Tony a large one before he asked for a Perrier for himself. He entertained them with stories of San Francisco while Tony competed with some of his father's old Irish jokes. While she went to the loo Burt offered them a ride home in his Jagwaar.

'Don't worry,' said Tony, 'we're going the other way.'
'You don't know which way I'm going,' said Burt.
'Which way are you going?'
'Any way you want to go.'
'It's no trouble. And I've got the Porsche outside.'
'Oh. OK. Well, have fun. Nice meeting you guys. And I'll call you at the office tomorrow,' he said to George.

It occurred to him only while he finished his cognac that he was not equipped for seduction. His wallet contained a few pound notes, a Barclaycard, a dry-cleaning ticket, an office I.D. card and an out-of-date raffle ticket for Louise's school fête. But the little compartment at the back had been empty since Alex went on the pill after Louise was born. What if George wasn't? What if she had none of the other devices? What, impossible thought with girls these days, if she'd never done it before? It wasn't the sort of thing you asked a girl before you took her home for the first time. I mean, he'd hardly had a chance to talk to her all evening. It was half past ten. Where could he go at this time of night? The hotel shop was closed. How about the all night Asian stores on the Earl's Court Road? Half a pint of milk, a vegetable samosa and a packet of three please. Unlikely, squire. His only chance was a buy-me-and-stop-one machine in a pub lavatory. And there was only half an hour until closing time.

It was the quickest pub crawl he had ever been on. Seven

pubs in twenty minutes. George was bewildered. The pace was killing. They burst into lounge bars and Tony looked frantically round for the gents. He ordered two brandies and excused himself. He rushed back, made her swig her glass and pushed her back out into the street.

'You haven't got bladder trouble have you?' she asked at the Marquis of Granby.

'I'm looking for a phone,' he snapped.

He could have had plenty of aspirin and in one upmarket place an impregnated toothbrush. At last, during drinking up time, he found what he wanted. They were black and she would think he was kinky but by then it would be too late. Now that the practicalities were taken care of he could concentrate on romance.

She closed her eyes and clutched his arm as they shivered in the damp chill of the summer night while he tried to remember where he had parked the car. He forced himself to concentrate. He had drunk three gins, several glasses of wine and half a dozen large brandies. Just as well. Dutch courage.

'I feel sick,' she slurred, 'I've never drunk brandy before. Only on Christmas pudding. Hic.'

He helped her into the car and fastened her seatbelt. Her spiky hair had gone limp and her panda rings were dissolving round the edges. 'Where do you live?' he asked.

'Dollish Hill.'

'No problem. My wife used to live out that way. Cricklewood actually.'

He bit his lip. That was stupid. He had avoided mentioning Alex all evening. Fortunately George did not pick up the cue. She slumped against the window with her eyes closed.

'I thought you said you had a Porsche.'

'You must have misheard. Listen George, ever since I first saw you that day in class I haven't been able to get you out of my mind. . . .'

She heard nothing. She was asleep. Oh God, not another A person. Why couldn't he meet a nice nocturnal girl for a change? He shook her awake when they got to the North Circular Road so she could direct him. They drew up outside a row of thirties semis. How many times in his youth had he brought girls home to places like this? More than he could remember. Hushed whispers in the hall; Mum and Dad upstairs in bed; petting on the sofa; half listening for creaks and footsteps upstairs; leave the door open so we can hear if someone comes down; or close the door so they can't hear us; giggle and slobber and grope on the stretch covers. He forced his eyes to focus on George's face and gave her his best smouldering gaze. But before he could take her in his arms she wrenched the door open and stumbled along the pavement to a low wooden gate marked Shangri-La. He caught her up when she was half way up the garden path.

'Aren't you going to say good night?' he asked.

She turned and looked at him. Her eye were moist, her gaze distant, her lips full and slightly parted. She held out her arms. He felt her young, supple body tremble in his embrace. Like lovers under a harvest moon they stood in the yellow light of the streetlamps. Gently he took her chin and raised her face to his. She turned her head away and in an impulsive, passionate surrender threw up over the lobelias. He held her head and breathed through his mouth until she had finished, looking round and pretending he wasn't there like holding a dog's lead when it's doing its business. He gave her his handkerchief and helped her to the front door. She gave him her key like girls do in old movies.

'I'm sorry. Reely I'm sorry.'

'Please don't be sorry. Love is holding someone's head.'

He drove back slowly, concentrating on the white lines and keeping his eye open for police. He didn't feel too great himself. The more he tried to force out of his mind the events of the evening the more they came back to taunt him. Was it just him? Or was adultery always so squalid?

11

'Are you practising to be a ventriloquist?' asked Alex.

'My head hurts when I move any part of it. I would regard it as a personal favour if you would show a tiny bit of sympathy,' he croaked, trying not to move his lips.

'You were in late last night,' she accused.

'Was I? How do you know? You were fast asleep.'

'I heard you come in.'

'Funny how when you're a kid you can never pretend to be asleep. Your eyelids quiver or you start to giggle. Then you get married.'

'You must have had a good evening.'

'Why do you say that? Please don't rattle those plates. Please.'

'You're going to have to cut down on your drinking.'

'Rubbish. I've been like this only half a dozen times in my life.'

'And all those have been in the last three months. What's the matter with you?'

'Nothing. Absolutely nothing. Something must have upset me. Probably the sausage. You know how sausages give me a hangover. Could you pass those Alka-Seltzer please.'

'You've had three already. Your clothes had all the signs of a good time.'

Oh so casual. Dropped just like that. She had been inspecting his clothes. He felt a wave of nausea and the vice on his head tightened half a turn. But at the same time he felt a tremor of excitement down where the brandy still churned. Lipstick on the collar, a long hair on his jacket, little bits of glitter sticking to his shirt front, perfume on his shoulder, make-up on his tie. Attack was the best form of defence.

'What do you mean?'

'There's sick all over your shoes.'

'It wasn't mine. I'm never sick. Not until I get home.'

'Whose was it then?'

'You've got a suspicious mind. What did you find with the bits of tomato in the trouser turn-ups?'

'Don't be disgusting.'

'You're the one who's disgusting. Fancy inspecting my shoes when I come in late. What on earth did you expect to find? Doctor Watson, sniff sniff, someone has been drinking champagne out of this man's shoe. Why didn't you just ask me where I'd been instead of pretending to be asleep so I wouldn't molest you?'

'I didn't go inspecting your shoes. I smelt them when I woke up.'

'What a fuss. This is unbelievable. What an inquisition. Guilty m'lud guilty. What of I have no idea. What is this? Look what I get just for getting back late. Anyone would think you'd come home in the afternoon and found panties on the chandelier. So what if there was a bit of sick on my shoes? I could just as easily have trodden in dogshit or sat in a plate of lasagne. They're the hazards of city life. I don't know why you're on at me. If you must know I was standing next to someone in a pub who was sick over my shoes. That's all. Finished. End of story.'

This was good. Fight back. Don't give her a chance to ask the real question: Who were you with last night?

'Are you going into the office today?' she asked.

'Why shouldn't I? I work there don't I? What's so

different from any other day? If I don't go in we all starve. It's not a hobby. Not like the occupations of some people I know.'

'What time will you be back?'

'I thought I'd pop into the wine bar for a couple after work and then on to Maxime's for dinner and then take in a show and on to a club. You needn't wait up. I'll see you at breakfast.'

'I thought we could go out for a drink or something. Why don't I see what's on at the Odeon?'

He dropped two Alka-Seltzer in his orange juice and watched them fizz. She did suspect something. She never suggested going to the cinema. She would be suggesting they went to bed in the afternoon next. What could have been in that sick? Why else would she suggest a quiet little evening together? This was the soft approach. The little chat, the needling questions. She had found something else on his clothes. She had found something in the pocket? But what? Cloakroom ticket? After Eight wrapper? He hadn't been near George except to hold her head. His handkerchief, that was it. He had given George his handkerchief and now it wasn't in his top pocket. Othello and Desdemona all over again. But this time it was the handkerchief that wasn't found that was going to start all the trouble. Lord she was crafty. Fancy going through his pockets to see what she couldn't find. He would have to tread very carefully now. Humour her. Don't let her suspect you suspect she suspects. For God's sake don't mention handkerchiefs.

'Great idea. Let's see what's on at the handkerchiefs.'

'What?'

'I said great idea. Let's see what's on at the Odeon. Great idea. Get a sitter. Go out together.'

'What was that about handkerchiefs?'

'What about handkerchiefs? Me? I never have handkerchiefs. Only when I've got a cold. They're all upstairs in the chest of drawers. Never use them. Unhygienic. I use tissues. Just throw them away. When did you last have to boil a handkerchief for me? Go on, tell me. I just don't go in for them. Silk hankie flopping over the top pocket. Pooftahs. I may wear one with a dinner jacket from time to time folded into zigzags. It's not a bad idea to have one for emergencies. Nose bleed. Soup on the tie. Sick on the shoes. My mother always said you should carry one to give to a lady if she cries. You don't meet women who cry these days. You're all too tough and capable. You never cry do you? Besides you've always got a roll of toilet paper in your bag to blow your nose on. I never carry a handkerchief. Gone the way of the corset and the codpiece I'm afraid. I wouldn't hold on to shares in a handkerchief company. And I certainly wouldn't thank you for a packet of three at Christmas, even if they had my initial embroidered on them.

Oh Lord. How could he have been so foolish. *The packet of three*. Buy-me-and-stop-one. His initial was as good as embroidered.

Where had he left them? If they were in his trousers they would have fallen out when he hung them up. No, they were in the inside pocket of his jacket. While she looked for what she couldn't find she had found what she wasn't looking for. How was he going to explain that away? Darling I have no idea whose they are. Darling someone must have planted them on me. Darling a black man asked me to hold them for him. Look you stupid cow, the packet's still full. It was no use. Compared with a lousy handkerchief this was the big time. What Iago could have done with a missing packet of three. Better know the worst. At the risk of regurgitation he drank the Alka-Seltzer down in one go and made for the door.

'Are you sure you'll be well enough to go out tonight?'
'Of course. Get a sitter.'
'Why are you guzzling Alka-Seltzer then?'
'Prophylactic.'

Although it made his head hurt he went upstairs two at a time. Breathless he stood in front of the wardrobe. Be bold. He stuck his hand in the inside pocket, next to his wallet, and his fingers found the slim, shiny packet. At least they were there. But had she found them? He would have to wait and see. He would soon know from the questions she asked. Right now he would remove the evidence by throwing them away. But where? What if the children started ferreting in the dustbin or the bag split and the dustmen scattered them over the drive? He looked desperately round the room. On the mantelpiece was a red collecting envelope for Save The Children. He put the packet inside, sealed it, and put it back in the suit pocket. He would smuggle it out and throw it away at the station. Downstairs Alex was talking to Joanna on the doorstep. It was her turn to do the school run.

'Tony needs a bit of relaxation. He was rabbiting on about handkerchiefs this morning. I think it's stress at the office. It makes him aggressive.'

'Aggressive with handkerchiefs? What is he? A folk dancer?'

'Why did you give me all that brandy? Were you trying to have it off with me?' She looked straight at him. Her eyes were a piercing blue, like Alex's.

'Yes,' he admitted.

'I should have puked over your suit. It would have served you right.'

'Tickets please.'

She flashed a bus pass while he dug through his raincoat for change. They were on top of a number thirteen. He knew the route well. It went past where Alex used to live. George did not come to work on the day after the dinner. She phoned to say she had gastric flu. Tony was glad he did not have to face her. It was the last day of the induction course and he found it hard enough to recall his script through his ravaged brain without the constant reminder of the previous night's fiasco. On Monday she began a month at South East Regional Accounts in the office over the road.

He waited for her outside but she refused to come for a drink. She had to be home early to change. He insisted on going home with her.

'Why didn't you just ask me?' she asked. The conductor handed him change and churned out a ticket.

'Just like that?'

'It would have saved you a lot of money on brandy.'

He had never asked anyone that. It had always been unspoken, an understood progression from the first fondle. More important, she was obviously giving him a second chance. As they pulled away from Swiss Cottage station he popped the question.

'Will you sleep with me?'

'No.'

A stooping, grey faced man in an unseasonal overcoat slumped behind them. He wheezed and gurgled and gasped with the effort of getting his money out. Two large ladies eased themselves into the seat in front and debated in East European accents the merits of getting off at the Odeon or Golders Green station.

'Would you have slept with me the other night after the dinner?'

'No.'

'Then what was the point of asking?'

'To save you the trouble of getting me pissed.'

'Tickets please.'

He unravelled the ticket which he had screwed up into a little ball and smoothed it out on his knee for the inspector, a sour faced man with inquisitorial rimless glasses. His gimlet eyes penetrated Tony's tortured soul and passed on down the bus.

'I wasn't trying to get you drunk.'

'Why all the brandies then? What satisfaction would you have got to have me in a stupor? Is that how you get all your girls?'

So that's how she thought of him. Not the shy, romantic, tender lover in his prime as he saw himself but a dirty old man who got kids drunk to molest them. He wished he wasn't wearing his brown raincoat.

'I am not in the habit of getting girls. You are the first I have taken out since I got married.'

'Tell me another one.'

'All right. If you must know we went on that pub crawl because I was looking for a contraceptive machine.'

The top of the bus went quiet. The two ladies in front were looking intently out of the window. The inspector gazed unseeing at a bus pass three rows ahead. Only the man behind seemed to ignore them. He was too preoccupied with drawing his next breath. George concentrated on a signpost to Finchley and Frognal station. Her shoulders started to shake. She rested her forehead on the glass. He was making a real fool of himself.

'I'd better get off. I can get a number two-B to Victoria.'

She turned round wiping the tears of laughter from her cheeks and put her hand on his arm.

'Reely? Did you find any?' was all she could say before being overcome by another spasm of giggling. He stood up but she pulled him down again. She doubled up as far as you can in a London bus seat, holding her sides.

'Don't go. I'm sorry for laughing. And I'm sorry for being sick the other night.'

'Let's get off.'

'We're not there yet.'

'Fares please.'

'It's impossible to have a conversation here.'

'Don't worry about them. You fancy me?'

'Yes. You're the most beautiful person I've ever met.' All the declarations of love he had ever made had been on top of a number thirteen bus. Some people's lives are ruled by the stars, others by the bus routes. 'I want to apologize for the other evening. And I promise not to see you again.'

'Come on. Don't take it so seriously. I'm flattered.'

'It was stupid of me ever to think you could fancy me.'

'This is our stop.'

Stooping he led the way along the swaying aisle and down the stairs. He walked in silence with her to the end of her street.

'I'll say goodbye then.'

'Don't be daft. Come and have a cup of tea.'

Shangri-La belonged to Effie, an old friend of her mother's. She was staying there until she found a flat of her own. She pointed out the lobelias that were no worse for their experience. The night's rain had washed away all evidence of her indiscretion. She sat next to him at the breakfast bar in Effie's bright orange formica kitchen chaperoned by the picture of a wanton gypsy woman. He decided to have one last try and put his arm round her shoulder.

'You needn't do that to prove to yourself that you're attractive you know,' she said, putting a spoonful of sugar in her flowery cup. 'I think you're very nice. You're silly and kind and good-looking. And you make me laugh. You're not macho but you're sexy.'

'What's wrong with me then?'

'You're married. And you've got two kids.'

'They don't care much for me.'

'Don't give me that rubbish.'

'It's true.'

'So what if it is? That doesn't entitle you not to care about them.'

Out of the mouths of innocents. It was all right for her, a kid, she didn't know what it was like. She was going to give him stuff about his responsibilities in a minute.

'I never knew my Dad,' she said. 'I don't mind screwing around but not with other people's fathers.'

'What if I said I was leaving them. That I'd decided to be single again.'

'I wouldn't like you any more.'

He puffed out his cheeks and gave a big sigh.

'Is your wife screwing around?'

'Certainly not. Not that I know. I don't think so. She couldn't be.'

'Do you love her?'

'I don't know. I honestly don't know. And I don't know if she loves me. We just sort of co-exist. That's not much fun. And not much to look forward to for the next forty years.'

'What does she say when you tell her all this.'

'All what?'

'All you've just said to me.'

'I don't know. It's not something we talk about.'

'Perhaps you ought to start there.'

He banged his cup down on the saucer and slapped his other palm on the bright orange daisies.

'Listen. When I need a marriage guidance counsellor I'll get an appointment. When I want advice I'll ask for it. I don't need the wit and wisdom of some born again little prig who thinks marriage is a succession of one night stands with the same bloke. It's not like that. And if you start to preach to me about responsibilities I'll scream.'

She stood up and carried the cups and saucers to the sink.

'Effie will be home in a minute. And I have to change. I'm being picked up at seven.'

'Don't let me keep you.' He picked up his brown gaberdine mac. 'I'll let myself out. Have a wonderful evening. And stay away from the lobelias.'

'No wonder you're in personnel. You reely have a gift for human relationships. At least you're lucky about one thing.'

'I don't want to know.'

'When you get the male menopause you won't notice a thing.'

Alex had to ring three times. Joanna opened the door, her eyes red and cheeks streaked. She led the way back to the stripped pine table in the kitchen, sat down and burst into tears. She passed Alex a piece of paper to read. It was covered in fine print and little boxes to put ticks in.

'What's this? Pee one tank temp? Alt reg zero?'

'Other side.'

It was a letter. The writing was small and cramped and loopy in black ballpoint, the shrivelled writing they use on letters from the library or the tax inspector. But there was nothing inhibited about the words. 'My darling darling passion fruit' it started. Alex blushed after the first sentence. Sometimes when she was buying a magazine in the newsagent's and she was sure Mr Patel wasn't looking she browsed hastily through the adult section on the higher rack. The letter could have come out of one of them. She wanted to ask what some of the technical terms meant but this wasn't the moment. The letter was signed Romeo Superfly but she did not have to ask who had written it or whether it was meant for Joanna. She sat down next to her and put her arm round her shoulders.

'Where did you find it?'

'In his uniform. That's a pre-flight check list.'

'I'll make some tea.'

'That's sweet.'

'I brought a lemon.'

'That's nice.'

'They have nice ones at Sainsbury's.'

She busied herself with the kettle and sliced the lemon.

'How long has it been going on?'

'I don't know. He denies everything. He says I planted it. Can you believe it?'

'Why would you plant it?'

'To prove his adultery and get a bigger settlement.'

Alex made no comment. This was not the first time she had lived with Joanna through a divorce. She knew better than to get mixed up in the details. In any case Joanna was an expert by now.

'Alex? How do you do it?'

'What?'

'Stay married.'

'I supose we have a good relationship.'

'But what about sex? Don't you or Tony get bored? Don't you look where the grass is greener?'

'Sex is a symptom. Not a cause,' said Alex smugly.

12

'Is your wife screwing around?'

'Certainly not. Not that I know. I don't think so. She couldn't be.'

It was like falling in love all over again. He could not get Alex out of his mind. When he closed his eyes he could see her familiar face, the laugh lines round the clear blue eyes, the puckish dimples when she smiled, the slightly parted lips of passionate women and incurable mouth breathers. He had seen that face every day for over a decade, he thought he knew it as well as he knew his own. At a quarter to eight on a Wednesday morning he saw it properly for the first time. It was suddenly unfamiliar and mysterious. It seemed that he had known her for five minutes, no, five seconds. He stared at her while she shovelled All Bran into her mouth, a drop of milk dribbling down her chin. Her features had become disembodied and disconnected objects. Picasso had been right all the time.

'What's the matter?' she asked, wiping the milk off her chin.

'A cat can look at a king.'

'Daddy used to say that.'

Looking at her was like saying a word over and over again until it becomes an alien thing rolling round the tongue. He stared harder, trying to make sense of the collage in front of him. Who was this woman? She was a total stranger. Until yesterday he had had a conventional image of her face, a pattern imprinted in a few thousand brain cells. Somehow they had got jumbled up.

'Are you all right?'

'Right as a trivet.'

'Daddy used to say that too.'

He could not concentrate at work. The memos and papers and chits on his desk were meaningless. Dot asked him if he was going to the staff meeting at eleven. He looked at her blankly and said nothing. She repeated the question. Still he said nothing. She shrugged and went back to her typing. Dot's face looked normal. No one had interfered with the components. The tea-lady came in and she looked the same too.

'Sugar love?'

'Please Aggie.'

'When did you start taking sugar?' asked Dot.

'You're right. I don't.'

'I've put it in now,' said Aggie, who didn't like being messed about.

Tony took his sugared tea without a murmur. Aggie, Dot, all the rest of them were made of cardboard. If only he could catch them unawares he could peep behind them and see they were just cut-outs. Only Alex had a third dimension. How can you live with someone so long and not realize who they really are? The way she spoke cut into him like razors, the way she poured the tea, combed her hair, bit her lip when she was concentrating. These details came flooding back and swamped everything else. He took out a felt tip and doodled over a scrap pad and tried to imagine what she was doing now, where she was, who she was talking to. He had been such a fool. How could he have deluded himself for so long. He ripped the top sheet off the scrap pad and jotted down furiously the clues that had been staring him in the face for the past six months.

*

Clothes. When she started at the poly she dressed as she had never dressed before.

Scent. She wore it every day. He had given it to her, which rubbed salt into the wound.

Hair. She had her hair done. She brushed it every night.

Telephone. The wrong numbers THAT HE WAS NOT RESPONSIBLE FOR.

Dinner. She had cooked supper just for the two of them and put candles on the table and Christmas napkins.

She made an effort to be nice to him. She talked to him for no reason. She looked up from her books and made conversation about nothing at all. She made him cups of tea and coffee when he didn't ask for them. And the pancakes. He slapped his forehead, making Dot jump. She made pancakes last Sunday for the first time since they were married and reminded him how much he liked them. How calculating can you get! She had duped him beautifully. She had made him think it was all for him. He dug the Indian letter opener into the palm of his hand and screwed it round and round like a fanatic longing for the stigmata.

And then the worst. He could scarcely bring himself to think of it. No wonder she was so much more fun in bed, no wonder she moaned and sighed and pretended to come at the same time. The little fox was thinking all the time about her Lover. She would come home from an afternoon with Lover and feel guilty. What was the best way to assuage that guilt? He had been getting the scraps from Someone Else's table for two. She probably brought Lover back home during the day while he was at work and before the children came home from school. She opened the front door, *his* front door, let in Lover, put the chain on in case poor old Tony came back unexpectedly. She went into the kitchen and poured two glasses from the wine box. She led the way upstairs, sensing Lover's eyes on her bottom and her calves and her ankles. As soon as she put the wine down on the bedside table Lover seized her in his arms and covered her face and neck with kisses, tumbling her back on the bed. She made sure that when Lover called it wasn't covered with unironed washing and wet towels and toenail clippings. They ripped at each other's clothes, flung the duvet aside, and did things which she only let Lover do. They did them on his mattress, on his sheets, on his side of the bed. Then they showered together, with a new bar of soap specially unwrapped instead of the coagulated slime the children had left the night before. They sat down in the bath and Lover kissed her freshly painted toenails and her freshly shaven calves while she teased the hairs on his muscular chest and ran her fingers over the kind of stomach she had not seen on a man since she first married her husband. They patted each other dry and Lover pleaded to do it again and she said there was no time and then let herself be persuaded. There and then in the bathroom, her head over the washbasin as if she were bending over to wash her hair.

They quickly showered again and dressed. Tony closed his eyes to shut out the vision and drummed his clenched fists against his temples. But he could see them on the landing, locked in a final, tender embrace. She looked out of the front bedroom window and again out of the peephole in his front door to see if the coast was clear. When he had gone she retraced her steps, covering up the evidence. She rinsed out the wine glasses and took them down to the kitchen, straightened the sheet and switched on the electric blanket to dry it out, opened the bedroom window, scoured the carpet for things that might have fallen out of Lover's pockets.

God I've been a fool. Such a blind fool. He stabbed the dagger into the hole in his desk. I bet she's with him right now. What do they say about poor old Tony then? He hoped they were laughing at him. He couldn't stand it if they were feeling sorry for him. He gulped down the sweet tea. It tasted like poison but it didn't matter. He felt lonely and cold. He resented Dot complacently hammering away at her typewriter, obsessed with the trivia of everyday life. His own life was at a turning point. Confrontation, separation, divorce, the pain, the rebuilding, it flashed before his eyes as he drowned in misery. He would be a better man, tempered by fire. Nothing was worth doing unless there was pain. And there was pain, he could feel it now like a colic you know is going to get worse and worse and worse. He had not felt passion like it since he first met her. It was like falling in love all over again, only the reverse.

There was not enough to confront her with. He needed proof. Not for himself, he was safe in the knowledge of her infidelity, but for something to confront her with. He wanted to see with his own eyes, feel with his own hands smell with his own nose the evidence of her treachery. Then he would throw it in her face and walk away for ever. She was clever. Very clever. But no one is clever enough. There must be some trace, some reminder, even if she did not bring him home but went to Lover's luxurious bachelor apartment. He would have given her presents or written her letters or lent her a key. There must be something that she kept by her to remind herself of him. All Tony had to do was search. There had to be evidence. There always was.

He started to look for the evidence that very night when she was in the bath, washing away her guilt. He sifted through her bag and her purse like a tramp going through a litter bin, amazed at the cast-offs of a profligate society but finding nothing to feed his appetite. He went through the pockets of her coats and jackets heaped on the hooks in the hall but found only screwed up tissues. She had been very careful. He needed a day in the house on his own to search it from top to bottom. In the back of a drawer, under the corner of a carpet, in the bottom of a case, he would find what he was looking for.

He heard the waste-pipe gurgle and the bathroom door unlock. She would be damp and fragrant. He could go up into the bedroom and pretend to be amorous. It would annoy her to get sticky again just after she had come out of the bath. She did not have the monopoly of mental cruelty. No. She might think he suspected something and was trying to win her back. Until he had searched the house he wanted to give nothing away. Anyway, the thought of lying next to that treacherous Jezebel was too much. Let her stew by herself.

'Are you coming to bed Darling?' she called down seductively.

'Ha!'

'What did you say Darling?'

'Ha!'

Shaking his head he went into the kitchen and poured a large whisky. He took it into the lounge and stood at the French window, staring out at the house that backed on to theirs. The lights were on upstairs and down. It looked warm and friendly in the dark night and very far away.

He watched her every move. He went through her handbag and her briefcase and her pockets every night. He listened for the phone to ring. He toyed with the idea of hiring a detective but the expense was a deterrent and in any case he wallowed in the masochistic anticipation of catching her himself. He browsed through magazines looking for advertisements for bugging devices for the bedroom and the telephone and the car. He was first down to the mail every morning. He did not expect to find vellum envelopes with her handwritten address marked Private and Confidential. They were too clever for that. It was the brown ones he did not trust. He peered through the windows of the envelopes at circulars from mail order houses and tried to peep down the narrow gap in the corner of those from the book club. He thought he had tumbled to them when the third summons came from the library for *Black Beauty* and *The Day The Dinosaur Died*. The flap wasn't even sealed. That was it. Why hadn't he guessed before? They got letters from the library at least twice a week. Surely nobody else got so many dunning letters for overdue books. She was having an affair with the librarian. She could go and see him every other day without suspicion. They were closed on Wednesdays so he could come to the house. Other times they sneaked behind the religion and philosophy shelves by the card index and read *Fanny Hill* together. Tony scrutinized the scrawly handwriting, but unless they were using microdots there was no obvious message. It was obvious that they had worked out some sort of code. He threw the envelope casually down on the counter while she stirred the scrambled eggs. He watched for her reaction, the blush, the tremble, the suppressed smile.

'Letter for you.'
'Uh huh.' (She was so cool.)
'I said there's a letter for you.'
'Uh huh.' (So very cool.)
'Aren't you going to open it?'
'It's from the library.' (Ha! She knows.)
'Don't you open letters from the library?'
'I know what it is.' (Ha! She knows I suspect she knows.)
'Why don't you want to open it? Shall I just throw it away?'
'If you like. It's only *Black Beauty* and *The Day The Dinosaur Died*.' (Ha! She must have seen him yesterday.)
'So you knew then.'

She dropped the wooden spoon in the saucepan, pushed him out of the way and stormed out of the kitchen. He wondered whether to go after her and follow up with a direct accusation or to carry on stirring the eggs so they didn't burn. Before he could make up his mind she was back again. She thrust two books into his chest.

'You take them back as you're so high and mighty the library's open on Saturday too you know why should I always be the one who looks after the children's things I would have thought a little participation now I'm out all day instead of nag nag nag it's not as if they're overdue more than a couple of weeks and you don't pay fines on children's books. . . .'

He took them back to the library to discover that it was

staffed by a large middle aged woman who scolded him for bringing them back three weeks late. 'What male librarian said it would be all right?' she asked. 'We don't have any male librarians at this branch.'

But he was not discouraged. He knew it would only be a matter of time. He would lie in wait, the wounded hunter, for them to fall into his trap.

Derek did not ask her for a drink again although she fussed round with her books long after the others had left while he carefully dusted his leather jacket with a yellow handkerchief. He walked out with a curt goodnight. In that case, Alex decided, I shall ask him. And I will not feel guilty, I will not feel guilty, I will not feel guilty. But I won't stay very long.

'Sure,' said Derek, with his I-am-dangerous-person smile, 'let's go back to my place.'

'Oh no, that's not what I had in mind at all, I imagined we would go to the pub round the corner where the students and some of the staff usually go and I would have a shandy or a lime juice and soda and we would banter lightheartedly about bookkeeping and world revolution and I would show you that although I wasn't going to be taken in by your anarchical nonsense I was not blinkered and bourgeois, not a housewife mother-of-two aged 35 like they would say in the papers, but an intelligent woman, a vibrant and attractive personality and full of entrepreneurial flair and ambition with radical and independent views who coped wonderfully with her home and family and didn't feel guilty at all about establishing herself as a person in her own right and was confident that the children would benefit from the example although they were cross when the school trousers weren't dry on time and she didn't have time to make puddings. I didn't imagine we were going back to your bachelor flat to open a bottle of something bubbly from Bulgaria and put on a record and sit on a long luxurious couch and light a fire so I would have to take off my tweed coat and wish I could take off my velvet waistcoat but that would be too suggestive and in any case the seam on my blouse is pinned up where I should have sewn it while you took off your jacket and sat beside me and put your arm round behind me and were a dangerous person, it's not what I had in mind at all.'

'OK,' was what she actually said.

Derek's flat was the ground floor of a Victorian house. One wall was covered with pine bookshelves carefully stained to look like mahogany. The other walls were covered with red and black flags and posters exhorting readers to support this and smash that. The chairs and couch were uncomfortable contraptions of wood and steel and simulated leather. In front of the gas fire was a thick white flokati rug. On the mantelpiece was an aluminium bust of Lenin crowned with a wreath of withered daisies. Derek put a Barry Manilow record on the music centre and asked what she would like to drink.

'Wine?' she asked, going over to the windows that opened on to an overgrown garden. They were protected by a curved iron grille armed on the top with sharp spikes. 'Why the iron bars?'

'Burglars,' he said, getting out glasses.

'You respect your own property then,' she said as he tussled with the perforations on a box of Yugoslavian Riesling. He milked a glass from the teat and handed it to her.

'Cheers.'

'Cheers. Is this OK?' he asked.

She held her glass up to the light. 'A bit revisionist but very nice.' She prepared herself for the cut and thrust of the class war, the swift swordplay of conversational dialectic, but he switched weapons.

'I saw your husband in the wine bar the other night.'

'Oh? On his own?'

'Not quite.'

'His trainees probably.'

'Probably.'

'What does he think of your going to college?'

'I don't know what he really thinks and it's none of your business anyway, who cares about what he thinks or what he gets up to when he says he's working late, your relationship is with me, I'm a person in my own right, why don't you ask me what I feel about going to college?'

'He's very supportive,' is what she actually said.

He filled her glass, stooped to light the gas fire and slipped off his leather jacket while she hummed along with Barry Manilow and contemplated a socialist-realist depiction of a mother hero of the Soviet Union. He came up behind her. She smelt after-shave and chalk dust. She turned and looked him in the eye.

'Before we go any further I should tell you that I am happily married with a husband and two children whom I love very much. I think you are amusing with your little boy expressions and funny ideas and you're attractive and I'm sure you're used to bringing back your students and ending up with them on the flokati in front of the fire. But I have a relationship with my husband based on mutual trust and I believe the promises and bonds and obligations of marriage outweigh physical desire and the pleasures of the moment. Can we just be friends?'

'There's someone at the door,' was what she actually said.

Derek put down his glass. She heard him open the front door.

'Darling,' he said, 'how wonderful. Put your coat in the bedroom.'

She heard them go down the corridor past the living room. Barry Manilow sounded flat and empty. The wine tasted sour. She ought to get back to say goodnight to the children. She would go to the loo and leave. She picked up her handbag, went out of the living room and down the corridor. She passed the open door of the bedroom and saw Derek locked in a passionate embrace with a man in a moustache dressed up as a cowboy.

13

From his hiding place in the bushes Tony gave her another five minutes after he saw her drive off. He felt guilty as he let himself in through his own front door. He heard a man's voice and stood paralysed on the doormat until the music started and he realized it was the radio. Alex left it on when she went out on the same principle as leaving the lights on at night. She said it made the house seem inhabited. Tony said it led the villains straight to the hi-fi. He went into the sitting room and switched it off. He stood in the hall and held his breath, listening with his eyes closed to the unnatural silence. He had the uncanny feeling he was being watched. It seemed like someone else's house. Ninety per cent of your villains come through the front door, Sergeant Willoughby had said. It's not having things stolen that I find abhorrent, it's the invasion of privacy, Alex had replied.

'Snap out of it,' he said aloud, 'you can't be a burglar in your own home.' His voice echoed up the stairs. He resisted the temptation to turn round and catch the next train to work. He had come so far and he would go through with it.

Where should he start? He went into the kitchen. Her briefcase was on the table, the old solicitor's black leather case his father had given him when he started day release. He had lent it to her when she started college because it was too big for him now he only carried the newspaper and an apple to the office. Hiding mementoes of her Lover in there would be the ultimate duplicity, like wearing Tony's tie to meet him for lunch. He jerked it open and pulled the contents out on the table. Half a dozen pink and blue and green folders, a stenographer's pad, a book about oil companies, a couple of dried up felt tips and a few screwed up tissues. He tipped up the empty bag and shook it and banged the bottom and looked for a secret compartment.

It was unlikely that he would find anything downstairs. There were many good hiding places but it was too public. He would start with the intimacy of the bedroom. He went upstairs, avoiding the creaking step half way up. He knelt down in front of the bedside table and opened the cupboard. They had bought the pair of tables in a junk shop when they were first married. The cupboard doors had ventilation holes because that's where you kept the chamber pot. There was nothing in there now except a few screwed up tissues, the Bournemouth Echo Slimmer's Guide, a knotted blue dressing-gown cord, a subscription form for the 1981 National Geographic, a crab shell and a set of decals for an Airfix Harrier Jump Jet kit. He slammed the door shut.

Her stripped pine chest of drawers was next. The top was a mess of miscellaneous objects and screwed up tissues. He stared at it, trying to make sense of the collection but there was no message to be gleaned. He opened a wooden jewellery box and inspected each item but he had given her all of them. He picked up their wedding photo in its silver frame and looked at the back but there was only the name of the photographer. The top drawer was a tangle of pants and tights and odd gloves. In a flash of irrelevant inspiration he realized the real reason why tights had eclipsed stockings. Once you found one leg in this mess you automatically found the other. His fingers groped through them, squeezing and palping in the cotton and lace and fifteen denier nylon, driven by urges he only half understood. There was nothing. He took out the drawer and threw it on to the bed. He pushed his hand into the dark cavity and felt round but his fingers found only dust which he wiped off with a pair of blue and white bikini briefs.

Hadn't Lover bought her a set of red and black lace underwear? A garter? Silk pants with a fly front? Their lust left them no time for that nonsense. The other drawers were equally unrewarding. Nightdresses, shirts and a collection of neatly folded plastic bags. Sweaters, scarves and rolls of crepe bandages. Terry nappies kept out of superstition. Neatly folded jeans, incapable of being fastened even lying on the floor, kept in hope. A chewed, threadbare, one-eyed teddy bear, kept out of nostalgia. But nothing to satisfy his craving for incrimination. She was more cunning than he ever believed.

His hand was groping in the space behind the bottom drawer when he heard the front door being opened. Someone with a key. He froze. The door slammed. He heard someone stand in the hall and go into the sitting room. He wanted to sneeze. Who had a key apart from Alex? No one that he knew. If it wasn't her, the intruder was moving round with remarkable confidence. She came out of the sitting room and stood at the bottom of the stairs.

'Hello-o-o,' she yodelled. He did not answer but as quietly as he could put the drawer back on its runners. It jammed. He was caught red-handed. He shoved and pulled. He relived the feelings of being found with his hand in the biscuit tin, his mother's purse, the pencil box when he wasn't pencil monitor. Thank God she did not come upstairs but went into the kitchen. The drawer slid back. He checked the others and tucked back in bits of material that stuck out. He listened again. She walked back out of the kitchen into the hall and slammed the front door. He tiptoed out of the bedroom and into Mark's room at the front. He watched her get into the car with the briefcase she had forgotten and drive off.

That was a close shave. She had just called hello out of habit, to quieten the apprehension of coming into an empty house. He watched from behind the curtain for a couple of minutes and went back to work. He would try the wardrobe next. He started by ferreting through the jumble of shoes at the bottom. He found half a set of garden bowls, a polystyrene hairpiece stand and the inside of a hairdryer. He stood up and pushed all her clothes to one end of the rail with a teeth grinding scrape and yanked them one by one to the other end like a shopper at the sales. All he found in the pockets were screwed up tissues. Surely the mean sod would have bought her something for which she was still trying to invent an explanation for her gullible husband. Of course. She kept her new sexy wardrobe at his place.

He stood on tiptoe to look into the graveyard of the top shelf. He took out the corpses of old handbags one by one but all they contained were bus tickets and screwed up tissues. He stuck his hand in moth eaten woolly hats. He wrenched from underneath the rubbish a flat brown cardboard box which he had to put on the bed to open. It was her wedding veil, yellow and smelling of mothballs. Bitterly he rummaged in the tissues and put the lid back, like putting back the lid of a coffin. He pushed his father-in-law's urn to one side and scrabbled in the back corners. He stood breathing hard with exertion and anger, cobwebs over his suit and his nose running from the dust and smell of camphor.

What about the urn? No. She couldn't have. But why else would she have kept it? How low can she get? Desecration. Sacrilege. Her respectable, middle-class, devoted-husband-and-father R.I.P. would be turning in his grave if he weren't an ingredient of the English Channel. He reached up again and took down the shiny brown plastic urn. He shook it and there was a muffled thump. Something in his solar plexus tied itself in a knot. Above the pounding in his ears all he could hear was the wailing of a distant police siren. He grasped the top and twisted it but his hand slipped. He tried again but it remained jammed. Salt water must have got in the threads. He stuck it between his knees like an incompetent *sommelier* and twisted and yanked but it still would not open. He tried to jam the top in the bedroom door but only succeeded in chipping the paint. He would have to take it down to the cellar and use the vice.

He was halfway down the stairs when the doorbell rang. The shadowy shape through the stained glass was not Alex, and in any case she would use the key. It was probably a tradesman. He decided not to answer it in case he told Alex he had seen her husband the next time he called. He waited on the middle step of the stairs, holding the urn at arm's length. The man rang the doorbell again, waited another few seconds and went away. It was a good reminder that Alex might come home before he had finished. He put the chain on the front door so she could not get in even with her key. He was in control now. He went gingerly down the rickety wooden steps, keeping his suit away from the coal dust and peeling whitewash on the wall. It smelt damp and musty, like a crypt. With a crunching noise he picked his way past old fruit bottling jars and the car roofrack and empty paint pots to the workbench under the gas meter. He turned the bar to open the vice, put the urn in upside down and tightened the steel jaws until they bit into the plastic. With both hands on the bottom he turned until it gave with a crack like old bones. He loosened the vice, took out the urn and with trembling fingers unscrewed the lid.

He had found what he was looking for. He had been right all the time. He shook out the bundle of letters and read the top one. The writing was old fashioned and neat. 'My Darling Darling Darling Darling.' His eyes smarted with tears, whether of rage or sorrow he was too confused to tell. He folded them up again, put them in the urn and closed the top. Like an anonymous alcoholic with a bottle of gin he trudged back up the cellar stairs, planning where he was going to hide and wallow in misery for the rest of the afternoon. My Darling Darling Darling Darling. He would go upstairs to the spare room. It was a dumping ground for boxes and suitcases and unwanted furniture but of all the rooms in the house it had the least association with the family life that had just come to an end.

He stopped at the end of the hall. Someone was at the

front door again. He could see his bulky shape. Then why didn't he ring the door bell? Because he had a key that he pushed in slowly and carefully. Tony stood transfixed, uncertain whether to attack or flee. If it wasn't Alex then there were only two possibilities. It was either a burglar or it was Lover. The door opened as far as the chain would let it. Above the thumping of his heart Tony heard a curse. The shape receded. He had to see who it was. Brandishing the urn like a weapon he ran down the hall to the door. The door came to meet him. He heard a shout and a crack and the splintering of wood and felt an irresistible violence.

Alex pushed past the policeman standing by the splintered door. Sergeant Willoughby and another policeman were looking down at the body at their feet.

'Daddy,' she cried, her hand in front of her mouth.

'Is that your father, Madam?' asked Willoughby, nudging the body with his shiny toecap.

'That's my husband. This is my father,' she said, standing the urn respectfully upright as she knelt down to cradle Tony's head in her lap. 'Get the doctor quickly. And take those handcuffs off him.'

Alex had remembered halfway to college that she had left her briefcase on the kitchen table. When she opened the door the house was very quiet and she was sure she had switched on the hi-fi when she left. She went into the kitchen and found half the contents of her case scattered over the kitchen table. She went back into the hall and called upstairs in case it was Tony. There was no answer and she heard a faint scrabbling sound. She ran outside and got in the car. She looked back and saw someone behind the curtains in Mark's room. She called the police. Sergeant Willoughby came in a squad car, surrounded the house and rang the bell. No one answered and he could see someone moving on the stairs. Alex gave him her key. When he tried to open the door it was on the chain. He saw someone moving again. He retreated a couple of paces and put his shoulder to the door.

Sergent Willoughby was not happy. A good arrest had been snatched from under his nose. But he had an instinct for the fishy. He had not risen to the rank of Detective Sergeant and Senior Crime Prevention Officer for nothing. He prided himself on his flair. He hadn't had a case of necrophilia before and he had never even heard of one involving the ashes of the deceased.

'Do you have any idea, Madam, what your husband was doing loitering in covert fashion with your late father's ashes?'

'He wasn't loitering. He lives here.'

'Then what are these teeth marks on the lid? Look. There's been a pretty powerful set of teeth round here. If you wouldn't mind holding his jaw down a bit, Madam, we could see if they fit. The dental pattern looks pretty similar to me.'

Alex looked at Tony's battered face. His eyes were closed. His mouth sagged open. There was congealed blood over his neck and shirt. He looked sinister as well as pathetic. The worm of suspicion started to wriggle inside her too.

'Don't touch him. I want our solicitor. You're not to put Daddy's urn in his mouth until he wakes up. I want legal advice.'

As if in agreement Tony stirred, half-opened his eyes and lapsed back into unconsciousness.

'Can you think why your father's ashes would have driven him to suspicious behaviour? Did he harbour illicit thoughts about them, to your knowledge?'

'The ashes aren't in it. We scattered them at sea weeks ago. He knows that. They got all over his suit. And all over the pedalo.'

The plot thickened. Willoughby shook the urn like a cocktail shaker. 'There's something in there now,' he said, sensing mystery. This was going to be a complicated case. He had come across nothing like this since he used to watch

Fabian of Scotland Yard on his Auntie May's television when he was a boy. It had a kind of flat goldfish bowl filled with water fitted across the screen to make the picture bigger. It did nothing for the picture but made the viewing experience even more mysterious and exciting, like peeping into another world from inside a bathyscape. The Case of The Empty Urn. He could see Fabian of the Yard now, swimming behind the magnifier in his long raincoat and trilby hat, getting out of the Riley with goggle eyed headlights and calling for a fingerprint check. Alex snatched it out of his meaty hand and unscrewed the lid. She shook out the bundle of letters. My Darling, Darling, Darling, Darling.

'I know what's inside. I put them there. They're letters belonging to my father.'

'But you said your father was dead.'

'He wrote them before he died. There's nothing mysterious about them at all.'

'Then why . . . ?'

He was interrupted by the arrival of the ambulance. Sergeant Willoughby left his question unfinished, shook his head and closed his notebook. He did not look very happy as he put it in his pocket. He brushed off Alex's apologies. All in a day's work. A good arrest would have rounded off the week but never mind. He nodded to the prostrate Tony.

'I think you should keep an eye on him,' he said churlishly as if he could do a better job of it down at the nick.

'I know. He's probably got concussion.'

'I was thinking about what he was up to before the concussion.'

Alex went with him to the front door. She was careful not to tread on the panes of stained glass on the floor. He helped her lift the door as she opened it. The top hinge had been torn out of the frame. On the other side the doorjamb that Tony had fitted was splintered where the chain mounting had been ripped out.

'I'd get that fixed as soon as you can,' said Sergeant Willoughby. 'Ninety per cent of your villains come through the front door. Know what I mean?'

Alex thumped the iron down on another shirt. She knew it was a bad idea to combine ironing and introspection. It could leave her miserable for days. She usually ironed in front of the television as the two mindless occupations cancelled each other out but she could no more get Tony's recent behaviour out of her mind than the mountain of unironed washing. His explanation was that he had come back to look for his life insurance policy which had to be sent off for endorsement and which had been lost in the move. He had searched through her briefcase in case it had got in there by mistake. He hadn't heard her come in or call upstairs because he was in the loft. He was looking in the wardrobe when he heard someone at the door and happened to have the urn in his hand. He must have still been holding it when he was ambushed. That's all he could remember. His case rested.

'Willoughby thought you were trying to break into the urn. Did you open it?'

'What on earth for? There's nothing inside, is there?'

'Of course not. I told Willoughby we'd scattered it all in the sea. Did you find anything else?'

'Nothing. Why? Have you lost something?'

She licked the end of her little finger and dabbed it on the iron with a malevolent hiss. She had not put the letters back in the urn after showing them to Willoughby. Since Tony had not found them there was no point in telling him about them now and having to explain why she had not told him in the first place. She would wait until he was back on his feet. The shock must have been greater than they thought. He kept grinning at her like a lunatic and saying Ha! She had half a mind to call the doctor back and have him look into his head again with the tiny little torch. She had made him obey the doctor's orders and stay quietly in bed for forty-eight hours. She was scared of knocking his plastered nose or his bruises with a flailing arm in the middle of the night so she made up a bed in the spare room. When she brought him meals or drinks or the newspaper he gave her a sly little smirk. The more attentive she was the more he smirked.

She picked up the yellow shirt that he insisted on wearing with his ghastly blue suit. She bashed it with the iron and scrunched the buttons to wear it out quicker. Perhaps he was having a nervous breakdown. He had started to work late regularly three months ago. They even rang him at home during the evening, although she could not imagine what crises of management training required urgent phone calls. For the first few weeks after they moved in he had been his normal self. In fact he had been more attentive to her than usual. He talked to her and bought her flowers for no reason and was perkier than usual in bed. Then things changed after her father's funeral. Could that have upset him?

She sighed and gave up. Men were fascinating creatures. There was no logic to their behaviour. They pretended to be rational and sensible but they reacted to their fantasies and emotions in such an unpredictable way. That's why it was so hard to get a man to talk about his feelings. They were incapable of expressing them in logical sequences. She could never imagine men sitting down together and telling each other what they felt. They expressed and suppressed them in postures and rituals. No wonder men were all messed up. But we love them. What would we do without them?

Alex rang Joanna's bell several times and was leaving when Joanna came puffing up the drive in a half shuffle, half trot. 'Sorry I'm late,' she gasped.

She was wearing a tracksuit, stretched tight round the bust and hips, adorned with a pattern of chequered footballs on the back and World Cup Mexico on the front. The toes of her green trainers stuck up independently of her feet. Her hair was scraped back from her blotchy red face under a damp headband.

'I kept all Sam's kit,' she explained, 'except the jock straps. Although he won't need them by the time I've finished with him.'

She looked no less of a wreck when she came down from the shower in a Penta hotel bathrobe and her hair wrapped in a towel.

'This is the last time, Alex. I've decided. Three husbands is enough. Now I'm going to do it my way. Lemon?'

'Lovely.'

'Alex. Let's set up a business together. By the time your course is finished I'll have Sam's money. It's our turn to wear the trousers.'

'I wouldn't be a man for anything,' said Alex, spooning sugar in the Chinese tea to take the taste away. 'How would you like to live up to that stereotype. Rough and tough and macho. The SAS hasn't got room for them all. They have to sit behind desks or push buttons all day. These days all work is woman's work.'

'I haven't noticed many wanting to swap places with us.'

'Women are starting to have a choice. They can stay at home and have babies or they can try and have a career. I know the system is stacked against women getting in but it's also stacked against men getting out. They have to stick it out until they retire or die of stress diseases.'

'Good riddance. Listen Madam High and Mighty I thought you were on my side. You wait until your hubbie finds a cute little air hostess.' She swigged her cup, grimaced at the taste and went to the tap for a glass of water.

'In the dim and distant past when you liked men, last month,' said Alex, 'didn't you prefer them rich and powerful and successful? How often do women get criticized for not being ambitious or aggressive? Think of the pressure.'

'You and I are going to be as rich and powerful and successful as the next man. On our own.'

'Most women feel good if they do as well as an equivalent man. Men don't feel good unless they do better than an equivalent man.'

'My God, Alex, who are you quoting? Have you been brainwashed?'

'Then when they come home from the office their wives resent them because they've been meeting people and going places and getting out of the house. They're made to feel guilty for not participating in the housework and bringing up the children. They force themselves on the streets to run round by themselves or bash a ball against a wall. You know how daft that is. Then at the end of the day they feel they have to play Superstud to keep us happy and the image going. All they want to do is collapse in front of the snooker with a beer. No wonder there are so many gays. It's the only way they can leave the game.'

'Gay? Who's gay? Tony?' Joanna's eyebrows rose so high that the towel heaped on her head flopped over her eyes. Alex laughed.

'No, silly. My accounting lecturer.'

14

Even when Tony was well enough to go back to the office she did not tell him about the letters. The longer she waited the more difficult it was. She waited for the right moment, when she could be reasonably sure he would not be patronizing or sarcastic but since the accident with the door those moments became fewer and fewer. It wasn't just what he would think about her father. She knew she was bottling up a lot of her own emotions about him and was frightened of letting them out. It was a long time since she had been able to trust Tony with her feelings. Nor could she just throw the letters away and forget about them. Above all she wanted to find out what Veronica was like. But how was she going to find her? All she knew was her name and that twenty years ago she lived in Birmingham. The personal column? The police? The Salvation Army?

It took a little less than a minute. One afternoon after she had fetched the children from school, given them each an iced bun for tea, quelled an argument about who had the most icing, made Mark give back the currant he snitched from his sister, wiped up the milk she had spilt on the floor, forbidden the television for the third time, taken her coat off and been to the loo she phoned directory enquiries. Without stopping to think she dialled the number the operator gave her.

'Yes, that's me.'

'I'm Phil's daughter.'
'Gerraway.'
'My father died a few months ago.'
'I know Lovey. I came to the funeral. Nice. I didn't stay for the eats. You know.'
'He left some things he wanted you to have. Letters.'
'Send them here. You've got the address, haven't you Lovey?'
'I'd rather bring them.'
'That would be nice. We'll have a nice little chat about your Daddy. I'm in most days. Give me a ring Lovey.'

That was all it took. All she had to do now was decide what to wear. Intuition was the only guide to the right clothes for visiting one's late father's ex-lover. She mentally emptied the wardrobe on the bed and selected a sober dress to impress her in-common-law with respectability. Telling Tony was more difficult. He was in a bad mood that evening. He started an interrogation about the telephone bill, how often she used it and who did she call because she hardly ever used it when he was there and there was something fishy about the whole thing. If it wasn't her there was a ghost round the house making phantom phone calls. She returned his accusations with vigour and they both lapsed into a smouldering silence. He drank three stiff whiskies and pretended to go to sleep on the sofa. She put the lights out and left him there. When he came upstairs to bed it was her turn to pretend to be asleep.

In the morning she decided to tell him about Veronica over the scrambled eggs but he started to make a fuss about reminder letters from the library. He shut up when she pushed the overdue books into his hand but he was sullen until he left for the office. If he didn't want to tell her what was on his mind that was his business. Let him snap out of it himself. Bloody men and their moods. The opportunity to go to Birmingham presented itself the same day. The college was organizing a trip the following week to the Office Automation Extravaganza at the National Exhibition

Centre in Birmingham. She could take advantage of the group train fare and would not miss a day's classes.

'I'm going up to Birmingham next Wednesday for the day. Mark's going to Richards and Louise is going to Maggies.'

'Don't worry about me. I'll get a sausage.'

'No. I'll be back for supper. I'll put a casserole on the timer.'

'I said I'll get a sausage.'

'It's no trouble. Then we can have a quiet little supper together when I get home.'

'I'm very happy with a sausage. Don't worry about me. You go off and do your thing.'

'I'll be home before you.'

'I said I'll get a sausage. I want a sausage, a sausage I will have. I don't want your bloody casserole. I want a sausage. Sausage, do you hear, sausage!'

'All right. Get a sausage.'

'Thank you,' he said, triumphantly stroking his nose splint.

As a routine investigatory procedure Tony phoned the college, supposedly on Alex's behalf, to check the arrangements for the field trip to the computer exhibition. She had not asked for tickets. Sorry. There must be some misunderstanding. Tony was not surprised. There was no misunderstanding. It was carefully contrived. And now she had made her fatal mistake. He put the phone down and waited for the deep glow of satisfaction to spread through his body that he had been right all the time and that it would soon all be out in the open. But all he felt was misery.

'I'll be out all day tomorrow, Dot.'

He offered to drive Alex to the station and take the car on to the office. She got out at the set-down point and he kissed her for what he knew was the last time. He watched her run up the steps and then drove round to the car park. By the time he had parked and sprinted up the escalator to the station concourse she had bought a newspaper and was looking up at the platform indicator. He hid behind a column until she walked away in the direction of the trains. He scurried along behind her, the collar of his brown raincoat turned up, wishing he had a hat to pull over his eyes. His nose-splint made him feel conspicuous. He had a few moments of self-doubt when he saw her join the queue for the train to Birmingham International. Could the college have made a mistake? He had no change for the platform ticket machine so he ran back to the ticket office and queued, nervously checking his watch and the departure board while the passengers in front asked for inaccessible destinations and offered the most complicated methods of payment. He ran back to the platform with a minute to spare. There was a queue to get through the gate. When his turn came to give in his ticket he faltered. Was this a dignified way to behave?

'You going or not,' said the inspector.

'Seeing someone off,' he said, taking back his ticket.

Walking down down the ramp. He felt disembodied, beside himself. His rage and misery had subsided to be replaced by a leaden coldness. He was the hunter on the trail of his prey. He ran to the end coach as whistles blew and a green flag was raised. He closed the door as the train moved off. The ticket inspector asked him where he was going.

'You tell me where you're going and I'll tell you,' said Tony.

'Milton Keynes, Coventry, Birmingham International, Birmingham New Street.'

None of those destinations were an obvious choice for a day of love and laughter and romance. 'Darling. I have zis little love nest in Milton Keynes.'

'But Darling, I'd set my heart on the Bridal Suite in The Coventry Station Hotel.'

'Zen we will compromise. I know a charmant little bistrot

in ze Bull Ring wiz a room upstairs for the patron's special guests.'

'Darling, you're so good to me.'

Somehow they didn't have the cachet of more traditional places of assignation like Brighton and Torquay, let alone Paris or Rome. He succumbed to a wave of indignation on Alex's behalf. Birmingham International Is For Lovers. It lacked that certain something. He felt indignant. She was an attractive and vivacious and stylish woman. She was his wife, dammit. She deserved better than that. He bought a ticket to Birmingham.

He had to be careful at the stations. He had to watch to see if she got off and if she did, get down himself without being seen. At Milton Keynes he gazed nervously at the people walking to the exit as the train drew out. To make sure she had not escaped him he left his seat in the rear carriage and walked carefully along the train, peering through the automatic doors from a distance in case he made them whish open and reveal him. He found her in the carriage next to the buffet. Opposite her was a man. It was him. Lover at last. No longer a creature of his fears and imaginings he was sitting with her, before his eyes. With brazen effrontery they were travelling together. They did not even have the decency to pretend they were travelling separately. He leaned over the table and said something to Alex and she laughed. He punctuated his words by flicking back his hair and tossing his head. Tony could not see his face but the back of his head looked familiar. The hair was swept back over his head in the suspicion of a ducktail. He was wearing a black leather jacket and a red scarf. Recognition began somewhere round Tony's navel, forced its way up like bile through his stomach and his chest and oesophagus to the brain that refused to digest it and retched in disgust. In the end he was forced to spit it out. Derek.

He watched them for a moment, getting in the way of passengers wobbling back from the buffet like tightrope walkers with cups of coffee and sandwiches. He left them to their intimacy and went back to his seat in the rearmost carriage, his nose throbbing. Desolation and anger were compounded with indignation. If she had to destroy their marriage with a Lover couldn't she have done it with someone better? He could understand her preferring a handsome, rich, macho, witty Lover to her husband, but a penniless Marxist accounting lecturer? It was an insult.

He took the risk of going back to their carriage as the train slowed down for Coventry. They showed no sign of leaving. Not many other people got out which made him complacent. He was not expecting the pandemonium at Birmingham International. There was a scrum for the carriage doors. He was carried by the mass towards the exhibition hall entrance. On the other side of the crowd he caught a glimpse of a tossing head and a red silk scarf. He jostled through the crowd to follow them. His bandaged foot and knee and elbow were targets for the throng, impatient to see the wonders of office technology at first hand. As he suspected the lovers were not going to the exhibition. He caught a glimpse of the red scarf at the top of the stairs that led down to the taxi rank on the lower level outside. By the time he got to the head of the stairs they had disappeared. He limped down, taking each painful step one by one. He came round the corner just in time to see Derek clutch the trailing ends of his red scarf and swing his briefcase into a taxi. The door slammed, the yellow light went off and it pulled away. But behind it there was a rankful of others. Tony staggered to the next in line and wrenched open the door as the driver started his engine.

'Follow that cab!' he said, collapsing into the seat.
'You what?'
'Follow that cab.'
'Why? Where's it going?'
'I don't know. That's why I want you to follow it.'
'But I want to know where I'm going. I'm off duty in half an hour.'

'I'm sure it's just going round the corner. Please start. We'll lose them.'

'Who do you think I am, tear-arsing round the country after other cabs?'

'But I have to see where those two in front are going.'

'That's none of my business, Squire. You give me a destination.'

'Oh God. Please don't be difficult. It's a matter of life or death.'

'Whose life or death?'

'Mine. Theirs. It doesn't matter. Please go.'

'Are you a copper?'

'No. Not exactly.'

'What do you mean, not exactly. Look mate, this isn't the movies. Follow that cab. How do I know it's any of your business what they're up to in front? You're just another bleeding nosey parker for all I know. Now give me a destination. I've missed three fares already.'

'Never mind.'

He wearily opened the door of the cab. His nose felt on fire. All the other cabs had gone. He limped back towards the exhibition centre. He would never find them now. In a few minutes they would be drawing up in front of some pretty little inn in the Warwickshire countryside, oak beams and gleaming brass and crisp white sheets. We'll go up now, thanks. What time is lunch? He would have sat downstairs waiting for them to come down, hand in hand, looking in each other's eyes. They would have stood at the bottom of the stairs gazing at him in amazement. With a gentle sad smile he would have kissed her on the cheek, told them to be happy together and limped out of their lives for ever. All he could do now was go to the computer exhibition. Then at least he could claim the trip on expenses.

When Alex woke up on the morning of her trip to Birmingham Tony was awake too. If this wasn't unusual enough he offered to make tea while she got dressed. He seemed full of excitement and tension like he did when he was planning a surprise for her birthday. His bizarre behaviour extended to driving her to the station, although it was out of his way. The suspicion nudged itself into her mind that he was making sure she got on the train.

'Goodbye Darling. Have a nice day in sunny Birmingham. Where are the others?'

'We're meeting on the train. Goodbye darling. Have a nice day.'

They exchanged Judas kisses and she watched him drive off from the top of the steps. She browsed in the bookshop, bought a newspaper and looked round the concourse for the other students. When she stopped to look at the indicator board she caught a glimpse of a familiar nose splint dodging behind a pillar. Her train left in five minutes from platform one. She had time to make a quick phone call.

'Hello Dot. How are things? Good. Is Tony there? Are you expecting him? Oh. He's out all day. The computer exhibition? Silly me, I forgot. Never mind. No need to leave a message, I'll see him before you will.'

What was he up to? He had the day off under a feeble pretext he had pinched from her and was now making sure she was out of town. She felt sick and tried to remember if she had had breakfast. What could she do? If she accosted him now he would make up some silly excuse. He probably had it all ready. If she turned round and went home what good would that do? And Veronica was waiting. She wanted to get that whole thing over with right now. She took a deep breath, forced down the heaviness rising in her chest and presented her ticket at the gate. She found a seat next to the buffet car and sat down with her back to the engine. She looked out of the window and saw, at the top of the ramp taking his ticket from the inspector, a man with a turned-up raincoat collar and a nose-splint.

'Alex! I didn't think you were going to the exhibition.'

Derek put his bag on the rack above her and sat down on

the opposite side of the table. Her heart sank. She had enough to think about without listening to revolutionary chit-chat all the way to Birmingham.

'I'm hitching a ride. I have to see a relative in Birmingham.'
'Crafty. Just what I'm doing. I'm going to see my old Auntie in Leamington Spa, poor old soul. . . .'

Why on earth was Tony following her? Bewilderment turned to anger. If Tony knew about Veronica why didn't he say? He had found the letters in the urn after all and he was waiting for her to tell him. That's why he had been in such a bad mood. Instead of coming out with it right away he had been lying in wait with a self-righteous little trap. But why go to all this trouble? She would never understand men. After Milton Keynes she told Derek she was going to the loo and walked to the back of the train. She stood in darkness and noise on the lurching link plates between the last two carriages and peered through the murky window in the sliding door. Tony was staring out of the window, huddled in his brown raincoat, fingering his nose splint. He looked thin and miserable and instinct urged her to go up to him and throw her arms round him. The thought of his petty deceit and mistrust enabled her to suppress the instinct without much effort and she want back to the buffet for a coffee and a slice of fruit cake, standing up, alone. At Coventry she was tempted to shake him off by leaving the train and jumping back on at the last minute. It probably wouldn't work but it would give him a few nasty moments. If she did that she would be descending to his level. She decided to retain her dignity. It was also descending to his level to pretend that she did not know he was on the train. The mature, sensible thing to do was to go up to him calmly and ask what he was playing at and resolve this silly situation here and now. He could then read the letters and come with her to see Veronica.

The train slowed down for Birmingham International and everyone around her got bags and coats down from the racks. They were actually going to the exhibition and not using it as an alibi. She wished Derek a lovely day in Leamington and composed herself to confront her husband. She rehearsed under her breath the modulated and sensible speech she would deliver to him before wringing a full and frank explanation from the little worm. For the first time that morning she felt calm and in control of the situation. She was therefore very disconcerted to glance out of the window and see that her husband had got off the train and was pushing his way through the crowd on the platform towards the taxi rank exit in limping pursuit of Derek's fluttering red scarf.

He was not on the train because of her after all. He was deliberately staying out of her way. He had not taken the day off work to follow her to Birmingham. She was an irrelevance, an inconvenience. But why? Did he have secret relatives too?

'Come in Lovey, goodness gracious I would have recognized you anywhere, you're just like our Baby, it's ever so nice of you to make all that effort you could just as well have put them in the post but I'm glad you've come, I saw you at the funeral you know but I didn't want to get in the way and to tell you the truth I was a bit upset and didn't really pay much attention, now your poor mother's lost a lot of weight hasn't she, that's more than you can say of me, when I knew your Daddy I had a good figure, you might say but I was a lot slimmer than I am now, I dare say you'd like a nice cup of tea and I made a bit of dinner in case you could stay, I did a cocko van it's ever so easy with that new stuff out of a packet you just mix it with water and stir it in, and how is she keeping, your Mom, I suppose it's all been a bit hard for her over the past few weeks and she's not used to coping on her own is she, I know your Daddy would have looked after everythink he tried to look after me but I was a wilful girl in those days, I never wanted to settle down, all I wanted was a bit of a laugh, your Daddy was a good one for a laugh though, he was always funny and had those jokes he used to make up, I used to do my Elizabeth Taylor impressions and he did Richard Burton and that Marx brother with the moustache and Maurice Chevalier and he could do those funny voices, now that was a long time ago now, twenty years, we've all changed but I bet he was still a bit of a lad wasn't he, he liked the old slap and tickle too, you don't mind me saying that do you, we're all big girls now aren't we and you look so much like our Baby that it doesn't seem like talking to a stranger, but he liked his bit of fun and so did I in those days, and we did have good times, I'm not saying it was right but he was a bit of a lad and you don't think then do you and I'd never met anyone as classy and funny as he was I mean he was in a different sort of class, your Daddy, but I'm sure I needn't tell you this you grew up with him, one day we dressed up to the nines and me in a big floppy hat and went to the Derby and he won quite a bit and we spent it all that evening, oh he was a bit of a laugh, and the best times was before we moved away and we was still in the shop, you mustn't get me wrong Lovey he tried to do the best by your Mom and he never let on until she came back and found us and if that made me feel terrible, think of what it made him, I thought he was going to throw me out on the street right there and then he was ever so upset, Lovey, but then he had a do with her and ended up throwing himself out on the street as well, I think it was because he was punishing himself, you know what I mean, just as much as wanting to come away with me, well I didn't understand that at the time, I just thought he was eloping with me and it was ever so romantic just like in the films and we left in the middle of the night, well it was early in the morning after we done the papers and we got the Green Line to Rickmansworth and then we went on to Milton Keynes, I was a bit miserable then and he did his funny walk, you know the Marx brother, the one with the moustache, over from the bus station to the caff and I had to laugh and I did my Elizabeth Taylor and that cheered us up a bit, he soon got a job doing the newspapers and I worked down at the supermarket and we had ever such a lot of trouble finding somewhere to stay but we managed and we had a bit of a laugh, but your Daddy never really settled down, he didn't like working for someone else but he didn't have the money to set himself up, all he took from your Mom was what was in the till the day we left so he couldn't even get the stock let alone the premises and I didn't like being down at the supermarket I mean it wasn't bad, we had a good time and a bit of a laugh for the first few weeks but I knew it couldn't last, he thought a lot of you and your Mom you know and I suppose I was getting a bit edgy myself, I mean, was this how I was going to spend the rest of my life, it was a bit of fun before we left but now it had got serious, you know what I mean, Lovey, anyway, I suppose I fell for a feller at work, I mean there was nothink going on I'm not like that except a bit of a cuddle sometimes in the loading bay if there wasn't a delivery but I wouldn't have let your Daddy down without telling him, nor was he so funny any more either, he'd sort of run out of his jokes, so I knew it couldn't last, and then after towards Christmas he got all morose so I put it into his head to go back home, I mean I was single and unattached and you and your Mom was by yourselves and it wasn't going to last and I didn't know I was expecting until your Daddy went back and I went to stay with my sister in Coventry but there was no point in him coming back it wouldn't have worked, listen to me talk your Daddy always said I was a talker and I haven't even given you your tea yet and the kettle must have boiled and switched off by now.'

Veronica heaved herself up from the armchair and waddled out of the room, the tops of her thighs squeaking as they rubbed together. Under her ample, flowery housecoat Veronica was short and fat and had the biggest bosom Alex had ever seen in real life. It formed a ledge a foot wide under her chin and ballooned down to her waist. She thought of her mother's two fried eggs. Her hair was dyed blonde and backcombed into a fuzz round her dimpled face, caked with make-up. She left the door open. Alex wondered whether she was expected to follow but was glad of a respite from the spate of talk.

The house was a three storey Victorian pile. A girl with bright orange hair, black string vest and purple tights had opened the door. Alex had given her a winning smile in case she was her half-sister but before either of them could say anything Veronica appeared and shooed Alex into the front room. She caught a glimpse of another exotic girl coming downstairs. What sort of house did Veronica keep? The front room was furnished with a hodge-podge of battered green and brown armchairs, each adorned with a plump silver lamé cushion, and a chrome and brass coffee table. At one end was a large bay window, curtained in bright blue velvet worn at the edges where people had drawn them. The window gave on to a prolific elder bush that crowded the glass with its tiny black berries. Three walls were papered floor to ceiling with the same enormous colour photograph of a Swiss Lake In Spring. Peppered over the walls were framed admonitions, some of them in Letraset and some embroidered like samplers, apparently hanging from the branches of the woodland scene or hovering in the blue sky. SAVE IT! WATCH YOUR STEP! ACCIDENTS WILL HAPPEN! SWITCH OFF BEFORE YOU'RE SWITCHED OFF! WATCH OUT THERE'S A THIEF ABOUT! HAVE A CARE!

Alex moved the silver cushion from the small of her back to under her arm and gazed at the distant horizon over the waters above the red tiled gas fireplace. She was not convinced that Veronica had been talking about the right man. She tried to superimpose her own memories of her father on the picture his old lover had painted of a funny, light-hearted philanderer and failed. Had Veronica had so many lovers that she had confused her father with someone else, a stand-up comic, a fill-in on the northern club and southern pier circuit? She couldn't remember her father making jokes or doing impersonations or funny walks. He was solemn and serious and earnest about getting up at five to pencil the addresses on the newspapers and worrying over the till ribbon and puzzling over her French homework. She had always thought that life had been a burden for her father.

Veronica came back with a brown plastic tray, breathless with exertion. She bent her pneumatic body enough to put it on the coffee table in front of Alex, who was surprised she could see where she was putting it down from behind her bosom. The tray bore a plate of fairy cakes iced in pink, two green china cups and matching sugar bowl. The milk was still in its bottle. She let herself back down into her armchair and squatted beaming like an obese nymph in her woodland idyll.

'Mustn't grumble must we, we have to make the best of it as we go along though it wasn't all that easy after your Daddy went back to you all and it all came home to me when Baby was born but you live and learn, I've done all right for myself and it's all been all my own work, that's what it's all about isn't it, there's no mortgage on this place and we live pretty well though we have to watch the pennies, the rates and the bills are somethink else, it's better since I just started having the girls they hardly eat anythink and they think of me as a sort of mother although I don't interfere in their private lives except they can't have boys back in the house, I'd lose my licence anyway, the council would be on me like a shot if they found out, most of my girls want to get into show business they send them along from the dance school down the road though there's a couple doing hairdressing down at the collidge, it was nice for our Baby, she had lots of friends though she was never interested in show business, I started her on ballet lessons when she was four but she didn't take to it, she never got her head out of a book, that's what she was interested in, your Daddy said both his girls was real little Einsteins, he thought a lot of you, you know, Our Alex this and Our Alex that, he used to come and see our Baby too, once a year, regular as clockwork, round her birthday, she never knew of course, she thought he was just her uncle, then she went to collidge you know, all through her own efforts, us girls can do it if we want, and then she got her degree and she couldn't find a job anywhere, your Daddy said he knew someone who could help and wangled somethink for her I don't know how and she got a job in London, that's why she's not here now, she's working down in London but she comes up once a month to see her mother, I didn't tell her about you coming of course or about her father, your Daddy, you know, that's up to you, I mean I don't mind telling her now, we're all big girls aren't we but I'll let you decide that because you're the only one who knows and it wouldn't be fair on your Mom if it got out, your Daddy wouldn't mind he often said you two would get on together, anyway here's Baby's address in London, I wrote it down, I suppose you don't remember Effie, do you, your Mom would, she lives down the road from where your Daddy's shop was, married that nice greengrocer and they have a lovely house now so I dropped her a line when Baby went down and they're putting her up for a bit until she gets herself fixed up, this is her picture look, I brought it in, I expect you wanted to see it, that's you to a T isn't it, here look at these school photos I got out as well, if there's one thing I can say about your Daddy is that he had strong genes. I don't think your Mom and I had a chance, mind you you're ten years older than she is so you wouldn't pass for identical twins but it's all there isn't it, you've both got your Daddy's eyes and his wicked little smile, it's extraordinry reely.'

The disorientation of the journey, her husband's peculiar behaviour, the meeting with her father's lover, were capped by seeing a perfect likeness of herself and someone else's name underneath it. Georgina.

15

Tony wandered round the exhibition in a daze. He drifted down thronging aisles like flotsam in a gutter. Arc lights blazed down and he sweated in the fug of people and machinery. On either side the stands jostled each other like market stalls. They all had the similar looking grey boxes and silent, blinking screens, glowing with numbers and letters and designs, logos like mystic signs and company names manufactured by computer. No one hawked, no one hollered. There was only the whirring and beeping of machines, the reverential hum of impenetrable conversation about bits and bytes. From hospitality rooms hidden behind partitions where computers were not allowed came gusts of laughter. He was washed up on an office of the future dominated by a grainy cardboard cut-out of Charlie Chaplin.

'This is our new pea-sea Sir, if you'd like to take a closer look . . .' said a fresh-faced youth, prematurely bald.

'What has Charlie Chaplin to do with this lot?' asked Tony.

'Sir, that's just an advertising theme. To communicate how user-friendly our equipment is. Can I ask what your application might be?'

'Application?'

'We have hundreds of tailor-made programmes. What is your business speciality?'

'Interpersonal relations.'

'Ah.'

'Don't you have a programme for interpersonal relations?

Ask him to design one,' he said jerking his thumb at the Chaplin cut-out.

Another stand was deserted except for user-friendly giant teddy bears propped up against the screens. Tony wandered into the hospitality cubicle. Six Japanese joked and chatted round a bottle of Scotch on a coffee table. They smiled as Tony gave a low bow, helped himself to a glass, drained it, bowed again and left. He kissed a teddy on the nose and disappeared into the crowd. He did the same on four more stands without being challenged. But neither technology nor hospitality could rub out the picture of a little Warwickshire inn.

'Are you user-friendly?' he asked a cardboard cutout of a girl in a low cut dress, sitting down for a rest in front of a word processor. He made an effort to focus on the screen.

CREATE DOCUMENT:	Separation
FORMAT:	Standard
FREQUENTLY USED TEXT:	We can't go on like this.
	Our marriage is a sham
	For the good of the children
	I want you to have your freedom
	I hope you'll be happy with him
	I'm sorry it didn't work out
	I couldn't give you what you needed.
	We can be civilized about this
	I'll be all right
	Thank you for the good years
	We don't love each other any more
	You can have the house
	I won't stand in your way

HELP
RUBOUT
SHUTDOWN

*

He decided against leaving a print-out propped against the tea-pot on the kitchen table. It would be cowardly to walk out of home and family and a ten year relationship without some kind of explanation or at least a goodbye. There was bound to be a scene. False puzzlement. Protestation. Indignation. How could you think? Rage. Tears. Pleading. Promises. Take me back. I implore you. New start. Fresh life. I'll make it up to you. For the sake of the children. But he would remain dignified and cool and stick to his position and leave the house right then and there. He had better make sure he had somewhere to go to and had packed all that he needed. It would spoil the effect to come back for his season ticket or his tie. Then there would be the parting speech, the last word. I'm doing this because although you don't love me I love you and will always want the best for you. Mulling all this over as he came back on the train he felt relieved and empty. It wasn't so bad after all. Plenty of people did what they were going to do. A third of marriages end in divorce. Among their friends and neighbours he and Alex were exceptions. Sam had done it twice, Joanna three times, Gordon twice, Rachel twice, Humphrey once. They all said it was terribly painful at the time but there must be *something* in it otherwise they wouldn't all let it happen and certainly not more than once in a lifetime. At the least it put an end to the agony of living together and if everything was true about starting afresh it could be challenging and interesting. He would soon find out.

What about the children? There were thousands of children of divorced parents around and they seemed to be all right. Children were very resilient. They adapted. It was better for them to know the truth and have a firm base on which to establish their own relationships than to live in a constant atmosphere of bickering and mistrust and unhappiness. Children only recently began to live in such close proximity and emotional dependence on their parents. In most other parts of the world children lived communally or with large families and didn't seem to suffer. It might even be positively bad for children to live in emotional incest. He would miss them, of course, but he would see them at weekends and birthdays and holidays and so on. He would go to all the school things for a change. Usually it was only the children of broken homes who got both parents to come to sports day and speech day. They would be all right. We will all be all right.

Whatever happened they would not descend to the sordid. He would start with the assumption that she was not cavorting with Derek out of lust. This was not about sex but about relationships. Relationships were based on trust and fidelity and communication and empathy and openness and sharing. Sex was irrelevant. Relationships had nothing to do with whether she liked kissing Derek more than him and if she liked him to tickle her whitest parts and if he was kinder to her and did it longer and was fun afterwards and did not have a fat stomach and a hairy back and had a bigger thing and she did not have to pretend at the end to make him feel manly. Nothing to do with that at all. Marriage was about self-realization and growth and mutual development and caring for each other and their children. Her affair with Derek was a symptom not a cause of the irretrievable breakdown, a bit on the side of the real issue.

He came out of the station into the main road and limped along a side street until he came to the Hotel Glamis, the first to advertise vacancies.

'Just for tonight. I may stay longer.'

'Luggage?'

He put on the desk a plastic bag containing glossy leaflets about computers and half an egg salad sandwich. These personal effects were not sufficient to guarantee the reservation so he had to pay a twenty pound deposit.

When Alex got back from Birmingham their largest suitcase was standing in the hall. Tony was already home. He was in the kitchen, spooning out alphabet spaghetti for the children and forbidding them to eat it with their fingers. He seemed cheerful. He had changed into his light blue suit. He had washed his hair and put new sticking plaster on his nose-splint. They forced smiles at each other.

'Hello Darling. Had a lovely day?' she said, unable to dull the edge in her voice.

'Lovely Darling. You? I was home early so I fetched the children.'

'So I see Darling. How was the office?'

'Lovely as usual Darling.'

'Darling.'

'Yes Darling?'

'I think we should have a little talk, Darling.'

'Little talks always end in tears Darling,' he said, licking sauce off his fingers, one by one.

She led the way into the sitting room. Talks in the sitting room were always about unpleasant things like the gas bill or school reports or what they were going to do for Christmas this year. They ended up with bad feelings and mutual recrimination. He stood with his back to the marble fireplace, his hands purposefully stuck in his trouser pockets. She took a deep breath and started.

'Darling, there's something I have to tell you.'

'I know.'

'I should have told you a long time ago.'

'I know.'

'But I didn't know how to bring myself to it.'

'I know.'

'I didn't want anything to come between us.'

'I know.'

'But it's all got to come out sooner or later.'

'I know.'

'For God's sake stop saying you know. If you knew, why didn't you say anything?'

'I wanted you to tell me. Also I wasn't sure. Not until I found the letters in your father's urn.'

'You did find them. You said you didn't. You lied to me!' she shouted.

'You're the one who lied! You said there wasn't anything in the urn,' he shouted back.

'Let's be civilized about this,' she said calmly.

'Let's be civilized.'

'I didn't want to say anything until I could tell you all the facts.'

'Better late than never.'

'I know her name now. I saw her mother.'

'*Her* name?' he said, surprised.

'Georgina.'

Tony blanched. What he thought was a confession had turned into an accusation. She knew all about Georgina. She had even been to see her mother. All those clues he had laid to an imaginary girlfriend had led her to the real thing. She was using Georgina as an excuse for Derek.

'Look Alex, you've got the wrong end of the stick. You're making a big mistake. It's a fantasy, a figment of your imagination.'

She took a photograph out of her handbag and handed it to him. It was Georgina standing outside Shangri-La, Effie's house. He could make out the lobelias.

'There's no mistake. That's her. She is as real as you are. She even looks like me,' she said, fighting back a sob. She brushed tears from her eyes with the heel of her hand.

'Alex, that's over. It's all over. It was nothing. Believe me.'

'How can you say that? Can you imagine what I feel like? After all these years? What if Mummy finds out? It will kill her.'

'She has to know the truth, Alex, we all have to face up to the truth. Georgina isn't the only person to come between us, you know that.'

'What are you talking about?'

'You know. I was on the train too this morning.'

'I know you were. I saw you.'

'And you carried on? Knowing I was there?'
'I was going to come up to you. I promise.'
She was lying. She was taking revenge for Georgina, flaunting her own lover in his face.
'It's too late now. Alex, I'm leaving for a while. I think we ought to have a trial separation. I think you know why. I don't blame you. Knowing about Georgina I would have done the same. But I can't forget Derek.'
'Derek? What about Derek?'
'Let's not play act. We both have to recognize that however much we loved each other in the past, when a greater love comes into our lives there is nothing we can do.'
'You're leaving?'
'Yes.'
'Because of Derek?'
'Yes.'
'I don't believe it.'
'Why not? What sort of man did you think I was?'
'Don't you feel anything for me, the children, us?'
'Of course I do. But I can't get Derek out of my mind. I couldn't continue to live here with you, knowing he was out there.'
Alex closed her eyes. She could see him running after Derek through the crowd. He wasn't on the train because of her, she had been an inconvenience, an irrelevance. Everything suddenly became horribly clear. She opened her eyes and looked at him. So simple. Words like any other words. She had no difficulty in keeping her face impassive and her voice under control. She knew she should be feeling tears welling up inside her but there was nothing, only an icy calm.
'If that's what you want,' she said.
'It is. I've decided to go right now.'
He looked out of the window at the unweeded flower beds. Was he waiting for her to say something else? What more was there to say? Nothing until she had had time to think.
'How long have you. . . ?'

'Have I known? I wasn't sure until today. Now I am certain.'

'I wish we could have talked about it before. Can't we talk now?'

'It's too late now. Perhaps when we have both had time to think about things we can work something out.'

'If that's what you want.'

'Alex we have to cut through this web of lies and imaginings and confusion. We can't go on living in fantasy and half truths. We should have been frank and open with each other. We owe it to ourselves. We can't go on living in the mind. We have wrapped ourselves in fiction, daydreams, unrealized longings. We have to face up to reality Alex. This is the truth.'

'Fine.'

'I'll get going then.'

'All right.'

'I've told the children I'm going on a business trip. For the time being.'

'Of course.'

'All right.'

He seemed puzzled, as if he had been expecting a different reaction. The poor lamb had probably primed himself with speeches. Well she wasn't going to give him the satisfaction of delivering them. Let him leave and be buggered if that's what he wanted.

'I'll be off then.'

'Goodbye.'

'I'll get in touch in a couple of days.'

'Fine.'

'I'll leave you the car.'

'Thanks.'

'Can you forward the mail to the office?'

'Sure.'

'I'll get going then.'

He left the room. She waited in the sitting room until she heard the front door slam. She ran to the door and looked out of the peephole. He was struggling down the drive with the heavy suitcase banging against his leg. She gave him a few moments to get clear before she went out to the children. They had finished their spaghetti and were arguing about what programme to watch. She surprised them by giving them an enormous hug and sitting between them on the sofa, arms round them, watching television until bedtime. Only when she got into bed herself did she burst into tears and weep into the pillow. When she got up that morning she was a married only child. When she went to bed she was a single parent with a sister. It had been quite a day.

16

'Where's my right shoe?' asked Mark hopping on his left foot into the bedroom. Alex stretched out her hand from under the duvet for her watch. Seven o'clock. At least she had slept for an hour. She stuck her right foot out and contemplated it with heavy eyes.

'It's not on my foot.'
'You must know where it is.'
'How should I? Where did you find the left one?'
'Have you been crying?'
'No. I've got a cold. I saw a shoe in the broom cupboard.'
'That was this one. I put it next to the mouse trap. Walsh says mice like the smell of sweaty feet. You must know where the other one is.'
'Yes. Where you took it off.'
'Where's Dad?'
'He had to go on a business trip.'
'What will he bring us back?'
'A surprise. Go and find your shoe.'
'I've looked.'
'Relive every moment since you got home yesterday.'
'What good does reliving things do?' he asked.
'No good at all.'

Louise came in wearing a bright pink T-shirt emblazoned with a message inquiring if readers of it fancied a quickie.

'You can't wear that to school.'

'Why not? There's nothing else.'
'You have to wear white or navy blue.'
'It's not allowed, fag slag,' brayed her big brother.
'Shut up wally pig,' replied his little sister.
'You have plenty of white T-shirts,' said her mother.
'They're yuck. They're all in the wash. You're always washing them.'
'Because you're smelly,' said her brother, 'and I bet you've hidden my shoe.'
'And you're a poncy poof.'

She hadn't got the energy for her standard lecture on family love and conversational etiquette.

'Take that T-shirt off right now. It was a present to me from your father.'
'Where is Dad? Don't tell me he's got up early.'
'He's gone on a business trip.'
'What will he bring us back?'
'A surprise.'
'Did he go on an aeroplane?'
'Possibly.'
'He stole the emergency instructions last time. Then he said they were a present. Rotten present.'

Alex dragged her leaden body upright and heaved her legs over the edge of the bed. Life must go on.

'Where does Dad sleep?' asked Louise.
'On the plane you wally.'
'With the pilot?'
'With the steward,' said Alex with resignation.
'Don't be a wally Mum. He's in a hotel.'
'Ah yes. He might be gone for a long time.'
'Good. Then he'll have to bring us back a really good present.'

She shook her nightdress down to her ankles and padded to the curtains. She squinted as a precaution against the glare but she needn't have bothered. The sky was overcast but last night's threat of rain had receded.

'It's a nice day. You needn't wear sweaters to school. And

look. Your shoe is in the middle of the lawn. It's soaking.'

'Yeah. He was throwing it at me last night.'

'Go and take off that T-shirt. I won't tell you again.'

Mark hopped out of the room to retrieve his shoe and Louise strategically withdrew to plan the next skirmish over what she was going to wear. Alex looked in the mirror. She lifted her lank hair and let it fall. She looked terrible after her sleepless night but the surprising thing was that she didn't feel anything. She would have expected to feel anger at least, and resentment and self-recrimination and guilt and self-righteousness and all the other things you are supposed to feel but she didn't. It had happened, he had abandoned her and that was that. She still had to get up, get dressed, get the children off to school, wash up the breakfast and go to college. She should be overwhelmed by stress. At three o'clock that morning she had looked up the stress table in her Behavioural Psychology text book. Psychologists had ranked the stress factors of various events on a scale from one to a hundred. Death of a spouse was top with a hundred. Christmas was twelve. Marriage was fifty. She totted up Death of Parent, Separation From Husband and Gain of New Family Member. She scored one hundred and sixty seven. Not a bad score for a beginner. No wonder she couldn't sleep.

Louise was right. She didn't have a clean white T-shirt. That was principally because she had used the week's supply to give her water colours and poster paints a good clean. Alex selected the least technicolour, scrubbed off what she could with a damp nailbrush, rubbed white chalk on what she couldn't, (burnt sienna was the worst) and ran the iron over it.

'Tell me, Alex, what was the first thing you did when you realized that your marriage and your life were in ruins?'

'Ironed a dirty T-shirt.'

'I see. And what were your feelings at the time?'

'Fear that my daughter would find out and throw a scene.'

'Then what did you do?'

'Hurried downstairs so I could fill the sugar bowl for the cereal. If the children do it they spill sugar all over the floor.'

'I see. And what were your feelings?'

'Satisfaction that I got there in time. Closely followed by self-recrimination when I dropped the bowl on the way to the table. However carefully you sweep it up it still crunches.'

'Then what did you do?'

'Sent my son to the front door for the milk for the cereal with instructions to carry no more than one bottle in each hand. The hall carpet smells enough of cheese as it is.'

'I see. And what were your feelings?'

'Pleasurable anticipation of smacking him when he disobeyed me. But he didn't. Because there weren't any bottles. The milkman had found a note on the step that was three days old and left only orange juice.'

'I see. And what were your feelings?'

'Fear that my son would throw a scene because there was no milk for his cereal. Then irritation at my husband. It's his job, it was his job, to put the bottles out and leave a note and destroy the old ones. We had to have toast.'

'Then what did you do?'

'Laughed uncontrollably at the picture of the family on the front of the cereal packet.'

'I see. And what were your feelings?'

'Ha ha ha ha ha ha ha. . . .'

Her class that morning was strategic planning. Every small business, every large business, every individual should have a strategic plan based on a long-term objective. First you have to be able to answer the question Where Do I Want To Be In Ten Years Time? Only when you answer this question can you begin to make an operational plan of how to get there. and without an operational plan you cannot make sensible decisions. You cannot make decisions at all. Now let's have an example of a Ten Year Goal. Anybody. Yes?

To be stinking rich. Yes, that's a start. Anybody else?

To overthrow the capitalist system. Ha ha. Anybody else?

To provide the best window cleaning service in south-east London.

That's more like it. Anybody else?

To be completely and utterly and totally independent from anyone and everyone else, financially and physically and emotionally. To be answerable to no one. To be a self contained and hermetically sealed island to myself so I can say to all you lot out there: bugger off, leave me alone, I'm all right. The only trouble is, that sounds like being dead. And that's not funny. Ha ha ha ha ha.

The hotel was too expensive for more than a couple of nights. He found a small room in a terraced house in Paddington that would do until he sorted himself out. He moved in one evening after work. He hung his suits on the back of the door and put away as many of his clothes as would fit into the small chest of drawers. He used his suitcase as a bedside table. He opened the bright yellow curtains and tried to open the window to let out the smell of cabbage and gas and old linoleum but it had been taped shut. The window looked out on to the back of another terrace and the small yards in between. The yard of his own house was filled with cardboard boxes splitting under their loads of brown bottles. Clothes were strung on a line, dripping in the grey drizzle. He decided it was more cheerful to have the curtains closed. For the first few days he spent a lot of time lying on the bed when he came back from the office. There was no room to do anything else. In the morning he switched off the alarm, closed the window, turned on the gas fire, put the kettle on, made a cup of tea and then got out of bed.

The landlady, Mrs Banks, lived in the basement. She lay in wait under the stairs like a troll for passers-by. As soon as she heard the front door open or steps coming down the stairs she would sidle out and shuffle along the hall on some mysterious errand, not looking at the newcomers with her red-rimmed eyes. Her genuine errands involved brown plastic shopping bags clinking with bottles. She wore a wig of tight red curls that fitted as well backwards and sideways. It was Itler what done it. The bombs made her hair fall out, whether gradually from anxiety or suddenly in the blast she would not specify. It was her job to clean the stairs and the bathrooms. She could be found on the stairs on her hands and knees in the middle of the morning, gasping for breath, red curls awry, scraping a patent tablecloth crumb sweeper across the treads. Notices, scrawled on the back of circulars from the Department of Health and Social Security, gave moral instruction such as Please Do Unto This Ablutions As You Would Be Done To When You Finish, By Order, Mrs Banks.

On the ground floor, in the largest apartment, two rooms with a connecting door and separate kitchen, lived two young men. Puck, a West Indian, lurked at home in leathers and chains while his white friend Lorry went out at nightfall in a white lurex blouson. They had many visitors, ushered in past the red-rimmed gaze of Mrs Banks. Tony met them both in the hall when he moved in. Lorry helped carry his suitcase in from the taxi. He must come in and have a drink when they weren't so busy, he said, teasing the lick of hair down the back of his neck. Nice boys, said Mrs Banks, very sociable. Always pay the rent on time. On the first floor were Tony's small bedsit and a larger room where Wing Commander Pitt lived. Fleet Air Arm old man. Torpedoes. Torps Away then Bang. One day it happened the other way round. Bang then Torps Away. D'ye believe it, old man, I don't have a bum? Call me Pitt. Bottomless Pitt. The bones there all right but bugger all to sit on. Bugger all is right. Not much use to the lads downstairs but they're civil enough to slip me a G & T when the going's rough. His face was yellow and lined and dry, like desiccated lemon peel. Sometimes when he was opening his own door Tony could hear the sound of retching from behind the Wing Commander's. A Gentleman, said Mrs Banks. Always pays the rent on time.

The top floor, two attic rooms and a tiny bathroom of its own, was inhabited by Mr Grosser, a little man with a scruffy goatee and gold rimmed spectacles. He tried to pass off suit jackets as sports jackets over his shiny grey trousers. Mrs Banks whispered that he kept snakes in his room which he fed with live mice every Saturday morning. She hadn't been up there in thirteen years. He scuttled to and from his room with brown padded envelopes. He says he's a littry critic, whatever that is, said Mrs Banks, but I think he's into something dirty, all those envelopes coming and going and him being so crabby. Always pays the rent on time.

On his first Saturday morning Tony sat on the edge of the bed stroking his nose-splint and wondering what to do for the rest of the weekend. He twiddled the knob on the gas ring that stood in front of the fire. That was no solution. North Sea gas wasn't poisonous. Alex had taken the children to her mother's for the weekend. They still thought their father was on a business trip. They had to be told sooner or later what was happening. He couldn't stay away indefinitely. Perhaps she would talk to her mother first. He could picture the poor widow, shimmering in mourning acrilan, unable to understand what was going on. She had had a cosy, conventional quiet and tedious marriage to an amateur pornographer. What could she know of the heady passions of infidelity and desertion? Alex would blame it all on him of course.

He slapped his forehead. He was a fool. She said she was going to take them to her mother's for the weekend. And where was Derek? In a bed-and-breakfast down the road, on the seafront. They would be there now while Mark and Louise were watching *Doctor Who* and eating Granny's indigestible rock cakes. Just going out for a walk, mother. Arm in arm along the seafront, free like the seagulls at last. Hurrying back to his digs. Sea-shell ashtrays, times of breakfast, sand in the bath, double bed with a slippery eiderdown, who cares, we've got our love to keep us warm.

'Darling I can't believe our luck, he walked out, just like that!'

'When are you going to tell the children?'

'Not yet. We must be very careful. I have to get the money first.'

'He abandoned you, remember.'

'I know. We must meet in secret still.'

'Can you slip out tonight?'

Derek with his leather jacket and red scarf and black wavy hair. The two of them were probably laughing right now. He drummed his fists into the pillow. Then he ran downstairs to the phone in the hall. He would spoil their little weekend. He would say he was coming to see the children and discuss their future and that he was catching the next train down. She could not refuse. Holding the receiver between his chin and shoulder he dialled his mother-in-law's number while rootling in his pockets for coins. Damn. He had put them all in the gas meter. Someone picked up the phone at the other end but the pips went before he could tell who it was. He slammed his own handset down on the cradle as Lorry came out of his room, dressed in an embroidered kaftan, escorting a sheepish-looking middle-aged man in a camel overcoat to the front door.

'Change? I think we can find a few pee. Come in for a seccy while I look.'

Tony followed him into the room and stood amazed. Stepping from the scruffy, brown and cream hall into their room was like stepping from the wings onto an exotic stage set. From the central rose in the ceiling hung swathes of delicate mauve and green diaphanous material that made the room into a circular and windowless tent. The door which he just stepped through was painted gold. The connecting door into the next room was hung with silver beads that tinkled behind Lorry. Tony caught a glimpse of brown legs and a scarlet jockstrap sprawled on the oval bed and looked away. The atmosphere was heavy with the scent of joss and marijuana. Soft light came from a large old fashioned lamp with a glass bowl shade and a base of pink and purple lilies. In the middle of the room was a round brass table. The only seating was low, flat couches spread with kilims and multicoloured blankets. There were two marquetry cabinets on either side of the fireplace. One concealed a stereo whose hidden speakers bathed the room in luscious Mantovani. Every flat surface in the room was covered in marble and porcelain and onyx eggs, alone or heaped in baskets. The word Orgy sprang to mind. The door to the hall clicked shut behind him.

Lorry tinkled back through the silver bead curtain with a Greek embroidered shoulder bag. His black hair was brushed flat round his small head into a cap from which the tops of his ears peeped out. Standing close to him Tony could see he was older than he first appeared, perhaps his own age, make-up covering the lines on his face and neck and his eyelashes helped with mascara. Tony thought of the white clown. He gave Tony sixty pee and brushed away the pound note.

'Now you're here we must have a little drinkie-poo. I mean we're neighbours, aren't we?'

'I really must phone, you know, I mean, thanks.'

'Now sit down and be a bit sociable. And don't look so worried. I mean, it may never happen.'

'It already has.'

Tony did not resist as Lorry put a hand on his arm and pushed him gently down on the sofa facing the fireplace. It was difficult to sit down. The wide seats and low backs were meant for sprawling. He sat on the edge of the sofa with his knees together like mother come to tea while Lorry opened one of the cabinets to reveal a small fridge and a shelf of bottles and glasses.

'This is the speciality of the maison. Puck and I invented it on Mykonos last year. Double-O. Ouzo and orange juice. Licensed to whatever. But what a way to go.'

Tony forced back the retching lump in his throat as he

took the clinking tumbler. A couple of weeks ago he would have brushed off Lorry. He must be losing his grip. Lorry sat next to him on the sofa, knees together too and shoulders hunched. If you touch me again, thought Tony, I'll smash your face in. Then he thought about the black man in the next room and eyed the distance to the gold-painted door into the hall. He closed off his nose inside, up by the soft bit where the bits of sick get caught, and sipped his drink. It actually tasted quite good. The aniseed blended with the orange taste and was lost. He unblocked his nose and took a swig.

'You didn't tell me your name. Is it a secret?'
'Tony.'
'How lovely. Is that short for Antony?'
'Antonia. My parents always wanted a girl.'

Lorry rocked back, raising his feet from the floor as if someone was going to sweep under them and laughed a deep throaty laugh instead of the giggle Tony was waiting for.

'Now tell Lorry what the matter is. I mean, whenever we've seen you I've said to Puck we have to cheer that poor man up. It wouldn't be the first time.'

I bet it wouldn't. Tony waited for him to edge closer along the sofa. You try to cheer me up and I'll smash your face in, Puck or no. He took another swig, the ice cubes falling in a rush onto his lips and splashing Double-O on to his chin and his nose-splint. He wiped his mouth with the back of his hand.

'I really don't think you can help me. It's personal.'
'Puck and I are very personal.'
'It's private.'
'Puck and I are very private.'
'It's none of your business.'
'You mustn't keep it bottled up inside. Come on, be a good boy, out with it.'

Tony sipped his drink and looked at the oriental carpet. Then fatigue and Mantovani and the soft light and the heady atmosphere and the exotic room and half a tumbler of ouzo began to have an effect. He lay back on the sofa, keeping his legs crossed, while Lorry refilled his glass. For the first time he said out loud, to another person, what had happened.

'I found out my wife was having an affair with someone else and it's probably not the first time and she doesn't love me any more and I've left home so she can get on with her own life and because I couldn't bear to live with her any more and I want to see my children and I don't know what to do. I don't know what to do.'

He snatched the glass from Lorry and took a gulp and spluttered because he felt deep embarrassment and uncontrollable sobs welling up from deep inside him. Oh God, not now, not in front of this fairy. He sat up and brushed Double-O off his trousers and the kilim and squeezed his eyes tight shut so the tears would not come. But they burned their way through the lids and on to his cheeks and down the plaster on his nose and more welled up when he burped the acid taste of orange juice. He put his head in his hands and wept.

'You poor dear,' said Lorry, and put his arm round Tony's shoulder. It felt warm and soft and he did not shrug it off or smash him in the face. When the spasm of sobbing had finished he felt a handful of tissues pressed into his hand.

'I'm sorry. I don't know, I mean. . . .'

'What came over you. Never mind. You poor dear.'

Tony put one hand back over his eyes while Lorry took the other in his. His nails were long and his hands were soft but they did not feel like a woman's. Their touch was different and not unpleasant.

'Hey man, what we got here?'

Tony looked up and snatched his hand away from Lorry's. Crouching in front of him was Puck, clad in nothing but his scarlet jockstrap, reflectively scratching his armpits. His hairless body was lean and muscular and an even tan colour. A gold cross dangled from his neck.

'Puck this is Tony and he's a very unhappy boy. Tony this is my friend Puck.'

'Hey what's this friend shit. We're a team. Lorry baits the hook and pulls in the catch and I puck the white trash.' He grinned and stretched out his hand to pinch Tony's cheek.

'Hush Puck. This isn't business. He's not in the mood.'

'Sorry guys. How was I to know? Talking dirty goes with the job. So what's the problem Tony?'

'Wife trouble,' said Tony, shaking his head. Puck tutted, stood up and helped himself to a Double-O. He came back and stood behind Tony, massaging the back of Tony's neck with a strong hand.

'Left home, right? Left her to stew, right? Make it on your own, right? Teach her a lesson, right? Wondering what the hell to do now, right? Don't know whether to stomp back and stick it to her, right? Or find a girlfriend and stick it to her, right?'

'Right.'

'Tell me the old, old story. You're not the first one to tell it right in this very room. Us whores hear that shit all the time. You know what I tell them? You can swallow your pride and go home or you can get out there and find someone else. The choice is yours. No use moping. Meanwhile, if you care for a little bit on the other side of the street. . . .'

Tony stood up and drained his glass.

'Not just now, thanks. But thanks for the drink. And everything. You're both very kind.'

'Pleasure.'

Tony handed the glass to Puck who opened the door for him. Their doorbell rang. Lorry followed him out into the hall and opened the front door to a fresh-faced young man in a blue blazer, green golf trousers and white loafers. He gave Lorry a large bunch of flowers and a big smile.

'Randy! How sweet!'

'If it were another woman it would be different.'

Alex stared at the snickering face of a desiccated Papuan.

The other heads behind the bar scoffed and chortled. Her shrunken reflection in the silver ice bucket looked like the latest addition to the collection. Joanna poked her slice of lemon reflectively with a long fingernail, making it bob under the surface. Although it was the middle of the morning and the lemon ritual still held they were drinking gin and tonic. Joanna thought Alex needed something stronger than tea.

'Didn't you have any clue at all?'

'I was awake all night thinking about that. He harped on about Gordon making a pass at him at your party. He wore that awful blue suit. I smelt scent on his face one day. I think he'd been wearing my lipstick. There were lots of wrong numbers and you could tell it was a man trying to make his voice sound like a woman's. He talked about someone called George in his sleep. Should I have noticed something?'

From experience at the receiving end Joanna knew when to be diplomatic. She shrugged her shoulders and poured them both another large gin.

'I know what my mother will say,' said Alex. 'I shouldn't have gone out all day. I should have stayed at home and looked after the children. Then this wouldn't have happened.'

'It's not your fault Alex. If you blame yourself, you're finished.'

'I thought homosexuality was something boys grew out of, not into. I drove him to it.' She drained her glass and held it out for a refill. A band round her head tightened and squeezed.

'I told you it's not your fault. Most women think they can show gay men what they're missing. Let them try.'

'But doesn't he think what he's doing to the children?'

'Men don't behave logically. They're incapable of controlling their emotions.'

'We lived together for over ten years. Suddenly there's a whole part of him I knew nothing about. He's a complete stranger. Where does that leave me? I don't even know who I am any more.'

'Pull yourself together Alex.'

'Yes. Pull myself together. See a solicitor. Find an au pair. Take the money out of the joint account. Change the locks. Get my hair done. Look for a house. Have a party. Get a job but only start when the maintenance is fixed. Join the tennis club.'

'That's more like it.'

'But it isn't. I like being married.'

'So what are you going to do?'

'I'm going to see him. Talk to him. . . .'

Joanna shook her head and poked around in the bucket for more ice, fishing for words of consolation and common sense, like 'don't waste your time'.

'. . . and then I'm going to boil his head and nail it to the bloody wall.'

17

'George something terribly, terribly momentous has happened. You see, I have no ties any more.'

He turned his head to show her a half profile, the nose-splint gone, tragic and aqualine, etched deeper by the candlelight. His eyes were dark pools of suffering and tragedy. She gave a little gasp, her perfect lips parted in surprise and compassion and she reached over to touch his hand, very gently.

'No, let me tell you all. It's all over with her. She has abandoned me. She left me long ago, when the flame of our love, always a cold flame, flickered and gutted. I was the last to realize it. But she knew, she is a woman.'

He took a deep, tragic breath and looked upwards. The candle between them cast their shadows on the ceiling, a tragic shadow-play of benighted love. She gave a little gasp, her perfect lips parted in surprise and compassion and she reached over to touch his hand, very gently.

'I don't blame her, George, how could I? Who can put blame or guilt on the turmoil of the human heart? I am glad, deeply glad that she has found a true soul-mate and love-mate after the barren years with me of pretence and dissimulation. She will bloom now, like a woman should.'

He turned to show his other tragic profile, and discreetly with his handkerchief, wiped a tear from the eye she could not see. She gave a little gasp, her perfect lips parted in surprise and compassion and she reached over to touch his hand, very gently.

'I can't pretend that at first I felt no pain and bitterness and despair. When you have loved someone, as I have done, passionately and whole-heartedly, and you discover that your love was never returned, the anguish can be like a white hot dagger plunged into your breast. But, George, one can grow and learn from such experience. With hope and courage it can be overcome and one is a better person, a more loving person, someone who has plumbed the depths of feeling.'

He turned and looked at her full face, a slight smile playing round his firm mouth, his left eyebrow slightly raised by the same muscle he used to wiggle his ears, his tragic eyes wide and limpid in the candlelight, filled with tears of happiness and pain. She gave a little gasp, her perfect lips parted in surprise and compassion and she reached over to touch his hand, very gently.

'And so I have come to you George.'

With a deft movement he pushed the candle to one side so he could look her in the eyes. The flame flickered like his flaring passion and left half his face in tragic darkness.

'George, come away with me. I love you, and now I know myself and the very depths of love. . . .'

'Aye thank you. Fares please.'

The bus conductor stood at his elbow like an impatient head waiter. He scrabbled in the pockets of his sodden raincoat for change and found a fifty pee. He had left the office at seven and decided to walk back to his room in the hope that the exercise would make him tired enough to sleep. He had stopped three times on the way for whisky and soda and lager and stout and red wine and a sausage with mustard and dry roast peanuts and a scotch egg and cheese and onion flavoured crisps and pork scratchings, all of which gave him another kind of white hot dagger in his breast. He had sloshed through the drizzle with masochistic satisfaction as he felt his feet and his cuffs and the back of his neck get wetter and wetter. Who cares? I don't. And nobody else does either. He arrived bedraggled in front of the house but did not go in. It was only half past nine. If he went in he would lie down on the bed and doze off and wake up at midnight and not be able to go back to sleep again. The only alternatives were listening to the Bottomless Pitt recount how they sank the Bismarck while he was lying on his stomach in Stoke Mandeville Hospital or taking a Double-O off Puck and Lorry while they relaxed between tricks. He wasn't in the mood for either. He stood on the pavement, swallowing air to make himself burp, undecided what to do. He should have stayed in the last pub and watched the television in the lounge.

He plodded off in the direction of Marble Arch. It would have been nice to walk on the Hyde Park side of the road under the whispering, dripping trees, at one with the dark shadows, like the pathetic something or other in poetry he dimly remembered from school, when nature is in the same mood as you. He felt pathetic all right. But he was scared of getting mugged and stayed on the bright side of the road. After half an hour he passed a request stop for the number thirteen bus. He used to take Alex home on the thirteen when he started to take her out. That was before he bought his first car. He stood at the stop and tried to resurrect memories of what it was like but they would not come. He remembered making her laugh with Charles Bronson imitations and nibbling her lips while the other waiting passengers looked away and groping under her sweater and fidgeting with hooks and eyes and standing so his erection did not show but the actual feelings were gone for ever. Poor kids.

The thirteen also went near where George lived. Since he had left home he had deliberately not called her. Leaving home was nothing to do with her at all. He had left his wife out of pure altruism. *Cherchez La Femme* the know-alls would say. Alex would tell everyone it was because of

Georgina but he was determined to prove her wrong. Three number thirteens, empty and bright, playing an elaborate leap-frog to avoid picking up passengers, appeared out of the rain. One of them stopped in front of Tony and he did not have the heart to refuse. Besides it was warm and dry. He climbed upstairs, his feet squelching, and realized how cold and damp he was. The top was empty. In the old days he sat right at the back with Alex where they could pet in privacy. Now he lurched to the front, diverting his thoughts to what he would say when he next met George.

'George, something terribly, terribly momentous has happened. You see, I have no ties any more. . . .'

He got off two stops before where Alex used to live. He had no wish to see the old shop, now owned by Mr Patel. He walked towards Georgina's. He couldn't arrive unannounced, just like that, late at night and dripping wet. On the other hand she might be taking a walk in the rain or be coming home or putting the milk-bottles out and he could wave and say he was just passing and how about dinner tomorrow? His hands in his pockets, hunched against the cold, he slouched along her road. He was twenty yards from her gate when a car drew up outside. The headlights blinded him until they were switched off. It was Burt's Jagwaar. He carried on walking. Through the rain spattered and rapidly misting windscreen he could see a couple locked in an embrace. He walked past and dodged into the shadow of an overhanging elder bush. He watched until the couple got out of the car and ran through the gate and past the lobelias and up to the door. She let herself in, kissed him once again in the light from the hall, and watched as he ran down the path, shoulders hunched, to his Jagwaar. The spray from its wheels spattered him under his bush. Shivering he walked as quickly as he could back to the main road. On such a night there was no hope of a taxi and he had to wait three quarters of an hour for a bus. He was very cold, inside and out.

*

Derek stood with his head back, mesmerized by the numbers flickering above the door.

'How's Auntie?' asked Alex.

He looked down in surprise. She looked as though she had been ill. Her eyes were unnaturally bright and she was breathing heavily.

'Hi Alex. Didn't see you there. Are you all right? You haven't been to my classes.'

'You're pretty cool, Ché. I asked how Auntie was.'

'What Auntie?'

'Leamington Auntie, Auntie Antonia.'

'Gladys.'

'Gladys? Ha ha ha. It suits him. Auntie Gladys.'

The lift stopped at the canteen floor. Derek stood by the controls with his fingers on the open button. He flicked his glossy hair back with the other hand. Alex stood in front of him, her feet on the crack between the lift and the floor. She flicked the Lenin badge on his lapel. She flicked the Wrangler badge on his shirt and the Pringle badge on his sweater and the Levi buckle on his belt.

'You're covered in labels Ché. You talk in labels. You think in labels. I bet you've got a label branded on your buttocks. Or shall I ask Gladys?

'Alex, are you all right?'

'Bitch.'

She walked away, head held high, leaving him stunned with his finger on the open button until the lift filled up.

Tony woke up in the middle of the night pouring sweat and with a pain in his chest. He groped for the handle of the white hot dagger but it was embedded too deep. The bright lights of the red Jagwaar burned into his skull, even when he had his eyes closed. The bed bucked and wallowed beneath him like a pedalo and the taste of ashes was in his mouth. Alex was standing with the children at the end of the bed but they disappeared when he turned the light on, although he shouted to them to come back. George gave a little gasp, her perfect lips parted in surprise and compassion and she reached over to touch his hand, very gently. He ran towards the centrefold girl kneeling on a shingle beach with her bottom on the air. She turned to look at him and she had Derek's face. Cathy pinned his head to the wall and smeared his mouth with lipstick and forced him to kiss his own woolly tie. He sat at a coffee table in the middle of his tiny room while Alex covered it with bunches of car keys. He shivered so his teeth chattered but the single blanket was unbearably hot.

He had to get outside where he could breathe. He forced his legs over the edge of the bed and crawled along the tilting floor to the door with his eyes half closed. He stood up to throw off his wet pyjama jacket, it must still be raining, and went out on to the landing. The bathroom was on the half floor above. If only he could get in a warm bath he would be better. He clutched the banisters, supporting his weight on the rail, and tried to pull himself up by his arms. He looked down into the stairwell to Mrs Banks's lair, two storeys below. If he could just get his legs over he would float gently down to her door.

'Hello Mrs Banks. Look, lighter than 'air, it wasn't Itler what done it, it was Love, perfect Love.'

He managed to heave one leg over the rail. He lay with his cheek on the warm wood, holding the banisters, his right foot dangling over the void. All he had to do was flick the other leg over and he could fly, up and down the stairwell and out of the door and over London and take her in his arms and over the roofs like Superman. He knew he could do it. There was a lightness and warmth in his body springing from round his crotch, a burner in a hot air balloon. But which 'her' would he take flying over Dollis Hill? He tried to get the face in focus but it wouldn't come. Unless he was certain he wouldn't take off, because there was no coming down again if you made a mistake, the power would be gone. He wanted it to be George's face, he could see the eyes already. Alex knew too much about him, she could see right inside him. The warmth was beginning to fade, the strength in his fingers was going, if he didn't let go now he would fly nowhere. With a delicious feeling of abandon and ecstasy he lifted both feet as high as he could, let go with his hands and drifted into the stairwell like thistledown.

It was Lorry and Puck's evening off. Wednesday was a rest day. They came back together at one o'clock, ready for an early night. As Lorry unlocked the door Puck tugged his sleeve and pointed up the stairs. Perched on the top of the banister rail were a pair of rosy buttocks coyly peeping out of a pair of blue pyjama trousers. From where they stood they could see neither head nor torso nor feet.

'Who that ass belong to?'

'Don't recognize it, man.'

'Is it a gift?'

'Interflora don't do that kind of thing.'

'Perhaps it's like a kissogram.'

'Or the Pitt sent away for a new bum.'

'Transplant. Male order.'

'Not competition I hope.'

'Not unless old Banksy has rented out the landing.'

'Is it real?'

'Soon find out.'

Puck took a long, slim handle out of the top of his right boot and flicked the stiletto out. He began to creep up the stairs, eyeing his target, trying to decide between the right cheek and the left cheek. But he got no further than the fourth tread when the bottom began to move towards him. Puck stopped. They saw hands and feet spread out on either side. The body gathered speed and they recognized Tony, his eyes half closed, a beatific smile on his face. Puck shouted and made a vain grab as he slid past. Lorry leapt forwards to break his fall. Happily the banister rail ended in a downward curl and not an acorn upright. Tony shot off the end into the arms of Lorry, Lorry staggered under the impact, tripped and fell backwards. They sprawled on the linoleum, feet in the air, Lorry holding Tony by the waist and clutching his bottom to his thighs. Puck whooped and sat on the stairs, clutching his sides. Doors clicked open. Mrs Banks emerged from her hole in a purple wool dressing gown, tugging her wig down. Wing Commander Pitt, yellow face and yellow pyjamas, peered down the landing. Mr Grosser, an old suit jacket thrown over a grubby nightshirt, peered over the well from the top floor and snorted in distaste. Lorry struggled to extricate himself from what should have been a familiar position.

'You bring the rum, I'll bring the lash.'
'Go back to bed Wing Commander.'
'He just dropped in, honest.'
'Not in the hall. It ain't decent.'
'Cover him up.'
'He's sick.'
'You're all sick.'
'He's nothing to do with us.'
'Stair rails turn him on.'

Tony stood up, clutched his pyjamas round his waist, breathing heavily and smiling in triumph at them all.

'I can fly,' he said, 'I can fly.'

The doctor came within the hour, chain smoking, bleary-eyed. He prescribed warmth and antibiotics and X-rays if he did not improve in twenty-four hours. Puck went to the all-night chemist and Lorry changed the sheets, lending him a pair of his own. The black satin felt slimy and the antibiotics were the size of gob-stoppers.

'In my day they'd have whipped him into horsepiddle. It's The Cuts what done it. Finished what 'Itler started.'

He lay in the dark for ages and waited for his life to pass before him but all he got was daydreams. When he was a child he could generate his own nightmares of scaly monsters and giant ogres before he went to sleep. Now he tried to bring back again his father-in-law, covered in shame and sea-weed to his bedside, his shimmering mother-in-law, his own mother holding out a tie, the girl he loved in the clutches of a Jagwaar with a gear-lever up her skirt, his forsaken children, his Jezebel of a wife. He expected that a brain in a state of delirium, alone, friendless, near to death from pneumonia and pleurisy, his family in ruins, covered in guilt and confusion and anger, would have conjured up more than the illusion that he was tossing and turning in a seedy bed-sitter listening to his left lung gurgle. All the romance had gone long ago. And now the comedy had gone too.

18

Tony sat on the bed, his back against the wall, trying to mesmerize himself in the gas fire. It was all he could think of to while away the afternoon. There was a pile of books by the bed but he could not concentrate. Wing Commander Pitt had lent him a few choice volumes on the War at Sea, Mrs Banks a couple of bodice-rippers and Puck the collected works of Albert Camus. He had started them all and they seemed equally absurd. He had not finished any of them. But then the antibiotics make you feel depressed, don't they Dear. I am not depressed, he snapped back at Lorry, the balance of my mind has never been less disturbed. I now see things calmly and dispassionately. I know exactly what I am going to do. He had to find a solicitor, a plumber to fix the feeder tank in the house before the central heating came on for the winter, and fix a meeting with Alex. He had to go to the office, clear his desk, say goodbye, write a note and jump off Tower Bridge to end it all. It was going to be a busy few days.

Self-hypnosis was interrupted by a ring at his front doorbell. Someone must have made a mistake. The only person who called was the doctor and he had made his final visit two days ago. It rang twice more. One of his neighbours must have forgotten their key. He heaved himself wearily off the bed and padded downstairs in his socks, slipping on the linoleum. He opened the door and saw Alex standing on the step. The shock of her presence was intensified by the shock of her appearance. Over the last two weeks he had imagined her blooming in the hothouse of an adulterous passion. She should not be looking pale and bedraggled. Her hair was brushed straight and dull to her shoulders. She looked thin and the flesh round her cheeks was sagging. She had bags under her eyes that careless making-up did not disguise. She was dressed in the kind of clothes she wore before she started college, her old tweed coat over a baggy-bottomed wool skirt and a nondescript shirt. A Harrods plastic bag dangled by her knees.

'I phoned the office. Dot said you'd been ill. She gave me your address.'

'I'm fine. Just fine.' He gave a deep, fruity cough.

He saw she was looking at him in the same way he was looking at her. He saw himself in her eyes like a mirror: four days growth of beard, grubby nose-splint, yellow shirt, the trousers of his light blue suit, a thick woolly cardigan of Lorry's, lime green and embroidered like a cottage teapot, odd socks. He opened the door for her and she came in, careful not to brush against him. He led the way upstairs, knowing she was noticing the threadbare linoleum and chipped brown paint. He gasped more than was necessary while he ushered her into his room and closed the door.

'Are you all right?' she asked.

'Just a bit of a cold. Nothing really.' He gave her another fruity cough in case she thought he'd just had a bit of a cold.

'Have a seat. There's only the bed. Sorry.'

'All you need, isn't it?'

She sat on the edge of the bed, still in her overcoat, hugging the Harrods bag on her lap for security. He stood facing her, squeezed between the gas fire and the chest of drawers. She looked round the tiny room. Lorry had decorated it with a large spray of pink silk flowers in an ornate vase and a little china bowl of onyx eggs. The black satin sheets and a pink satin pillow were still on the bed.

'A friend of mine lent me those. And this cardigan. He took all mine to the laundry.' Fruity cough.

'You didn't go to Derek's,' she said.

'Ha! Waiting for me was he? Don't worry. I won't cause trouble. Has he been round to the house yet?'

'He wouldn't have the nerve. I brought you some clean socks. I know how your feet get sweaty when you're ill. And some lemon barley water.' She took them out of the bag and put them on the bed and neatly folded the Harrods bag for something to do with her hands.

'Thanks. How are the children?'

'Fine. They keep asking when you're coming home. They still think you're on a business trip. That can't go on forever. They have to be told something.'

'Of course.' Fruitier cough.

'Have you got any linctus for that cough?'

'I save it all up for the evening. It helps me to go to sleep.'

'I'll tell them you're coming home soon then. You can explain.'

'Me? What have I got to explain? Haven't you told them about Derek yet?'

'I thought that was best coming from you. How much do you want them to know about him?' She breathed the last word, as if Derek were standing outside the door, listening.

'They have to be told the truth. The whole truth,' said Tony wrapping himself tightly in his cardigan.

'They'll be devastated.'

'Children know more than you think. They talk to their friends, they watch television. It's only an affair with another man. They'll take it in their stride. You see.'

'How can you be so brazen?'

'What do you want us to do? Sweep it under the carpet?'

'They can be spared for a little while. Until they grow up. Until they can handle it better.'

'And what about me? Do I come home like a lamb, play lovey-dovey for the next ten years?'

'If necessary, yes. You can have your private life.'

'Oh. Very convenient. Our private lives go on, do they, Derek or whoever else waits round the corner until the bell goes for playtime. Well let me tell you something right now. For me it's all or nothing. All or nothing, do you hear?'

She started to sob, looking down at the Harrods bag twisted in her hands. Ha! Crocodile tears. How pathetic. If she thought she could get round him with a few mealy mouthed words to get him home while she carried on with her lovers she was very much mistaken. A nice little set-up. He brought home the money and played Daddy to the children and stripped the front door and took the rubbish round to the dustbins and loaded the dishwasher while she popped out twice a week for a work-out. Private lives. Separate holidays. Marriage of convenience. Her convenience.

'Pah!' he said. 'Pah!' and reached over her for the lemon barley water.

'I'm sorry,' she sobbed. 'I drove you to this. I thought we were making a decent enough job of it for all these years. But our marriage was just an alibi.'

'At least you have the decency to admit it. That's something. It's the first word of apology I've heard from you yet.' His words were strained from the effort of trying to unscrew the top of the lemon barley water. They brought her to her feet. He flinched and jerked his shoulder up, thinking she was about to hit him.

'Apology!' she hissed. 'You walk out and destroy our home and you talk about apology? What a nerve. I suspected you needed a psychiatrist but now I'm convinced.'

'You mean you have no intention of changing your way of life? You want it like it was before? You expect me to accommodate you? No way, brother, no way.'

'Don't call me brother, you pervert! I'm your wife. You're the one who's got to change.'

'Me? Change? Why the hell should I?'

They were standing nose to nose with nothing but the bottle of lemon barley water between them when Lorry knocked on the door and came in without waiting.

'Yoohoo, Tony-pony, it's me-ee. Whoops. Sorry.'

He was looking nonchalant today in a knitted white cashmere three-quarter length coat and an off-the-shoulder T-shirt printed with the words, 'If you can read this you're on the wrong side so get thee behind me you devil you.'

'I'll come back.'

'No it's all right. Lorry, this is my wife, Alex. Lorry looked after me when I was ill. He was tremendous.'

Bending at the knees Lorry put on the bed a couple of plastic bags from the cleaners and a paper bag of groceries.

'We boys just need a bit of mothering when we're poorly. Well I'll be going, leave you two in peace.'

'Don't worry. I have to go.'

Tony grabbed her arm and she made no attempt to shake him off.

'You can't just scoot off like that. Typical. You come in here, stir things up and then run away.'

'I'm in a hurry. I have a lot to do this afternoon.'

'So have I.'

'Don't bother to see me out.'

She pushed past Lorry while Tony became absorbed in the task of opening the lemon barley water by jamming the cap in the top drawer of the chest. Lorry followed her downstairs and opened the door.

'He's a still a bit under the weather. He's not himself you know,' he said.

'He's himself for the first time in years,' she said.

'Oh good. By-ee.'

'Ha!' he cried and with a masterful flourish threw Lorry's embroidered cardigan across the room. It hit the wall, hung suspended for a second, and then fell dead on the pink satin pillow.

※

'If you think you can drive me mad with loneliness and despair, you've got another think coming.'

He grabbed Alex roughly by the arm and pulled her on to her feet. He leaned over behind her and with a violent tug ripped the blankets off his bed. He bundled the satin sheets into the plastic bag that had come back from the cleaners.

'I'm not taken in by that helpless, cringing pose. It's another of your ploys. I know all about your deceitful web of intrigue!'

She was cowering against the mantelpiece in front of the gas fire. He grasped her shoulders, shook her hard so her teeth chattered and threw her back on the bed.

'I shall come back but not to plead, do you hear? Not to beg. Not to fawn like a whipped puppy.'

He jerked his fisherman's jersey from the pile of clean clothes and forced his arms masterfully through the sleeves.

'If you don't like it, too bad. Clear out. Thanks for the memories. But if you think you're getting the children or the house or so much as a penny out of me you're mistaken. The decision is yours. If you stay, it's on my terms.'

He pushed her out of the way so he could sit on the bed to put his shoes on. He was wearing odd socks. He ripped them forcefully off and got out a clean pair from the pile.

'Don't think I don't need you. I need your support and help and solace when I come wearily home. What I do in the world is all for you and the children. You mean everything to me. Without you I am nothing. From now on you are my wife, not some kind of live-in companion.'

He peeped out behind the yellow curtain to see if it was raining. It wasn't but the clouds were heavy and dark and he didn't want to risk catching another chill. He took his raincoat down from the hook behind the door and took out his woolly scarf.

'I realize where I went wrong. Yes, I admit my guilt. I share the responsibility. I've been too soft. If I had put my foot down from the start, if I had shouldered all the responsibility, taken all the decisions, kept you barefoot and pregnant like you really wanted to be, none of this would have happened. But it's not too late. It's time for me to stand up and be a MAN.'

She struggled up from the bed but he slapped her down with the back of his hand across the cheek. She fell back and touched the weal with her fingertips.

'From now on you listen to me. You're never to see Derek again. Never do you hear? I'm going to see him. By the time I've finished with him he won't dare show his face again. And you're leaving that college. You never really believed in it all along. It was just a decoy. Your place is in the home with me and the children. You belong in bed and in the kitchen. You don't want to be treated as an equal, you want to be treated as a WOMAN.'

He knelt down on the floor and groped under the bed for his shoes. They were covered in fluff which he masterfully wiped off on a satin sheet. She watched his every move wide-eyed with surprise and fear.

'That's why the sex has been so rotten. I was trying to be considerate, to let you take the initiative, to give you an equal part. But if I waited for you to be in the mood every time it would drop off through lack of use. You want to be wooed and seduced and, yes, raped. I know what you want.'

He reached across her prostrate body for the books to give back to the Wing Commander and Mrs Banks. *Cockleshell Heroes*, *Warriors Of The Deep*, *The Men Of Squad 90*. Tough, dangerous, masculine men, like Mrs Banks's bodice ripping males in *Cavalier Romance*, *The Master of High Tor*, *Scarlet And Lace*. It wasn't only Mrs Banks who liked her men raw and passionate and masterful. He had browsed through enough women's romances on the station bookstall to know what women really wanted. Dark, tall men with experience and a tragic past who would as soon spank a girl as talk to her about caring and meaningful relationships. As long as she deserved it, they always have to deserve it, and Alex certainly deserved it.

'And now we've got that straight I'm going to give you the hiding I should have given you months ago.'

She cowered against the headboard, tucking her knees up to her chin. With one fluent and masterful movement he leaned over, grasped her by the wrist and pulled her towards him so she sprawled face downwards on the bed. Her scream was muffled by the mattress. He kept hold of her wrist, twisting it behind her back so she was pinioned to the bed. The hem of her skirt was round her thighs, revealing her stocking tops and suspenders and the soft, white milky flesh. He picked up the leather belt that was hanging conveniently on the bedrail. . . .

*

There was a knock on the door. 'Yoo-hoo, Tony?'
'Come in.'
'Everything all right?'
'Yes thanks Lorry. Here's your cardigan. I'm on my way to the laundry with your sheets.'
'Look after yourself. By-ee.'

Alex went down into the cellar for one of the large cardboard boxes in the cellar left over from the move. She was struggling back up the steps with one marked KITCHEN UTENSILS when she saw the porno magazine behind the gas meter. She took it out and made herself look at every picture. She threw it in the bottom of the box in disgust. What some women will do for money and men. At least she knew it didn't belong to Tony. She carried the box up to the bedroom and dropped it in front of his part of the wardrobe. She bundled his clothes and dumped them in on top of the magazine. The sensitive, tactile brown cord suit. Varnish covered jeans. Squash kit. Office suits with pink handkerchiefs in the breast pocket. A sealed Save The Children envelope dropped out on to the floor. She put it in her handbag to mail. She emptied the chest of drawers and the mantelpiece of his belongings, tipped them into the box and dragged it into the spare room.

She went back to the cellar for another cardboard box. Into it she dropped all the clothes out of her own wardrobe except a couple of pairs of jeans and her father's old overcoat. Last to go were the velvet skirt and grey silk shirt and purple tights she used to wear to parties. She hesitated over the brown box with her wedding veil. Louise might want it for a school play. She put it back in the top of the wardrobe next to her father's urn. In the chest of drawers she left only essential underwear. With particular venom she threw into the box the French panties he had brought her for Christmas. She dragged the box downstairs, out of the front door and round to the side gate by the garbage cans.

Oxfam had promised to pick it up by lunchtime.

Later that morning she stood in front of the department store window in sweater, jeans and her father's old overcoat. The window was empty except for three naked dummies, erect and proud. They had piercing blue eyes and the slightly parted lips of passionate women and incurable mouth breathers. Their heads were bald, their breasts had no nipples, their smooth, cream bodies had no hair. They were sexless like the dolls she had loved when she was little. Over them hovered her dim reflection.

'All off,' she said to the hairdresser, clutching her hair in both hands and shaking it. 'I want it half an inch all over. Then I want a blonde rinse, eyelash tint, steam bath, body massage, arm wax, leg wax, body wax, manicure, pedicure, full facial, make-up consultant, the menu. The full menu.'

'That's quite expensive, Madam.'

'My husband will pay.'

Her husband also paid for three Dior silk shirts, a navy pinstripe cashmere trouser suit, a Burberry trench coat, two pairs of black shoes with tiny gold buckles, Gucci briefcase and matching handbag and a long black umbrella with a cane handle. She left her old clothes in the changing rooms. When the store closed she walked down Knightsbridge looking at herself in the shop windows. Then, over a Pernod and a dish of toasted almonds in the Berkeley Hotel, she studied the Businesses For Sale in the *Financial Times* and savoured the admiring looks of men and the critical looks of women.

Tony stood in front of Men's Toiletries pondering the aftershave. Changing the habits of decades wasn't easy. For years he had taken the piss out of aftershave advertisements, pretty boys from a model agency posing against jeeps and wind-surfers and horses, denim and leather, lantern jaws and broad shoulders. Now he realized that when he made fun of them he was suppressing his own manliness. Never again, even if it did sting like hell when you slapped it on. Nor would he find an excuse to do something else when the men talked dirty while the women did the washing up. Nor would he avoid the little corner at the end of the bar in the pub round the corner from the office where the men told jokes. He would write them all down in a notebook and memorize them so he could join in. Forgetting dirty jokes was just another symptom of his flight from masculinity. He picked a box from the shelf decorated with a chunky man in a dinner jacket staring out of the picture at him while a sexy blonde girl clinging to his arm looked up at his perfumed cheeks.

Now that it was all over with Alex there was no reason why he shouldn't have a sexy blonde girl clinging to his arm. 'You are a woman and I, well, I'm a MAN.' After all, he was owed one, wasn't he? Alex had been unfaithful to him often enough. It would even things up a bit. He was entitled to his fling. What's sauce for the gander. While he queued to pay he eyed the packets of contraceptives out of reach behind the counter. Menswear for Women. Be gentle with me. To hell with all that. To hell with Gossamer and Fiesta and Featherlite. It was Rough Rider and Macho Man from now on, studded and ribbed. The picture on the front of one packet was like the picture on the aftershave, a blonde wrapped around a dark tough guy. He ground his teeth at the memory of the fiasco with George.

'Next,' said the girl behind the till. She looked about sixteen years old. She chomped gum between her back teeth. Behind him was a stern middle-aged woman with a Margaret Thatcher hair-do. In front of him two older women browsed among the laxatives. He was surrounded by women. Now was the first test of his masculine nonchalance. Let these women know what sort of a MAN he was. But now that contraceptives were above board and over the counter, why did they always make you ask for them? Why didn't they just put them in Men's Toiletries with the shaving cream and the baldness cures and the mansize cotton balls? He handed over the aftershave and felt a burning on his cheeks as if he had just slapped some on. He leaned over the cash register. He smelled spearmint and saccharine and ashes of violets and heard the slurping sound of cud chewing. He coughed a fruity cough and pretended he had a sore throat.

'Apaktermatchm'n.'
'Youwah?'
'Apaktermatchm'n.'
'Carnear.'
'Apaktermatchm'n.'
'Youwah?'
'A PACKET OF MACHO MAN. THOSE THERE.'

She slipped it discreetly into a small paper bag and he handed over the money, avoiding her eyes by developing a consuming interest in the indigestion tablets. He stuffed his purchases in his raincoat pocket, took his change and ran.

The next stop was the hairdresser. His composure recovered and his raincoat pockets stuffed with virility he gave his instructions with masculine assurance.

He was stern with the girl at the desk. 'Shampoo and Cut. Nothing fancy please.'

He was firm with the girl at the sink. 'No conditioner please.'

He was strict with the girl at the chair. 'No waves or flounces. Blow dry it flat please.'

He waved away the manicurist like a man who does his nails with a Bowie knife. With suave self-assurance he tipped them all fifty pee when they helped him on with his raincoat and his woolly scarf. He wished he had a hat. It was chilly round the back of his neck and he wound the scarf as high as it would go, leaving enough at the ends to cover his poorly chest.

He walked home through the jungle of the city streets feeling dangerous. He moved lithely on the balls of his feet, every nerve alert, exuding the animal musk of his mounting desire. He appraised the girls he passed and if they returned his predatory stare, provocatively turned up the corners of his mouth. Waiting for the little green man at the crossing he sucked his stomach in and eyed the cute blonde on the other side of the street, transfixing her with his irresistible masculinity. She rewarded him at the refuge in the middle of the road. 'You arter summink?' she said and he just flaunted his provocative smile.

He unlocked the door to his room feeling a weight had lifted from his shoulders. He had come to terms with himself at last. He threw off his raincoat and scarf and lit the gas ring to make a cup of tea. He unwrapped the aftershave and put it on the mantelpiece. He kept the other little packet in its paper bag and put it in the inside pocket of his best dark blue suit. Perhaps the pain had all been worth it for the self discovery. Tomorrow he would be scintillating and witty, civilized and seductive, but there would be no doubt that here was a MAN. 'Ha!' he said as he poured himself a spoonful of linctus.

He took off all his clothes and went up to the bathroom in just trousers and a sweater, carrying his tea. As well as manly he felt young and single and free. He shivered while he put coins in the water heater and swilled out the hairs and scum of the previous occupant. While the water trickled out of the roaring heater he admired his haircut in the pockmarked mirror over the towel rail. Beneath it was a notice handwritten in green ballpoint on the back of a pension book cover. PATRONS ARE KINDLY REQUESTED TO WIPE MIRROR IN THE EVENT OF SQUEEZING SPOTS BY ORDER MRS BANKS. The mirror had developed an acne of its own underneath the glass but it showed enough to be pleased with. He twisted his head, admiring his half profile and, squinting out of the corners of his eyes, gave himself a masterful smile.

19

Georgina suggested the Cock. It was half way between her office and Alex's college. It was a jewel of Fifties pub architecture. In its application of the straight line, deployment of the right angle, juxtaposition of primary colours, use of painted concrete, implementation of formica, it was a showcase of the period. Alex arrived fifteen minutes early. She decided to hang round outside and found a convenient bus stop on the other side of the road where she could loiter intent on everyone who went into the pub. She wanted to size up Georgina before she met her, get over the initial shock. She imagined a clone of her mother, overweight and garrulous, dressed for a seaside outing, like a beach chair. Also she did not want to look too keen, too anxious. This wasn't her idea. Veronica had set it up out of sentimentality and a vague idea of keeping an eye on Georgina. When she phoned Alex could not think of a good excuse for refusing.

By half past twelve Georgina had still not arrived. Shows how much the little madam thinks about getting together she muttered as she crossed the road. She arrived at the swing door at the same time as a tall, slim girl with black spiky hair. The shock of recognition was like coming across a mirror in an unexpected place. 'Are you er. . . .' They each held open a wing of the door for each other and resolved the etiquette by squeezing through together.

'Were you hanging round outside?' asked Georgina.
'Me? Whatever for?'

'I did. I wanted to see what you looked like. I was nervous.'

'What will you have?'

'Oh. Thanks. Large gin and tonic. I'll bag a table.'

The bar was filling up with men released from offices, cheers, first of the day, standing rounds and flourishing luncheon vouchers at the barmaid behind the perspex sandwich shelves. Alex elbowed her way through the pot bellies to the bar for the drinks and a packet of dry roast peanuts, holding her nose against tobacco breath and acrid aftershave. She tried not to let her new clothes touch the beer-swilled bar. Lemon love? A question expecting the answer no. A man with tartar stained teeth and a walrus moustache touched her bottom. The peanuts were plucked from the right nipple of a pouting blonde stuck up over the wine cooler, the sister of the busty tart on the beer mats. She reached past a racing paper and an egg-stained waistcoat for the ice-bucket in which a few clinking shards wallowed in cold water. Someone bellowed a punch line in one ear and guffaws rang in the other. The barman wiped his fingers under his armpits before he worked the till. She left the few pee change on the bar where he put it in a puddle of beer. Fanks love.

Georgina had found a small table in a corner made by a partition of what looked like artfully assembled beer bottle bottoms and a wall of fibreglass Cotswold stone tastefully decorated with elegant hunting prints. She had pushed the ashtray, brimming with cigarette ends and screwed up crisp packets, to the side of the table and was mopping the red formica with a tissue. Alex sat gingerly on the edge of her chair, avoiding as much as possible of the beerstained and cigarette burned upholstery.

'Nice place.'

'Just handy reely.'

'Cheers.'

'Cheers.'

'I worked over the road for three weeks. I was mastering

the art of simulating old fashioned knots in the end of reconstituted soyabean sausages.'

'Fascinating.'

'I had to sign a paper saying I wouldn't tell anyone how it was done.'

'Peanut?'

'No thanks. They put sulphuric acid in them.'

'Ah. I didn't know.'

Georgina's suit was the same vintage as the Cock. Long tight skirt tailored over the hips, pinched waist, padded shoulders, with a cream blouse and single string of pearls.

'I like your suit. Did you get it at Oxfam?'

'It was me Mom's. She kept all her clothes.'

Alex tried to picture the inflated Veronica as a slip of a girl but failed. Her father knew that suit. Was that why she'd worn it? A bandy-legged man in pinstripes, gut hanging over his belt and a pint of Guinness in his hand came over to ask for the third chair at the table. May I have the pleasure of intruding on the Ladies? He breathed stale beer and smarm and strained to show how he could lift the chair with one hand.

'You go to college then.'

'Until I qualify. A friend and I are buying a business.'

'Great. What sort of business?'

'Drop forgings.'

'Oh.'

'What do you do?'

'I work for a multinational. We're in the food industry.'

'My husband's in Edible Fats.'

'Reely? You're married then.'

'I'm not sure.'

'What's that supposed to mean?'

Damn damn damn damn. Why can't I keep my big mouth shut? I was going to talk about drop forgings and aluminium castings and jobs and strategic planning and the economy and the current business environment and life in London and the theatre and Wimbledon. I am a professional woman. I was not going to talk about husbands and babies and boyfriends and families and mothers and fathers. And what do I blurt out in the first thirty seconds? My bloody husband's left me.

'What? Nothing. A joke. One is never sure.'

'You and I ought to know I suppose. I saw him a few times, you know.'

'Who? My husband?'

'No. Not your husband. Our Father.'

'Who art in heaven.'

'I like it. Knowing him he might be in the other place. He used to come round when I was little. I thought he was my uncle. He was ever so funny wasn't he? He used to tell jokes and make funny faces and he had that red rubber clown's nose. He used to make me laugh.'

'You must be thinking about someone else. He was never like that with us.'

'It was him, reely. Uncle Phil. Uncle Philander my Mom used to call him.'

'You're mixing him up. Did you have lots of uncles?' Alex drained her glass in one gulp to drown her malice and fought the resulting burp. She tried to imagine her father in a clown's nose, making everybody laugh.

'Same again?'

She watched Georgina slip into the crowd of men. When they weren't telling jokes with punch lines they were talking about sales and production and football and cars and do-it-yourself. She felt a pang of envy. Talking about that garbage was a lot easier than the True Life Confessions that women got into. The men at the bar made way for Georgina's return with exaggerated courtesy, sucking in their paunches like matadors as she passed through with two glasses and a packet of crisps.

'Cheese and onion. Is that all right?' said Georgina.

'No thanks. They're full of monosodium glutamate.' Alex forced herself not to take any although they were her favourite.

'You're lucky, you know, having a Dad. Everyone should have one,' said Georgina.

'Like those over there? Which one would you choose? Go on. Pick any one you like. Look, the one on the end of the bar's got a red nose. A real one. He'd be good for a giggle.'

'That's not fair. 'They're not like that when they're at home.'

'No they're not. You're right. They're either mute and crabby, sitting in front of the telly and expecting to be humoured or they're telling their wives what a better job they could do of running the house if they didn't have more important things to do like go out to work and tie knots in plastic sausages.'

'That's ever so cynical.'

'It's the truth. Oh yes, say the Dads, I'll load the dishwasher and I'll read the children a story and I'll put the milk bottles out but I'm doing you a favour. A big favour. Just don't try asking me to clean the lavatory or sew the name tapes on or iron the shirts, that's all.'

'The men I meet aren't like that.'

'That's because you don't meet them at home. Look at them now. Not a care in the world. Life and soul of the party. They go back to a comfortable office and act the big I Am with female slaves bringing them tea and typing their letters. They are so busy and managerial and important and they love every minute. Why? Because they don't have to talk to their wives and children or anyone else like human beings, that's why. And then they come home and look weary and it's such a burden being the breadwinner and I've had such a hard day at the office Dear but I don't mind because I do it all for you. Puke.'

Alex drained her glass and stared at the men at the bar as if she had lost the power to turn them to stone.

'I like men.'

'You wait till you marry one. They're different people then. Do you think my mother would recognize your Uncle Phil? Funny faces? Jokes? Pornographic magazines? You can live all your life with a husband and never realize that when you're not there he's a completely different person.'

'What about your husband?' asked Georgina.

'Why should he be any different?' She wanted to be calm and collected about it all. She certainly wasn't going to tell this stranger, this kid, even if they had the same eyes and the same nose and the same father. She was only her little sister, after all. She stood up, holding on to the edge of the table. Her face felt hot.

'Same again?'

'I couldn't. I haven't had any lunch.'

'Come along old boy. One for the road. Put hairs on your chest.' She drew a deep breath of the moist, smoky air and took a bearing on the sandwich counter. She returned with the drinks and two crusty yellow rolls filled with crusty yellow cheese.

'Enough to give the ploughman anorexia,' she said but they both bit into them like navvies.

'So tell me about you,' said Alex, swallowing hard and reaching for her glass.

'I'm getting married next month. Only because I have to, mind.'

'I didn't think anyone had to get married these days.' She glanced at Georgina's waist. Georgina giggled with her hand in front of her mouth.

'No, not for *that*. He's an American called Burt. B.U.R.T. Like Reynolds. He's going back to California and I'm going with him. We're getting married so I can get a visa.'

'It's a good a reason as any to get married.'

'We'd live together if he was staying here. It just makes it easier. I can get a job when I'm over there. And his company will pay for me to move as well.'

'Good luck. I'm sure you'll be very happy.'

'Burt's family are coming over. We're having a church wedding. For his Mom's sake. They're Catholics.'

'Enjoy it Dear. Just cross your fingers when you make your vows.'

'Alex?'

'Yes?'

They were interrupted by an old man in navy blue trousers and waistcoat and collarless shirt collecting glasses. He kept his gums clamped shut on his brilliant white dentures to stop them clicking.

'It'd be ever so nice if you came to the wedding.'

'Me? After all I've said? It'd be like asking the wicked fairy.'

'Go on. My Mum's my only relative. Burt's got all his lot coming over. There's only my Mum's friend Effie who I'm living with. It's going to be a small do. It would be nice if you were there. Sort of tie things up.'

'Thanks. I'd love to make up the numbers. I'll have to see. But my mother must never know. It would kill her.'

They dedicated themselves in silence to cheese chewing. Alex regretted her churlishness and realized with anger that she wanted to cry. She should never have come. The little bitch had no right coming into her life like this. It was her own stupid fault for tracking her mother down.

'Who's giving you away?' asked Alex.

'You what?'

'Giving you away. There's got to be a man to hand you over. Like giving something to a jumble sale.'

'I hadn't thought of that.'

'You could always walk down the aisle by yourself. Or hire a morning suit for Effie. That would be great. The Father of The Bride wore Drag.'

'As long as the groom doesn't.'

'Don't bank on it,' said Alex, chomping on her lemon peel and flooding her mouth with bitterness. 'Isn't there an Uncle in Acocks Green?'

'I don't want any of them. I'll think of something.'

Alex picked up her bag from the floor and put it on her knees as a signal that it was time to go.

'It's my round. Don't you want another one?'

'Another time. I have to get back to college and you have a

job to go to. It was lovely. I'll try and make it to the wedding but if not I hope it all goes well.'

'Do you think your husband will come? I'd love to meet him.'

'We don't live together any more. I left him. He's gay. He lives in a house with other gays. I threw him out in case he gave the children Aids.'

'Drop forgings,' panted Alex to Joanna's knees. Joanna squatted down to look her in the eye. Dangling upside-down from the exercise machine her open mouth looked like a hole in her forehead.

'You need your tiny shaven head looking at,' said Joanna.

'I've been round the factory. It's a gold-mine. Only thirty people for all that turnover. Undervalued I promise.'

'What are drop forgings anyway? False earrings? Counterfeit money?' Joanna leapt in the air and squatted again.

'Hot metal that's hammered into shape between two dies.' She took a deep breath and reached up to touch her toes while Joanna did another bunny jump.

'Listen Alex when I suggested we went into business together I meant a dress shop or something. What do you know about drop forgings.'

'Enough. You get this powdered metal, heat it up and bang it into shape between two dies. It's like making waffles. The present owner invented a computer controlled die. He's got a long term contract for the airbus. He's got no relatives. He wants to keep a majority stake for three years and then get out and be rich. He'll stay on to handle the technical side. In three years we take over.'

'Then who will do the technical side?' panted Joanna.

'You. You're a mechanical genius, Joanna.'

'Me? I can just about put a bag in a vacuum cleaner.'

'That's all you need. In three years even you can learn enough to hire some man.'

'Where's the money coming from?'

'We have to find twenty per cent now. Mummy will lend me a third. Daddy had lots of life insurance. You wring a third out of Sam as part of your settlement. The bank will lend us the rest. In three years we'll float it on the stock exchange.'

'But we'll have to run the company. Manage all those people.'

'Anyone who can run a house and kids can run a company, Joanna. You treat the men like children and the women like the cleaning lady. Don't worry. Management is a big mystique invented by men. It's a substitute for personal relationships.'

'You've got it all worked out. When do we start?'

'As soon as you show me how to unhook my feet from this damn machine.'

Tony suggested the Cock. It was half way between Georgina's office and the training centre. He arrived fifteen minutes early. He downed a large gin and tonic for courage and nursed the second in the comforting press of men at the bar, watching the swing door. The man next to him struck a manly pose with one foot on the rail and two hands on the bar, his scotch and soda between them.

'Seen the new Ford?' he said. Tony was not sure who he was talking to as he kept his eyes on the mirror behind the bar. He darted a quick glance in Tony's direction.

'No. Good is it?' said Tony.

'Anti-lock brakes.'

'Really?'

'Fuel injection.'

'Great.'

'It talks to you all the time too. If you want it. Slow down, change gear, that sort of thing.'

'Wonderful.'

'Saves listening to the wife.' The man looked Tony in the eye for the first time, gave a brief guffaw, and looked back at the mirror. Before he could hear more about this stunning advance in automobile technology Georgina came in.

'Gin and tonic?' he asked.

'Perrier thanks. I've still got a headache from the gin I had here yesterday.'

He bought the drinks and a packet of dry roasted peanuts ripped from the upper thigh of a pouting blonde stuck up over the wine cooler. He left the few pee change on the bar where he put it in a puddle of beer. Fanks Mate. Georgina found a table in a corner made by a partition of what looked like artfully assembled beer bottle bottoms and a wall of fibreglass Cotswold stone tastefully decorated with elegant hunting prints. She had pushed the ashtray, brimming with cigarette ends and screwed up crisp packets, to the side of the table and was mopping the red formica with a tissue.

'Cheers.'

'Cheers.'

'Peanut?'

'No thanks. They put sulphuric acid in them.'

He tore a hole in the peanut packet and shook some into the palm of his hand. Alex used to tell him off for swigging them straight from the packet.

'You're getting married then,' he said. 'Congratulations.'

'Thanks.'

'New job, new life, new country. I wish I could get a meal ticket like that.' He put his hand on her forearm to stop her throwing her Perrier in his face. 'I apologize. I really didn't mean that. I was thinking of my own life.'

'Don't take it out on me.'

'You asked me once if she was screwing around. She was. Love letters, little country hotels, the works. She admitted it. Her accounting lecturer. Probably not the first.'

'I'm sorry. Reely.'

A bandy-legged man in pinstripes, gut hanging over his belt and a pint of Guinness in his hand came over to ask for the third chair at their table. He appraised Georgina and caught Tony's eye with a man-to-man wink.

'You also said that you wouldn't like me any more if I left my wife and kids.'

'I've stopped making judgements. I've learned a few things since then.'

'Who from?'

'My Mom. My sister. I do like you. So much so that I'd like you to give me away at the wedding.'

'Me? How can I give away what I've never had?'

'You know what I mean. It would be nice to have you there. It was because of you I met Burt.'

'With my views on marriage it would be like asking the wicked fairy.'

'Go on. Burt's got all his lot coming over. There's only my Mum and my sister and my Mum's friend Effie who I'm living with.'

'And you don't know any old men, right?'

'You'll like my sister. Half sister really. Her marriage has just broken up too. She looks like me. Her name's Alexandra.'

'What?'

They were interrupted by an old man in navy blue trousers and waistcoat and collarless shirt collecting glasses. He kept his gums clamped shut on his brilliant white dentures to stop them clicking.

'She's ever so glamorous and she's got this reely short blonde hair.'

'Oh.'

'She runs her own business. Drop forgings.'

'And she's single? Introduce me. I'm the one who's looking for a meal ticket.'

'Her husband was having an affair with a man. She kicked him out of the closet and into the street.'

'Poor girl. So now she's looking for a real man.'

A fresh faced man of about forty in horn rimmed spectacles,

button down collar and tassels on his loafers held open the gilt lettered door for Alex as she entered the shop. She smiled graciously as he followed her inside. A man in a morning suit shuffled to meet them.

'I'm looking for a hat,' she said superfluously, as the shelves on either side contained nothing but hats on polished wooden heads.

'We don't stock ladies' hats, I'm afraid Madam,' said the aged retainer.

'Then I'll have to take a man's hat, won't I?' She handed him her tightly furled umbrella and her trench coat. He raised his eyebrows at the American who shrugged.

She tried bowlers and trilbies, tweed caps and shooting hats before settling on a dark blue fedora. While the fedora was being wrapped and boxed she telephoned Georgina from the manager's desk. The American, who had bought the right kind of hat to go grouse shooting in, pretended to be engrossed in the flies on a fishing hat.

'It's Alex . . . I'm coming to your wedding . . . I have to now. I've just bought a hat. . . . Have you got someone to give you away? . . . What makes you think I'll like him? . . . You sound like you're trying to fix me up . . . His wife's fault was it? . . . That's what they all say.'

The American held open the door for her and followed her out. He adjusted his hornrims.

'I'm glad you were there,' he said on the pavement outside.

'Stores like that makes me nervous. They're not like that in Slippery Rock Pa. I guessed if they didn't throw you out I'd be OK. Care for bite to eat? The Ritz is around the corner.'

'We haven't been introduced.'

'I'm Wayne. Hi. And you're Alex. I promise it's just for lunch. I have to get back to the bank for a loan committee meeting.'

'The bank? Would you like to be propositioned?' she asked.

*

Gordon tilted back his Leatherette executive chair as his secretary put a tray down on his desk. He adjusted his Rotarian cufflinks and beamed and rubbed his hands together.

'Who's going to be mother?' he asked. Joanna and Alex smiled and kept their hands folded on their laps. He poured the coffee and handed them each a cup.

'Well ladies. You're going into business together. That's good news.' He put on a listening bank manager's expression. 'What can we do for you?'

'Lend us money,' said Alex. Gordon stopped beaming as soon as she started to outline the deal.

'But ladies, what do you know about engineering?'

'As much as we need to know. Does the chairman of Ford know how to design a carburettor?' She slapped on his desk a feasibility study, financing plan and the last five years' accounts.

'What do your husbands think about this?' he asked.

'What the hell difference does that make?' asked Joanna. 'No one ever asked me what I thought about my husbands' businesses.'

'But this is an industrial enterprise.'

'What did you think it was? A souvenir shop? A cuddly toy co-operative?' asked Joanna.

'Drop forgings isn't the sort of thing, you know, I mean. . . .'

'That women do, Gordon?'

'Alex, I have the greatest respect for women in business, you know that. The bank is a major employer of women. I have many women colleagues.'

'They're all cashiers and secretaries. How many women bank managers are there, Gordon?' asked Joanna.

'These things take time.'

Alex picked up her files and put them in her bag. 'Let's not get into sexism, Joanna. That isn't the problem. The first problem is that the loan we're asking for is outside Gordon's lending limit. The second is that Gordon knows what a souvenir and a cuddly toy is. But he wouldn't recognize a forging if it dropped on his foot.'

Outside in the car Joanna sighed as she turned the ignition.

'We blew it. We should play them at their own game. Gordon was our only hope. Where do we go now?'

'The Bank of Pennsylvania. I had lunch at the Ritz with their industrial lending manager yesterday. He thought we had a great deal. He said he'd fix us up to see the branch manager this afternoon.'

'You fox. Why didn't you tell me? Let's go. I hope his boss isn't like Gordon.'

'She's not.'

20

'I'm going to trip over this dress I know I will,' said George as they waited in the church porch for her mother and Effie to find their seats in the front on the bride's side. 'I hope Burt's Mom appreciates this. I feel a right wally.'

'You look absolutely lovely. I wish I were waiting for you up there,' he said, annoyed that his genuinely heartfelt words sounded so trite. It's all so bloody trite, that's the trouble, even what's genuine. She looked up and kissed him on the cheek. Her lips felt like the brush of a rose petal through the fine lattice of her veil. She looked exquisitely beautiful and happy. She put her small, pale hand through his arm and gently squeezed.

'Have you got all the right things? Something old, something new, something borrowed, something blue?'

'Don't give me that garbage. Does rented count as borrowed? This dress is. I've got nothing blue though.'

He dug in the pocket of his tailcoat and found a screwed up number thirteen bus ticket. It was white with blue printing on it, fare scale C. He had intended to take a taxi but as soon as he got to the main road four number thirteens came along together and he waved them down with his top hat. Off to the races Guv? He pressed the ticket into her hand under the orange blossom bouquet. They peered anxiously through the stained glass of the door at the altar. He had paid for the two vases of carnations. He wished he'd spent a bit more. There didn't look very many. His knees felt weak and he wondered if he could make the long walk down the aisle and through the rest of the service. He caught a whiff of his new aftershave, making him want to puke and sneeze simultaneously, but he had forgotten to bring a handkerchief. His stiff collar rubbed against his neck and his morning coat felt even more ill-fitting than it had in the hire shop. He batted his top hat nervously against his leg in syncopation with the organ music. The organist was showing off that he knew something other than 'Here Comes The Bride'. It sounded as if he was tuning up with lots of fanfares and twiddly bits.

'Are they all there?' he asked.

'Burt's there and Andy. And his family. Effie and Mom and my sister.'

He peered through the stained glass again. It was like looking into a soupy green aquarium. Her sister Alexandra must be the tall, slim woman in the fedora.

It was ten years since he had walked down the aisle with another Alexandra. Alex had looked just like this bride, same blue eyes and wicked smile and laugh lines round the eyes. It was hard to believe that so much had happened in those ten years. It was as if he was simply taking up where he had left off. Marriage, job, and home had been ripped out of memory, leaving only a dull ache. George was fifteen years younger than he was but they could be equals. He felt as self confident and gauche and young as he had at his first wedding. He wondered where Alex was now, what she was doing, what she was thinking of. Certainly not white weddings. The organ stopped with a discordant flourish. There was an expectant silence in the church, like waiting for a pneumatic drill to start again. There was a clattering on the stairs that came down from the organ loft.

'Ready?' asked the organist and clattered upstairs again.

The organ changed its tune. 'Here Comes The Bride'. Tony struggled with the door and his top hat and his gloves. The congregation stood and coughed and banged their kneelers and rustled their hymnbooks. The priest walked towards the altar and looked expectantly to the back of the church. Tony felt his chest thumping with sadness and pride. He gave her a smile and squeezed her hand against his body with his arm and started the long, slow walk, pacing in two movements like soldiers do on television at a state funeral, as if they were picking their way over dogshit. With every step his antibiotics rattled in his trouser leg pocket but there was nothing he could do about that now. The groom and his best man resolutely faced the front. Tony felt a spasm of anguish that Burt looked so tall and slim and erect and had a neck that showed lots of white collar over the back of his jacket. He thrust his own shoulders back and George looked up at him, startled by his sudden movement. The rest of the congregation turned sideways in their pews and gazed down the church at them, eyes only for the bride.

It was then that Tony knew he had finally gone mad. During the agonies of the past few months he had been astonished that he had kept his sanity. He had been proud of his resistance to emotional and physical stress. But the body is not a machine. He had lost a family, a home, a wife and now he was giving away the girl he loved to another man. He had been seriously ill and was still on antibiotics, as everyone in the church could hear from the rattle in his pocket. No wonder he was having hallucinations. He closed his eyes for a second, squeezed them tight shut but it did no good. He could still see his wife standing next to Effie and George's mother. She had a new dress and her hair was cut short and her dark blue fedora was pulled down on her forehead and she looked ten years younger but there was no question in his tortured mind that it was his wife he was imagining. The only consolation was that he knew it was a delusion. He had not been sucked wholesale into insanity.

He forced his eyes away and concentrated on the altar. He would not have been surprised to see her face popping up behind the tabernacle or out of the carnations but for the moment his self-control worked. As they passed their pew

George grinned at her relatives and shrugged her shoulders and waved her orange blossom. Tony implored whoever was sitting up there in the tabernacle to save his mind, just for an hour, but there was no mercy. When he looked again Alex was still there. The only odd thing was that she stared at him in horror and incredulity, which was a funny way for a hallucination to behave. He would have expected anger or sorrow or hatred or malicious delight. He decided to bluff it out. He winked at her. Instead of disappearing in a puff of smoke her eyes turned to venom and she turned away.

What if it was all an hallucination? He squeezed George's arm and looked down at her as he delivered her to the altar rail. She had eyes only for Burt who was sidling up beside her. He stared at the priest to see if he was really his father or his boss or the ticket inspector or another figure of authority. He clutched his top hat and fingered the sweaty barathea of his coat. His knees began to tremble and perspiration poured from under his neck and his arms. Was he in the middle of a terrible nightmare? He implemented the classic test and pinched his thigh as hard as he could under his stripy clown's trousers. This hurt so much it made his leg jerk and he banged his knee against the altar rail. The pain shooting through his leg made him drop his hat. He grabbed at it with his other hand and dropped his gloves. The hat rolled in a perfect circle and came to rest at his feet next to the gloves. Hoping he would not be noticed he stooped down quickly to snatch them up and banged his forehead on the top of the altar rail. It was like walking into a lamppost. He reeled under the unexpected blow and clutched at the nearest object for support. This was the bride. Oblivious of the growing pandemonium at her side she had been gazing into her beloved's eyes. Caught unawares she staggered sideways, catching Burt off balance as he stooped to kiss her on the cheek. She headed him in the mouth. He rocked backwards in surprise and pain and barged into the best man. The best man was making sure yet again that he had the ring and was putting it carefully back in his waistcoat pocket when Burt jogged his arm. The ring went flying up in the air. The priest tried to catch it like snatching at a fly but it tumbled on to the altar rail and bounced on to the floor. The best man tried to trap it with his foot but instead kicked it in the direction of the side aisle where it disappeared down the central heating grating under the fourteenth station of the cross, Jesus is Laid in the Tomb. The honorary father of the bride clutched his knee and his forehead, the bride rubbed her temple, the groom dabbed his mouth with the back of his hand while the best man scrabbled after the ring on his hands and knees and gazed down through the holes of the grating into the nether world below.

'Ahem,' said the priest, 'would anyone happen to have a spare ring?'

Alex came out of the front pew, pursing her lips and twisting something in her left hand with obvious effort. She held out her wedding ring to the best man who stuffed it thankfully into his waistcoat pocket. She walked back to her pew resolutely ignoring the hallucination of her husband standing at the altar rail in ill-fitting morning suit rubbing his forehead.

During the agonies of the past few months she had managed to keep a grip on herself. With remarkable composure she had coped with her husband's infidelity and bisexuality and desertion, her father's public death and secret life and the revelation of her sister. She had been surprised that she had kept her sanity. She had been proud of her resistance to emotional and physical strain. But the body is not a machine. The stress of starting a new life, coming to this wedding by herself, reliving the memories of her own wedding was the last straw. No wonder she was having hallucinations. When she turned round to see George coming down the aisle and saw her husband by her side she closed her eyes for a second, squeezed them tight shut but it did no good. She could still see him. He had a different hair cut and looked less pathetic than when she had seen him but there was no question in her tortured mind that it was Tony she was imagining. The only consolation was that she knew it was a delusion. She had not been sucked wholesale into insanity. She forced her eyes away and concentrated on the altar. She would not have been surprised to see his grinning face popping up behind the tabernacle or out of the carnations but for the moment her self-control worked. But she knew he was coming closer like an ogre in a nightmare. She could hear a sinister rattle getting louder with every step he took.

As the couple passed their pew she dared to look at them again. George grinned at her mother and shrugged her shoulders and waved her orange blossom. Her husband was still by her side. She implored whoever was sitting up there in the tabernacle to save her mind, just for an hour, but there was no mercy. He was still there, staring at her with malicious delight. He had the effrontery to wink at her. Hallucination or no she scowled at him as if he was real.

What if it was all an hallucination? She held tightly to the pew as Tony delivered George to the altar rail and Burt sidled up beside her. Alex stared at the priest to see if he was really her father or Derek or Lorry or another figure of male duplicity. Was she in the middle of a terrible nightmare? She felt dizzy and the tall, cavernous church seemed to close in on her. She was about to implement the classic test and pinch herself when events at the altar rail convinced her that she was part of a hideous reality. She saw the vision of her husband jerk his left leg, kick the altar rail, drop his top hat, bang his head on the altar rail, barge into Georgina who shunted the groom who barged the best man who threw the ring into the air and kicked it down the grille in the floor underneath the fourteenth station of the cross.

'Ahem,' said the priest, 'would anyone happen to have a spare ring?'

Yes, I have a spare. Take it and welcome. Nothing would give me greater pleasure. She handed it to the relieved best man and walked back to her pew with the grim satisfaction of having sealed the irrevocable. She stared straight through Tony as he retreated thankfully from the altar rail and entered the pew behind her. She tried to shut her ears as he leaned over and hissed in her ear. She could smell moth balls and acrid aftershave.

The Lord be with you

'And also with you. What the bloody hell are you doing here?'

'Don't blaspheme in church. Amen.'

Father, you have made the bond of marriage a holy mystery. . . .

'I've a right to be here. I'm her sister.'

'Since when?'

'It's none of your business.'

'It is my business! She's my sister-in-law.'

. . . they pledge their love today. . . .

'Not for long. You soon won't have any relatives by marriage.'

May their lives always bear witness to the reality of that love. . . .

'And what are you doing here?'

'She asked me. We're still friends.'

'Was she wearing trousers when you met her? Amen.'

There was a scuffle and a rustle as everyone sat down. Burt's father, resplendent as a compère in his silver tuxedo and scarlet bow tie went up into the pulpit to begin the readings but he might as well have been talking to himself. The bride and groom stared up at the altar, the best man fingered his waistcoat pocket and the new in-laws eyed each other across the aisle. Tony leaned forward in prayerful contemplation, hand over his eyes and mouth next to Alex's left ear.

'Why won't you let me see the children?'

The Lord fills the earth with his love.

'In case you give them Aids.'

Tony slumped back into his bench as if a divine seizure had come upon him. This was worse than any nightmare.

Not only was she a shameless adulteress but she had gone completely off her rocker. He gazed up at Burt's father as if the gift of tongues had made him suddenly incomprehensible to any but Outer Mongolians. But another kind of enlightenment was seeping into his confused brain. If *this* was the woman George had been trying to set him up with then *he* was the husband she had thrown out of the house.

Let us love one another as God has loved us. . . .

Burt's father stepped down and the priest took his place. They stood for the Gospel. As they sat down for the sermon Alex turned and they exchanged looks of consummate loathing. She sat bolt upright and felt his eyes like lasers on the back of her neck.

They drilled into her confused brain the glimmerings of a horrible suspicion. If *this* was the man her sister was trying to fix her up with then *she* was the wife who had driven him out of the house with her sleeping around. Had the priest looked down at her while he preached instead of trying to hypnotize the clock at the back of the church he would have thought he had been blessed with the gift of prophecy, her expression was so inflamed. He returned to the altar and began the rite of marriage. They all stood up.

Are you ready freely and without reservation to give yourselves to each other in marriage?

Tony: I wouldn't give her a toenail off the bathroom floor.

Alex: No, I take it all back. All, all, all.

Are you ready to love and honour each other as man and wife for the rest of your lives?

Tony: I'd rather be dead.

Alex: I'd rather love and honour a cockroach.

Are you ready to accept children lovingly from God and bring them up according to the law of Christ and his Church?

Tony: As soon as I get them away from her.

Alex: As soon as I get them away from him.

Tony: I do solemnly declare that I know not of any lawful impediment why I may not kick the cow out of my life for ever.

Alex: Good riddance.

Will you take this woman here present for lawful wife, according to the rite of our holy Mother the Church?

Tony: I'd rather marry my landlady.

Alex: I'd rather clear up the playroom.

'I call upon these persons here present in their hired suits and funny hats to witness that I (full name including surname) do take thee (full name including same surname as me but only for the time being) to be a loathsome and despicable worm not worthy of the name of human being let alone wife/husband. And all this stuff about for better for worse, for richer for poorer, in sickness and in health, to love and to cherish, till death do us part can come out of a dog's bottom as far as I'm concerned.'

What God has joined together, let no man put asunder.

It was the best man's moment. With visible relief he handed Alex's ring to the priest who blessed it and gave it to Burt. George stretched out her left hand and he slipped it on. It was a perfect fit.

'George, take this ring as a sign of my love and fidelity.'

The priest led the way to the sacristy where the civil papers were to be signed. Effie and Veronica were quick off the mark to get in front of Burt's mother and father. All Burt's relatives trooped behind, under the mistaken impression that the service was over and wondering what had happened to the 'Wedding March'. Tony and Alex were left alone in the church.

'What's this you've been telling George about me being gay?' he hissed. Alex turned round. Her face was fleshless and pale, all her energy transformed into the hatred that poured out of her eyes.

'Are you frightened of the truth? I've seen you and Puck and Lorry and the rest of your little commune. You try to cover it up with those lies you've been telling her about me sleeping around. I'm promiscuous and an adulteress am I? You are despicable.'

'Oh yes? And what about your affair with Derek? I saw you with my own eyes, sneaking off to the country.'

'You're stark staring mad! Derek's as gay as you are. I saw you leave the train with him.'

'I went to the computer exhibition. It was you who got in the taxi with Derek!'

'Rubbish. I stayed on the train to Birmingham to see Veronica.'

'Who's she? Another of your alibis?'

'She's here. She was my father's mistress. Georgina is their daughter. At least Daddy chased girls.'

'But those letters in the urn?'

'They were the ones Daddy wrote to Veronica.'

'You didn't know about me and Georgina?'

'What about you and Georgina?'

'Nothing.'

Their words dropped like stones into a deep, deep well. As the bride and groom, now wife and husband before God and the Home Secretary, led the procession back into the church, looking unreasonably cheerful, both Tony and Alex felt like they did when the first saw each other in the church, a disorientation as if something had come loose inside their heads. The priest began the final blessing but his words seemed very far away.

'... *May your children bless you, your friends console you and all men live in peace with you.* ...'

The Happy Couple turned and walked down the aisle to the 'Wedding March', grins over their faces, as trite and worn a cliché as the same old buds appearing on the same old branches every boring old spring. George's mother and Burt's mother jostled for position again and Burt's Dad had to settle for Effie. The Best Man took the arm of sequined Granmaw followed by Burt's brother and sister. Tony and Alex came last, ten yards behind the others. They walked side by side, not daring to speak to each other or touch each other. They hovered on the edge of the party while the photographer fussed and waved and forced their faces into smiles that would later beam with all the others from coffee tables in Acocks Green and Cricklewood, Slippery Rock and Punxatawny. Have you met my sister Alex? Have you met my friend Tony? asked George. While the rest were getting into the beribboned cars Tony drew his wife back into the privacy of the church. They stood by the collecting box for the Souls In Purgatory and faced each other.

'We've been complete fools.'
'We have to talk to each other.'
'We have to listen to each other.'
'I don't know you at all.'
'I'm not the person you married.'
'You may not like what you find.'
'I'll take that risk.'
'We have to trust each other.'
'It's worth a try.'
'What happened to us?'
'What happened to love?'
'Who knows?'
'Can we find it again?'
'If we believe in it.'
'We can only hope.'
'I love you.'
'I love you.'

The church was quiet. The altar server had put the candles out. Only a tiny red light shone on the sanctuary, a pinprick in the gloom. They did not notice the central heating grill start to jiggle under the fourteenth station of the cross or a flickering light below cast shadows on the vaulted ceiling. There was a whoop, the grill clanged open on the stone and the best man's head, begrimed with soot, popped out. 'I found it' he whooped again, holding up the bright, gold ring in his blackened hand.

Even this did not disturb their passionate embrace.